ALSO BY SHANE KUHN

The Intern's Handbook
Hostile Takeover

THE
ASSET

SHANE KUHN

SIMON & SCHUSTER
New York London Toronto Sydney New Delhi

Simon & Schuster
1230 Avenue of the Americas
New York, NY 10020

First Simon & Schuster hardcover edition July 2016

SIMON & SCHUSTER and colophon are registered trademarks
of Simon & Schuster, Inc.

For information about special discounts for bulk purchases,
please contact Simon & Schuster Special Sales at 1-866-506-1949
or business@simonandschuster.com.

The Simon & Schuster Speakers Bureau can bring authors to your
live event. For more information or to book an event, contact the
Simon & Schuster Speakers Bureau at 1-866-248-3049 or visit
our website at www.simonspeakers.com.

Interior design by Lewelin Polanco

Manufactured in the United States of America

10 9 8 7 6 5 4 3 2 1

Library of Congress Cataloging-in-Publication Data has been applied for.

ISBN 978-1-4767-9621-5
ISBN 978-1-4767-9623-9 (ebook)

For all who have died at the hands of terrorist cowards. May those who have silenced you never be heard.

THE
ASSET

PROLOGUE

We're all going to die.

This thought is the ice pick in his head, a cold metal truth penetrating, splitting his synapses, bleeding his sanity dry. He is languishing near the end of one of many TSA checkpoint lines pooling into a seething crush of humanity. It's the busiest travel day of the year, at the busiest airport in the world, and families are assembled en masse, shuffling inches at a time with their screaming kids and overstuffed hand luggage so they can make it to Grandma's house in time for turkey and pumpkin pie. Outside, a light rain under an iron-gray sky is hindering low-altitude visibility, and a red rash of delays begins to spread across the flight status screens.

He hasn't slept in days, as evidenced by the steamer trunks under his bloodshot eyes. He fights off the shakes, palpitations, and brain fog of hypoglycemia, going on nearly twelve hours since his last meal. With his dirty, oversize raincoat and sweat-stained baseball cap, he's fresh meat for the airport cops methodically patrolling the security clearance area with drug-sniffing German shepherds. He can't afford to be singled out, searched, questioned, or detained. He looks at his watch.

Forty-five minutes.

His mind, despite his body's withering fatigue, speed-shifts from scenario to scenario, hoping to collide with a viable solution . . . anything that will relieve him of what he's there to do, what he *must do*. He sees his reflection in the obsidian eye of a video surveillance dome staring in wide-angle suspicion at the traveling hordes. He barely recognizes himself, a warped caricature on the verge of doing the unthinkable. He looks at his watch again. Its relentlessly ticking second hand juts like a middle finger, mocking him.

Forty minutes.

Move, you fucking coward, he bellows inwardly, hoping his command will echo down to what's left of his guts and stir decisive action. Scanning his surroundings in a way he knows damn well looks like the scheming fidget of a novice criminal, he sees standing fifty heads behind him the one man he was praying he wouldn't see—his crisply pressed Atlanta Police Department uniform a black monolith in the noise of vacation color.

"Fuck," he says out loud, forgetting himself.

He draws immediate scowls from a gaggle of parents attempting to wrangle restless children. But their silent admonishments don't arouse shame or guilt, only an acute awareness of the thousands of mothers, fathers, and kids living and breathing around him, lined up like lambs led to slaughter. With every smile, every peck on the cheek, every hand held, every baby comforted, and every anticipatory moment of holiday cheer, his heart beats faster in his chest and sweat soaks his clothes. He checks his six. The uniform is coming for him, working his way through the crowd with an eager hand on his holstered service weapon.

Time's up.

He unbuttons his raincoat and moves, walking quickly toward the TSA checkpoint, head down, eyes in a predatory squint, hands stuffed menacingly in his pockets. Within seconds, he hears the first scream. It rises quickly to full-panic pitch and incites more, spreading like wildfire. Those who aren't cowering in fear at the sight of him are pointing and shouting, trying to get the attention of the authorities. He breaks into a jog and throws off his overcoat, fully revealing the source of panic. A collective gasp sucks the air out of the room.

"He has a bomb!" a child shrieks, her tinny voice echoing.

He's wearing a vest with what appears to be thirty sticks of dynamite, blasting caps, and detonation cord duct-taped to it. Armed response officers sweep into the area, ordering everyone to get down. He only has a few seconds to make it to his target, the TSA checkpoint, before he gets a bullet in the head. He lowers his shoulders and breaks into a full sprint through the blind, stampeding chaos of the crowd. The terminal is hemorrhaging humanity into the concourse while the metal detector and body scanner alarms burst into an earsplitting crescendo.

He looks back. The dark uniform pursuing him snakes through the stumbling masses and draws the inky blur of a semiautomatic pistol from its holster, taking aim with the measured stance of a marksman. He ducks and runs toward the gaping mouths of more guns. The gray sky parts, igniting the scene with the white fire of sunlight.

1

L adies and gentlemen, in preparation** for landing . . ."

The flight attendant chirped apologetic Cockney while Kennedy snored in his British Airways business class flatbed seat, a coveted upgrade on the Heathrow–JFK leg of a fifteen-thousand-mile work odyssey that began five days ago in Los Angeles. As a two-hundred-plus-days-per-year business traveler, this was home, or, as Kennedy liked to call it, "the master bedroom." In fact, he had grown so accustomed to it, he wasn't able to sleep in a normal bed but drifted off like a baby in a metal and composite tube traveling six hundred miles per hour. While the smartly dressed crew tidied up the cabin, Kennedy was dreaming—another thing he could only do at thirty-three thousand feet.

The dream was what his former shrink called *recurring* and it was about his sister, Belle, whom he loved dearly but who had been dead for fourteen years. As always, she sat next to him on the last flight of her young life—American Airlines Flight 11, traveling from Boston to Los Angeles on September 11, 2001. Belle was sixteen and had gone to Boston to help their nana while their grandfather was in the ICU recovering from bypass surgery. Belle hated to fly, but that time she was especially nervous because it was to be her first time flying alone. Kennedy had accompanied her on the first leg of the trip, but had had to return to school before her.

Their father, Richard, an air force captain, had treated the situation in his usual hard-ass way, telling her to buck up and face her fears head-on. Their mother had passed from cancer shortly after Belle was born, so Richard decided he was going to raise them both in the school of hard knocks. For a highly analytical and somewhat emotionally unavailable child like Kennedy, this worked perfectly. But Belle was like their mother, Grace, the polar opposite. She had complex emotions from an early age and vexed her father with her inability to look at the world like he did, as a colorless grid ruled by mathematics.

The night before the flight, Belle spoke to Kennedy about it over the phone. The two of them were very close, relying on each other for advice and shoulders to cry on. Kennedy was nineteen at the time and every bit the protective big brother—feigning apathy but loving Belle more fiercely than himself.

"You're going to be fine. Just put your headphones on and sleep and the next thing you know you'll be home."

"What if I'm not fine?"

"What do you mean?"

"You seem so certain I'll be okay, but how do you know? How *could* you know?"

"I just know. There are literally tens of thousands of flights in the US alone every day. Statistically speaking, the chances of you dying in a plane crash are nil."

"Yeah but, statistically speaking, if my plane does crash, the chances of me dying are one hundred percent."

"Belle, riding in the back of Dad's car while he drives you like a maniac to ballet class is exponentially more dangerous, but you're not afraid to do that."

"I am now! Jesus, you're a big help. I'm more worried now than before I called."

"You don't need to worry at all, Belle. What good would it do anyway?"

"Oh, here we go with your patented *We're all doomed so screw it and have another beer* philosophy."

"I find it comforting."

"Which is why you never get any dates."

"Whatever. I get dates."

"Yeah, in your granola."

"Ha-ha. Pretty funny for someone supposedly experiencing mortal terror."

"It's how I cope."

"Coping implies the existence of an actual problem."

"I know this makes no sense to you, but this doesn't *feel* right to me. Like that time my hair stood on end before lightning struck Mrs. Garcia's oak tree."

"That wasn't a feeling, it was static electricity."

"Stop trying to make me feel better by telling me I'm full of it!"

"You know what? I don't have time for this right now. I have a tournament this weekend and an anthropology midterm I haven't even thought about studying for. Call Dad and tell him to come get you."

"Dad will tell me to buck up and get on the plane, just like you. You come."

"There's no way I can fly back to Boston right now. Absolutely no way."

"You'd be back in less than twenty-four hours. Come on, it'll be fun—"

"Belle, you're living in a fantasy world. I'm living in the real world and I can't just fly to Boston to fly you home because you're nervous."

"I'm not just nervous. I'm really scared! All you care about is your stupid golf and Stanford nerd friends! I'm your sister . . . I don't want to go alone."

Belle's aggressive tone disappeared on her last line because she was fighting tears. Kennedy angrily interpreted this as an attempt to manipulate him.

"At least I'm not a little princess who thinks the world revolves around her! Call me when you decide to grow the fuck up."

He hung up. Belle tried calling him back several times but he didn't answer out of spite. That was the last time he ever spoke to her.

———

In the dream, Belle was always the same age as when she died. Her strawberry hair and faint pixie dusting of freckles taunted him with their eternal innocence. Like when she was alive, she always had the mirthful expression of someone up to no good. As they sat next to each other on the flight Kennedy never took, Belle talked incessantly, blithely cruising through subjects both relevant and tangential, while he waited to get in his own edgewise word that would never see the light of day. But it didn't matter. Her manic narratives endeared him.

"I wish you would shut up," he joked.

"Then we would both have to listen to you, and that just wouldn't do, Monsieur Ennui," she politely chided, punching him in the arm.

"Maybe I have something important to say."

"About which of your noble yet hideously dull pursuits? Golf, er . . . Sorry, I need a second to yawn."

She played like she was yawning out of extreme boredom, eyeballing him for a reaction. Belle's truth serum. A teaspoon of sugar and you're stretched out on the cross.

"I don't have to take this kind of abuse. I'm going to sleep."

"Fine, you big lug. I have better things to do anyway, like the in-flight magazine crossword puzzle."

He could see she was getting nervous, so he gently patted her arm while she fidgeted with the folds of her skirt.

"Brother?"

"What now?" he asked with phony annoyance.

She didn't answer. Her face looked ghostly pale, as if the blood and wit had drained from it. Her slender fingers were perched tightly on his forearm, like a bird in a gale. He always tried to wake himself up at that point in the dream but never succeeded.

"What is it?" he asked.

Tears welled in her eyes.

"I don't want to go alone," she said.

Before Kennedy could be a good big brother and say something to reassure her, he was violently interrupted by the bone-crushing force of impact with the World Trade Center's North Tower. Belle disappeared in a blinding flash as the airplane's fuselage disintegrated into white-hot cinders. Bodies—gasping, burning, convulsing, and clinging to nothing—were blown and scattered through a maelstrom of glass and concrete, bloody dandelion florets seeding the mouth of blackness. After the last of the aircraft debris exploded out the building's exit wound, Kennedy always ended up sitting on the edge of the building's smoking maw, looking down on a rain of fire.

"Sir?" a voice called, cutting through the dream.

Kennedy awoke with a start. Teary-eyed and disoriented, he was staring into the face of a young female flight attendant with a cruelly similar swath of freckles.

"So sorry to disturb you but we're preparing the cabin for arrival."

———

Before landing, Kennedy went to the lavatory to do what he always did after having the Belle dream. The crying wasn't the most difficult part. The most difficult part was stopping. The hollow of anguish he felt for Belle had not changed in all the years she was gone. Even in that moment, crammed in an airport lav fourteen years later, he could vividly picture everyone in his college dorm watching Belle's plane hit the World Trade Center. He had just gotten up, and after breakfast he was going to call her to apologize. Instead, he watched her die, and all that was left was a profound sense of helplessness and the one emotion that would drive everything he did in his life from that point on: regret.

2

Terminal 7 at JFK always smelled of cheap, overboiled coffee and stale cologne. As Kennedy took a brisk walk along the concourse—his version of going to the gym—he stretched his legs and contemplated Manhattan. It was the fourth week of September and the city would be singing the crisp overture of autumn. Of course, he was never going to see or experience any of it during his brief visit. Like on most of his business trips, the only sights he'd be taking in were those of Duty Free, Wok & Roll, Dunkin' Donuts, and all the other apostrophic, postapocalyptic airport landmarks he vagabonded past countless times a year.

People often made envious remarks about his business travel, not realizing that the homogenous scenery endemic to virtually every airport in the United States made one susceptible to what Kennedy half jokingly called "Terminal Illness"—a chronic frequent-traveler disease brought on by extreme isolation, fatigue-induced delirium, fast-food malnutrition, excessive consumption of bottom-shelf booze, and diminished social equilibrium. He likened it to extended space travel, but with inferior cuisine.

Kennedy lived in the rarefied atmosphere of the consultant—a hired gun on the payroll of power opening its deep pockets to address deeper fears. The client he was visiting that day was his biggest, the US government, or his rich Uncle Sam, as he often joked. Kennedy was an aviation security specialist, and the TSA paid him to train their officers with his own trademark curriculum at airports around the country. Just like contracting Blackwater and G4S mercenaries to fight his wars, Uncle Sam found it was a lot easier, and cheaper, to outsource airport security—especially since before September 11 it had been nothing more than an FAA afterthought.

In college, Kennedy had studied to be an architect. But after his sister's death, he withdrew from the things that had defined him—the golf team and his academic pursuits—and nearly flunked out of school. He thought constantly about hurting himself back then but never followed through. It would have been completely selfish compared to what Belle had suffered. All he could think about was doing something, *anything*, to help prevent something like 9/11 from happening again. Rationally, he knew that would never bring her back. But in his heart he felt if he made a difference somehow, she would forgive him for what he'd done and there might be a slight chance he could forgive himself.

He explored the military at the suggestion of his father, but the idea of killing people indiscriminately in conflicts that serviced political ideologies or protected corporate revenue streams only made him feel worse. The intelligence community was a natural choice for someone with his IQ and work ethic, so he applied to the CIA, thinking a career in the clandestine service might be a way to stop terrorists before they started. But news started coming out about how interagency bickering between the CIA and FBI may have paved the way for the 9/11 terrorists to pull off the worst attack on American soil in history, and Kennedy burned the thick pile of application documents that had taken him weeks to complete.

One of his friends at school, the son of a senator, landed a job with the newly formed Transportation Security Administration, an organization that piqued Kennedy's interest. To him, the front lines in the war on terror were at the nation's airports, and TSA would put him in the trenches. Lockheed Martin recruited and trained the majority of new agents for the TSA at the time and Kennedy used his friend's connections to get an unpaid internship after graduation. His father was furious that he would shoot so low when he was armed with a degree from one of the most prestigious universities in the country. Kennedy didn't care. He had no interest in working anywhere else and was committed to doing whatever it took to get on staff. He spent all the money he had saved since he was a kid, supporting himself during his internship and even completing an elite aviation security training course in Israel. When he came back from Tel Aviv, he had earned a foot in the door.

By twenty-five, Kennedy was one of Lockheed's top trainers, a specialist in Behavior Detection, something the Israelis had practiced for years but that was a relatively new field in the United States. In addition to training officers, he also became well versed in screening equipment and learned how to write grants for federal research facilities like Lawrence Livermore to develop new tech. At twenty-seven, he was in such high demand it no longer made sense for him to be a Lockheed employee. He hated corporate culture anyway and it seemed like the more he got promoted, the more they wanted to take him away from his boots on the ground and make him a high-paid desk jockey standing around eating birthday cake on Friday afternoons with the rest of the drones.

A few weeks before his thirtieth birthday, he became an independent consultant and inked a specialized skills contractor agreement directly with TSA and the Department of Homeland Security. Back then, it was extremely rare for individuals to have direct contracts with DHS and TSA, and this status expanded Kennedy's reputation in the airport security industry worldwide, winning him contracts with foreign governments.

As they did every year on Kennedy's birthday, he and his father had dinner in Los Angeles at Morton's. Richard was beaming with pride, a very rare condition indeed, but Kennedy thought he looked tired and underweight, a stark contrast to his usual robust self. When he asked Richard about it, his father said he'd had the flu and was on the mend. Six weeks later, Richard was found dead in his home. Unbeknownst to his family and friends, he'd been battling lung cancer for over a year. He had tried to hide that, like he used to try to hide his pack-a-day Marlboro Red habit from Belle and Kennedy. At least with the cigarettes, they could smell the evidence. With this, there was only the stink of death. His own father had not had the decency to allow him to say good-bye, something he was also denied with Belle.

Kennedy had already been struggling to assimilate himself into some semblance of a normal life. Richard's death killed that for good. Work became the false idol he worshipped nearly every waking moment. It was the only thing that made him feel safe from the constant betrayals of people and the outside world. He stopped calling friends and broke off a six-month relationship with a young woman he'd met and fallen for at Lockheed. It was impossible for him to imagine connecting with anyone beyond the superficialities of the job. For Kennedy, it all came down to a choice. He could allow his pain to swallow him up into the same dark mire he'd been in with Belle—and run the risk of suffocating to death—or harden his heart and channel his rage into his work. He never looked back. Now, at age thirty-three, he was making a very high six-figure salary, consulting with every major airport in the United States and many in Europe and Asia, and living in the hermetically sealed, disposable world of the frequent flier.

————

"Good morning," he said to Lizzy, the young Starbucks barista who knew him by name and his order by heart.

Despite the line of caffeine junkies snaking all the way around the kiosk, she waved him over to the pickup counter to get the latte that was already waiting for him.

"Damn, you look tired," she said.

"You forgot old."

"Shut up"—she laughed—"or I'll call out your embarrassing order in front of all these people."

"You wouldn't dare."

"Double tall coconut half caff cinnamon dolce latte, extra whip!"

Teenage girls pointed and laughed.

"Thanks, Lizzy, you're a mensch," he said, handing her a twenty.

"Anytime," she said. "But when are you going to really show your gratitude and take me out on the town?"

"When I'm not old enough to be your . . . cool uncle," Kennedy said.

"Eleven years is not that far apart."

"Maybe not in Utah."

She laughed again, and Kennedy was eager to change the subject.

"Seen any of my sworn enemies?"

"You mean like that massive toolshed from Homeland Security?"

"That's Mr. Massive Toolshed to you, young lady."

"Haven't seen him. And my boss isn't here either, so you can kiss me now."

"Maybe I should go to Peet's," he said, blowing her a kiss as he walked away.

"I better not catch you cheating on me!" she yelled across the con-course.

————

As he walked to the TSA office, dreading another training session full of recently unemployed 7-Eleven clerks, his mood took a nosedive. In the past few months, he had begun to hate his job, something he had never dreamed possible. His career had always given him purpose where he had none, and it was one of the few things in his life he genuinely felt proud of. That was back when he thought he could make a difference. But that buoyant illusion sank like a stone when he saw the recent TSA "progress" reports all over the national news saying the agency was failing on an epic scale.

As much as he wanted to nail himself to the cross, he knew the situation was completely beyond his control. Equipment suppliers who skipped testing and oversight because they had half The Hill in their back pockets, bureaucratic interference, and an overworked, underpaid officer work-force that was never given enough time to train and mentor in real-world situations—these were enough to destroy the TSA long before Kennedy arrived on the scene. Put simply, Washington and its parasitic fauna sucked the life out of a program that, in the beginning, had great promise and was formed for all the right reasons.

The end result for Kennedy was a monkey on his back telling him that his life's work was a complete waste of time and taxpayer money. His passion for traveler safety had increased over the years, but his sense of purpose was beginning to ebb. The only thing that kept him going was knowing *they* were still out there, plotting their elaborate schemes to burn the good old US of A to the ground and stomp on the ashes. When he focused on that, and thought of all the time, money, and manpower ter-rorists were spending to get the upper hand, it didn't matter how fucked up DHS and TSA were. All the cynicism, laziness, and pointless internal bickering weren't going to change the fact that passengers still needed to be kept safe.

As he often did when he was facing a crisis in his life, Kennedy turned to Noah Kruz, a "life mastery coach" who had published a dozen best-selling books and spoke all over the world on the art of creating a life that

reflected a person's true self versus one that reflected the demands of others. Kruz believed that the egos of people around us had the power to influence and control everything we did, from romance, to career, to health.
Once a person was able to filter all of that out and identify what it was that
they wanted in these areas, getting it was a far simpler and more rewarding
process.

Kennedy could relate. His father had lorded over his life for so long, it
took estrangement and, ultimately, death for him to get clarification about
his own dreams.

Kennedy had a Noah Kruz app on his phone and referred to it regularly for inspiration. That day, he selected PICK ME UPS and the app pushed
him a quote:

> There is no escape. Life has you in its clutches and you can either
> struggle in vain to free yourself, inviting the world's predatory forces
> to tear you to pieces, or you can allow yourself to be swallowed whole
> and join them in the hunt.

On that note, it was time to get to work.

As he walked in to train a crop of TSA agents, he was carrying a new
sense of purpose in the form of a Homeland Security threat memo sent to
all TSA chiefs three days prior. "Global intelligence sources" were warning of a "large-scale, coordinated attack on an indeterminate number of
US airports." Kennedy had seen a lot of threat-level-orange bullshit issued
by Homeland, usually when they needed free Fox News PR to get their
bloated budget rubber-stamped before the holidays, but this was different.
It wasn't just Homeland. *Global intelligence sources* was what made the hair
on the back of his neck stand on end.

3

When Kennedy got the memo, he'd been in London so he hit up his college buddy Wes Bowman from the CIA to pick his brain. Wes came from a wealthy Boston family, which had pretty much disowned him when he refused to be a paper doll exec in their restaurant food service empire. Working at the CIA, and having to live on a middle-class wage, had put some city miles on him. Even though they were the same age, Wes looked more like Kennedy's much older brother with his retreating hairline and box-cut Men's Wearhouse suit.

He was an IT geek servicing global field offices—not a master spy by any stretch of the imagination—but his security clearance made him privy to agency workings. Kennedy had taken him out to one of the best steak houses in town, hoping to butter him up for information. After polishing off a couple of bone-in rib eyes and nearly three bottles of French burgundy, Kennedy awkwardly brought up the memo.

"You didn't have to wine and dine me, dude," Wes said. "I could have told you over the phone that Langley and all the cousins are in a tizzy about this so-called threat."

"True, but I already know that."

"What you *don't* know are the specifics of the threat, which you think I might have. And now you're greasing my wheels with prime-cut marbling to get what you want. Does that about sum things up?" Wes said, taking a large draught of wine.

"Think of it more as a bribe," Kennedy said. "I really want to get a jump on this for my TSA chiefs if I can."

"I don't blame you. They don't jump very high, do they?"

"No, and after their F-minus report card, they're poking one another's eyes out pointing fingers."

"Shocker. Can't imagine this is doing much for your business."

"Let's just say I need to maintain a high level of relevance these days."

"I wish I could help you, man, but that information is north of my clearance. I can tell you what I've heard round the watercooler as long as you promise to take it with a grain of salt."

"Anything will help."

"We've been butting heads with the bureau for weeks about this. We don't think they're doing enough. And we definitely don't think Homeland is doing enough."

"Which makes this much more than speculation," Kennedy said.

"This is intelligence. *Everything* is speculation, even when it's happening right in front of you. What is it about this one that's got your panties in a bunch?"

"Gut feeling, I guess. And *global intelligence sources*."

"Sounds like they're trying to differentiate it."

"TSA gets too many warnings and no one's paying attention. I doubt that little bit of language is going to help," Kennedy said.

"Can I see the memo?" Wes asked.

"That would be a violation of my employer's NDA," Kennedy said. "Unless you came by it accidentally. Like if it fell out of my jacket."

Wes looked at the floor under the table and saw the memo.

"Promise me you'll never try to be a spy." Wes laughed.

"Ha-ha. Going to take a leak."

Kennedy went to the restroom and waited long enough for Wes to read the memo. He felt a little silly doing it this way, but he couldn't risk ruffling feathers at Homeland for breaking his NDA. They were already questioning his role and asking for more detailed accounting of his work with TSA. When he got back to the table, the look on Wes's face told him perhaps he had not been cautious enough.

"How about a cigar?" Wes asked.

"I could murder one," Kennedy said.

He paid and they went for a walk. Wes took a long drag on his cigar, looked around to confirm they weren't being observed, and handed the memo back to Kennedy.

"What's up, Wes? You look a little spooked. No pun intended."

"Based on what I've heard, this memo grossly underplays the potential threat."

"Shit," Kennedy hissed. "In what way?"

"Let's just say at this point I should probably see if I can dig up some actual facts for you."

"You'd do that?"

"Yeah. You're the only person who's going to take this seriously and you might be the only person who can get *them* to take it seriously."

They stopped by the river. The sluggish, murky green water looked like the back of a snake.

"Do me a favor?" Wes said.

"What's that?"

"Don't be a hero. You got lucky with that JFK thing years ago. Could have gone the other way and scrubbed all those people you were trying to save."

"What's your point?"

"I get why you're doing this," Wes said. "And I'm willing to stick my neck out a little to help you. But remember there's a reason even we separate the spooks from the cleaners. You get in over your head and you call in the cavalry. Dead is for martyrs and movie stars."

4

The TSA training center was a dank, fluorescent cinder-block hole
that could easily pass for a CIA torture cave. Kennedy surveyed his
pupils—newly recruited Transportation Security Officers, or TSOs,
to staff the checkpoints at JFK and LaGuardia. All he could think was
that if the country could see the people sitting in front of him, being
hired to protect them, they would never set foot on another airplane.
Many of them wouldn't cut it as crossing guards, let alone critical gate-
keepers to the world's airways, expected to observe hundreds, sometimes
thousands, of travelers in a ten-hour shift and spot the ones that just
might manage to fly another commercial jet into the Pentagon. Glenn,
their fearless leader, inspired even less confidence as he sat on a stool
at the back of the room and dunked a stale cruller in a cup of swamp-
water coffee. With his swinish build and beady eyes, Glenn looked like
a freshly shaven migrant from Middle-earth. Kennedy hated Glenn. The
feeling was mutual. So he dispensed with pleasantries and got right to
the PowerPoint.

"Good morning. Who's ready for a pop quiz?"

A collective groan passed through the room. Kennedy pulled a .45 caliber handgun from his pocket and pointed it at them. They all gasped,
screamed, and hit the ground for cover. Kennedy laid the gun down on the
table in front of him.

"That, ladies and gentlemen, is a successful act of terror in a nutshell. It happens quickly and unexpectedly, and it induces panic and chaos. By the time you realize what's happening, you've got a bullet in your head. Which is why in this business, an ounce of prevention is worth far more than a pound of reaction."

He allowed them to settle back into their seats and observed. Those still dwelling on the outrage they felt from the gun stunt were not going to make the cut. His Israeli instructors had taught him that emotional control is the most important characteristic of a good security screener. You had to keep your head.

"Prevention begins with knowing your enemy. I'm going to show you pictures of actual weapons that TSOs—people just like you—found at airports around the country. Then we'll look at traveler surveillance photos. See if you can guess which weapon belonged to which person."

Kennedy switched off the lights and fired up his laptop projector. The first image he displayed was a photo of the .45 he had just pulled on them.

"You're familiar with this item. When it was confiscated, it had a full fourteen-round magazine and one in the chamber. Anyone know where it was found?"

"Iraq?" someone joked.

"Right here at JFK," he said. "Last week. If you read your confiscation logs, you would have known that. Perhaps Glenn will make that a job requirement."

"It's posted every morning at seven. Right by the doughnuts." Glenn grunted.

"Outstanding. Then at least I know *you're* reading them."

Kennedy projected a new image on the screen with the same .45 and three surveillance photos of travelers—a young black man, a Caucasian man in his fifties dressed like a Hells Angel, and a middle-aged Hispanic man with a neck tattoo. Murmurs among the mostly black recruits vibrated through the ranks, followed by playful banter between them and a few Hispanic recruits.

"Anyone care to guess who this weapon belonged to?" Kennedy asked.

No takers. Most had the *Please don't pick me* look on their faces.

Kennedy pointed to a young woman immersed in her phone screen.

"How about you, Facebook?"

Roars of laughter. The young woman looked up defiantly.

"Take your pick," she spat. "I'd pull every one of them out of line."

The laughter quickly turned to grumbles of contempt. Kennedy displayed his next slide—a sixty-year-old grandfatherly man with thick glasses and a sweater-vest.

"And you'd be wrong every time," Kennedy said.

"Ah hell no," one of the young black men blurted out.

"How many times have you been stopped by the police without probable cause?" Kennedy asked him.

"I stopped counting," the young man said cynically.

"Profiling. Many of you have experienced it because of your race. The majority of cases that involve police using excessive force are with minorities—"

"And the cops doing it are usually from the same minority groups," a young black woman chimed in.

"Good point. So there's prejudicial thinking that goes with it. And let's not forget gender bias," Kennedy said to Facebook girl. "Why do people profile?"

The room was silent, but he could see many were itching to answer.

"Come on. I know you have an opinion on this."

"Racist motherfuckers," one of the Hispanic men said boldly.

"That's only part of the problem. What else?"

"It's easier to just blame it on a brother than to do any actual work to find the guy that did it," another young black man said.

"Especially when you think all brothers look the same!" his friend added.

"Exactly," Kennedy agreed. "People are lazy and always take the easy way out."

Kennedy switched the screen to a collage with pictures of Ted Bundy, Dennis Rader, Charles Whitman, and Timothy McVeigh—candid shots from their earlier lives, not mug shots or police blotter photos. They looked very normal.

"Does anyone know who these people are?"

Crickets. Kennedy placed a red laser pointer dot on the forehead of each person as he spoke about him.

"Two of the worst serial killers in US history, one of the most lethal school shooters in history, and one of the worst domestic terrorists our country has ever seen."

"They look like perfectly good white people," someone joked.

"That's the point. The smartest criminals don't broadcast their intentions. The only people who make bomb threats are the ones who do not have a bomb. No one knows a shooter's plan until he's already opened fire. A real terrorist has one goal and that is to kill as many people as possible with one act. This is why they strike when we are at our most vulnerable, when they know our guard will be down."

Kennedy clicked through more slides of confiscated weapons, matching them to pictures of their owners. Not one person looked the least bit threatening.

"Credit card knives, hairbrush ice picks, stun gun canes, live smoke grenades, incendiary and corrosive chemicals, and an endless parade of loaded firearms and ammunition—all very bad things that get a lot worse at thirty-three thousand feet. You cannot afford to allow even one of these items to ever make it onto an airplane. Does anyone here know what the September eleventh hijackers used?"

"Box cutters," Facebook girl answered.

Kennedy displayed a picture of the North Tower of the World Trade Center, the one his sister died in, taken just before impact.

"Correct. Something anyone can buy at the local hardware store and, more important, something that will raise no suspicions when purchased. Only an idiot or a mental patient is going to try to get a firearm on an airplane. Finding those will be the easiest part of your job. But someone with truly bad intentions and half a brain will show up with something they think you will overlook—not a box cutter, because now we have in-flight security in place to deal with cockpit attacks. If we learned anything from 9/11 it was that weapons by themselves are not the end-all for a successful terror attack. Our scanning equipment is sophisticated enough to identify weapons of any significance. You have to think *beyond* technology and get into the head of someone who is trying to outsmart you, getting creative, doing hours and hours of research, devising something they are certain you will not notice. But, in the end, the key is the attacker himself. Even if you can't see his weapon, you have to be able to see his intent."

Kennedy showed them a photo of Richard Reid and the shoe that he packed with explosives and took on American Airlines Flight 63 in December 2001.

"I thank this asshole every day I have to take my shoes off at the checkpoint. The only reason he didn't bring that plane down was because he knew nothing about explosives. He had enough C4 in his shoe to do the job, but by the time they took off, his foot sweat had soaked it through and then he tried to light the det cord with a match."

Everyone laughed.

"You know what's even funnier? The security checkpoint officers in Paris who screened him the first time he tried to fly refused to let him on the plane. They accurately analyzed his behavior, which was textbook amateur terrorist—fidgety, noncommunicative, unwilling to make eye contact, et cetera. So, he just came back the next day and the new screening crew let him on the plane. Did he change overnight? No. He just got lucky with screeners who didn't give a shit and didn't read the fucking logs from the day before. His photo was in those logs."

Murmurs of disgust. Kennedy could feel them orienting to him, like a magnet pulling iron filings out of the sand. He was making *them* give a shit.

"Whatever you think you know about how to identify a threat, forget it now. The truth is that you know nothing."

"Sir, all due respect," a quiet, white doughboy in the back said sheepishly. "We've been studying the manual for weeks. We're not clueless."

"Have you ever been trained by me before?" Kennedy asked.

"No, but—"

"Then you *are* clueless."

More laughter from the room. Doughboy looked for Glenn to back him up, but Glenn was staring at his phone screen, mentally checked out.

"What makes you so special?" Doughboy asked.

"I'm not special. The people who trained me are."

"Who trained you? God?" he said, laughing, but no one joined him.

"The Israelis. They're surrounded by enemies and have been at war since their country came into existence in 1948. Yet, not one plane has ever been successfully hijacked from Ben Gurion Airport, and the only attacks that ever disrupted air traffic came from outside the airport when groups like Hamas fired rockets from Palestinian territories or Japanese Red Army gunmen receiving weapons from Palestinian soldiers opened fire on passengers *outside* security checkpoints. Those were military offensives that airport security could not control. One plane was hijacked in Vienna in 1972 and forced to *land* there. Anyone know what happened?"

"I think you know by now we don't," a recruit said glumly.

"Israeli commandos stormed the plane, killed two terrorists, captured the other two, and one passenger was killed. One passenger. In the entire history of the airport! Two thousand, nine hundred and ninety-six people died on 9/11 and thousands more as a result of the wars triggered by that attack. We are, statistically, the worst in the world when it comes to aviation security. The Israelis are the best. And I'm pretty sure God himself must have trained them."

"What do they have that we don't?" Facebook girl asked. "I can't even pick out Israel on a map."

"It's not about what they *have*. Screening tech in developed nations is all pretty much the same. It's about what they don't have: trust. They trust no one. In the US, we're sheltered. We want to trust people—little old ladies, unassuming bookworms with glasses, the next-door-neighbor dad who rocks a great sweater-vest, moms with cute babies, and the list goes on. Profiling works both ways. There are people we've been trained to trust, just like those we've been trained to treat with suspicion."

Kennedy played a video showing people's faces—a wide variety of ages, ethnicities, socioeconomic groups, and everything in between—cycling through in the same position in the middle of the screen. As the video sped up, they appeared to morph into one another, creating the illusion they were all the same.

"Over fifty million travelers go through Kennedy Airport every year. That's roughly one hundred and forty thousand a day. But it only takes *one* to pull off an attack that could be as devastating to our country as 9/11. Anyone know the recent nationwide failure rate of TSA agents?"

"We don't need to go into that right now," Glenn started.

"It was in the *New York Times*, Glenn. And on CNN. Talking about it is the first step to fixing it."

"Ninety-five percent," one of the quieter recruits said in back, silencing the room.

"At least one of you reads the news. Ninety-five percent of fake weapons, explosives, and contraband that undercover DHS Red Team agents attempted to smuggle through TSA checkpoints at airports around the country—including this one—made it through," Kennedy pointed out.

"Holy shit," another recruit said.

"That's not all. Seventy-three TSA agents were on terror watch lists."

The room erupted. Kennedy liked what he saw. Most were pissed off, shocked, embarrassed, the whole range of emotions he would expect from someone who had chosen a career in airport security. Those who didn't react would not be coming back tomorrow. Glenn scowled at Kennedy from across the room and shuffled back to his office. *He* was the problem. It was easy to blame the TSOs, with their youth and lack of experience, but Kennedy likened it to the military. When you see a Marine, you are not seeing any of the shortcomings he or she brought into the corps. Good leadership and training shapes the minds of even the most stubborn youth. Kennedy felt a strong obligation to help shape young officer recruits, but the TSA was not supporting him with their team leaders, and that was why the system was failing.

"You can change that score. You have to want it. And you have to listen to me and do exactly what I tell you. If you do, when I'm through with you, you'll see *everyone* the way I do, as a potential threat. You'll trust no one . . . and nothing will get past you. In case you haven't noticed, World War Three has begun, but it isn't nation versus nation. It's individuals and groups versus whoever or whatever they hate. Add modern technology and the global availability of advanced weaponry—like rockets that can shoot down a commercial airliner at cruising altitude—and tell me: who can you trust?"

"No one!"

The group sounded off like a boot camp platoon. For some, there was hope yet. For others, there was a pink slip and a doughnut.

5

fter the group dispersed, Kennedy sat down to chat with Glenn. His office looked and smelled like it belonged to a high school football coach with a tendency to hoard old newspapers and novelty coffee cups. The tension, along with Glenn's ripening armpits, was palpable.

"Seen this?"

Kennedy set the recent DHS/TSA threat memo on his desk.

"Yeah," Glenn lied, glancing at it.

"And?" Kennedy asked.

"We get ten a those a day."

"Not like this one."

"What the hell're you talking about?"

"You haven't read it, have you?"

Glenn tried to cheat a sneak peek at the memo and Kennedy pulled it off the desk. Glenn's face turned cartoon red. The only thing missing was steam coming out of his ears.

"You come here to bust my hump? You enjoy fucking with me?"

"I'm here to help you protect your passengers, Glenn."

"Oh yeah," Glenn said sardonically. "Like you helped me before?"

Before he could stop himself, Kennedy was in Glenn's face.

"Would you rather have killed two planes full of people and become the national poster boy for criminal stupidity?"

"You done?" Glenn snorted.

"Just getting started," Kennedy said. "Red Teams breezed through here too, buddy. Three fake handguns and two leg-strapped bombs. Five of your planes would have gone down in flames."

Glenn just shrugged.

"I'll give you one thing, Glenn. At least you're consistent."

Glenn got up and left his own office, in much the same way he had three years back when Kennedy discovered a glaring security breach exposing him for what he was—an incompetent moron. DHS had warned TSA chiefs of a potential terror threat coming out of Somalia. JFK had seemed a likely target, and Kennedy was concerned Glenn wasn't taking the threat seriously, so he stuck around New York for a couple of days and kept his eye on the checkpoints. Eventually, one of Kennedy's TSA trainees pulled two men traveling with South African passports, carrying what they said were transplant corneas and human tissue donations. Their paperwork looked solid, and X-ray images of their cases didn't reveal anything overtly suspect, but Kennedy had felt they were *exhibiting* suspect behavior patterns and had them moved to a private room for additional questioning.

When their passports were scanned, the system came back matching their pictures to known Somali Al Qaeda operatives—but with only 70 percent accuracy. Kennedy practically sprinted to Glenn's office to celebrate having potentially bagged the threat operatives. But to his bewilderment, Glenn opted not to question them.

"Glenn, it's a seventy percent match. We have to question them."

"We?"

"You, I mean. Why don't I get someone from the bureau over here to do it? Then you can just let them handle it. I'm sure they wouldn't want you to just let them go."

"We're not calling them. Anything less than a ninety percent match and they'll chew my ass for wasting their time."

"Is that what you're worried about?"

"Yeah, some of us have jobs, buddy, and we want to keep 'em."

"At least search their medical cases."

Glenn had already started packing up to leave. He had his hockey bag and Kennedy knew he was in a hurry to make his beer league game.

"And run the risk of contaminating human tissue donations dying people might be waiting for? You want to pay for that lawsuit?"

"Then call the sending and receiving hospitals. If they verify it, we're good."

"That's proprietary medical information. Ever heard of HIPAA?"

"How are the names of the hospitals proprietary? It's not like we're asking the addresses of the recipient patients."

Glenn looked at Kennedy impatiently.

"We got protocols here, ways of doing things. I'm not about to just throw all that out the window on a hunch."

"A hunch?" Kennedy practically yelled. "It's the best lead anyone has had on this threat to date. We can't just let them go!"

Kennedy knew immediately his forceful tone had been a huge mistake.

"There's that 'we' again," Glenn said with a cynical grin. "I think you need to call it a day, CSI Miami. Let us do our job."

"But you're *not* doing your fucking job."

"You have a good night," Glenn said and left.

Smug Glenn thought he had put Kennedy in his place, but after he left, Kennedy went straight to the containment room to search the medical cases before the men were cut loose. It was an incredibly risky move. Defying a TSA chief and doing an unauthorized search was a breach of trust that could have easily landed him in jail, but he could live with all the consequences of being wrong, and none of the ones that came with being right. When he cut through the sealing tape on the medical cases, his hands were shaking. And what if a bomb was inside? He might accidentally detonate it and do the terrorists' work for them. He had to make a game time decision. If he did nothing, the cases would end up on two different planes in a matter of hours.

Kennedy opened them. He had seen donor tissue packs before, and what was inside looked nothing like those. In the dry ice there were six aluminum cylinders with safety-locked aerosol tops, like the aerosol triggers on mace cans. On the bottoms of the cylinders, there were stickers with nondescript medical insignias. When Kennedy peeled one off he found Syrian characters laser-cut into the metal. Someone had unsuccessfully attempted to file them off. He texted a picture of the cylinders to one of his father's old air force buddies, a guy who'd worked with his dad at the Missile Systems Center in LA. The guy wasn't 100 percent sure, but he thought they might be gas canisters. Kennedy wasn't going to risk it, so he called in an airport shutdown protocol, using Glenn's office hotline.

When the NYPD bomb squad arrived, they immediately turned the

case over to the feds and cleared out the entire terminal. Military muni-
tions experts later determined the canisters contained sarin gas, a deadly
nerve agent. Minuscule amounts of the toxin can kill several people and
they had enough in their two phony transplant packs to kill a thousand or
more. They had rigged the canisters with locking aerosol tops that, when
activated, would continue to spray long after the terrorists themselves were
dead. In addition to killing everyone on board and bringing down both
planes, the gas would have made the crash site a lethal hot zone, killing
emergency first responders as well.

The two men were taken into custody as enemy combatants and became honored guests at the Gitmo country club. Kennedy was given a
lucrative contract renewal and a big fat hush bonus, and Glenn was still
trying to clean the egg off his face. His decision to let the men go was a
matter of record and his superiors were well aware of it, but they didn't fire
him, for fear he would leak the incident to the press. It all got swept under
the proverbial rug, along with other, less egregious terror attempts Kennedy had thwarted at different airports over the years. Glenn, of course,
learned nothing from the experience and made no attempt to improve
himself. Instead he got fatter on the government dole and perfected the art
of resenting Kennedy.

———

Kennedy left Glenn's office, just like he had three years back, deeply worried about what would happen in the event of another, larger attack. The
problem was, there were too many Glenns in other airports around the
country, and now it was a matter of public record that US airports were
patently unsafe. The notion of trying to stop a threat being organized by
anyone with half a brain filled Kennedy with the sharp bile of anxiety. As
he zombie-walked through the airport, his mind was racing in so many
directions he could scarcely remember the departure time for his flight
home. He passed a Hudson bookstore, his version of a local library, and
saw a rack with Noah Kruz's new best seller, *The You in Universe*. He had
read it twice already but dropped in and cracked it to his favorite passage:

*If you view your enemies simply as antagonists, you narrow your vi-
sion and create a self-fulfilling prophecy of defeat. When you see your*

*enemies as emancipators, freeing you from the rigid perceptions that
create needless conflict, your mind will open to infinite solutions, and
the entire concept of defeat will cease to exist.*

Reading the passage made Kennedy realize he would never be able to
rely on TSA to respond to the threat because the "self-fulfilling prophecy of defeat" was festering at the core of their organization. *They* suffered
from the narrow vision that creates needless conflicts. Not Kennedy. Many
times he had proven he didn't need their help rooting out vermin. Alone,
he could move quickly, unencumbered by bullshit policy and rampant employee apathy.

In a world of infinite solutions, he was one.

6

Welcome home."

Gil, the British concierge at Hotel Bel-Air, was waiting by the curb when Kennedy's Uber SUV arrived from LAX a few minutes after midnight. The Bel-Air was one of Kennedy's favorite hotels. It was an oasis of Mediterranean architecture in the Westside hills, with sweeping views of Los Angeles, from the heat mirage of downtown all the way to Malibu. Although it was one of the most exclusive hotels in the city, it had managed to avoid becoming a celebrity petting zoo. For Kennedy, it was an exquisite escape, allowing him to turn the volume of LA down to zero and breathe.

"Thank you, Gil. Miss me?"

"Of course. This place is never the same without you."

"Like Jack Nicholson in *The Shining*."

Gil laughed as he slid Kennedy's garment bag from the back of the SUV. Aaron, the doorman, opened the tastefully gilded entrance, giving Kennedy a familiar smile.

"Nice to see you again, sir."

"You too. I see you guys kept up the old dump in my absence," Kennedy joked.

"We managed to chase *most* of the rats away," Gil flipped back as they walked into the lobby.

"Hi, stranger," said Julia, the front desk manager.

She gave him a hug and an air-kiss on the cheek.

"Welcome back—"

Gil shot her a look.

"I mean welcome *home*," Julia corrected herself.

"What's with this welcome home business? Did Walmart buy you out?"

Julia and Aaron laughed.

"Say good night to the children," Gil said and led Kennedy down the arched hallway.

Kennedy preferred the Canyon Suite because its warm wood and stone interior made him feel like he was in a well-appointed cave, protected from the meat eaters outside. On that evening, the glittering sea of lights from Hollywood and West Los Angeles radiated through the wide picture windows. Gil brought a basket full of papers from the kitchenette and gently placed it on the dining table.

"How about a drink?"

"What's all this?" Kennedy asked.

"Just your mail," Gil said somewhat tentatively as he escaped into the kitchen.

"I can see that. How did it get here?"

Gil emerged with a full tumbler of Japanese whiskey swirling around an ice ball.

"Funny story that." Gil seemed a bit nervous. "The Mailboxes n' More down on Santa Monica, where you had your post office box, went bankrupt. And you had listed this hotel as a physical address when you were shipping something that didn't allow PO return, so they sent everything here before they shut down."

"Bankrupt." Kennedy sipped his whiskey.

"That's what they said. I took the liberty of putting dinner in the oven," Gil said, attempting to change the subject.

"The whole welcome home thing makes sense now. Looks like you figured out my dirty little secret."

"How do you mean?" Gil said, walking into the kitchenette.

Kennedy followed him and leaned against the counter while Gil pulled dinner from the oven.

"That smells unbelievable."

"Porterhouse steak, medium rare. Asparagus. Béarnaise on the side. Do you want to eat on the patio? The weather is still behaving reasonably."

Kennedy set the basket of papers down. "I should have said something about this. I hope it wasn't any trouble."

"No trouble at all," Gil said.

"I guess I was embarrassed about not having an *actual* home," Kennedy said, shooting the elephant in the room. "That's why I told you guys I was from out of town. It's weird, I know. Everyone should have an address, right? I did for a while—a great place in Westwood. Amazing view. But the dust, you know. After three weeks. It's like a quarter-inch thick. And things would happen while I was gone. Water leaks, a smoke alarm the police had to shut off. My neighbors left hate mail under my door. And when you get there, it's empty. A big fat echo. Being on the road so much, I'm just used to this, you know, hotel life. It's more home than home was."

"Thank you for telling me," Gil replied. "Of course, it's none of my damn business, but I do appreciate the courtesy. And for what it's worth, I think you made the right choice. Why should you have to deal with all that nonsense when we can take care of you right here? Better than you can take care of yourself, I would guess."

"I'll drink to that," Kennedy said. He poured Gil a drink and they toasted.

Gil took dinner to the patio and set it up, then came back inside and refreshed Kennedy's glass.

"Is there anything else I can do for you tonight?"

"No. Gil, this is great. The whiskey. The dinner. Not judging my weird life. Way beyond the call of duty. Thank you."

Kennedy reached into his pocket and Gil held up a hand.

"Please, I deal with a universe of assholes every day, if you don't mind me saying so. Being a real person is gratuity enough. And from now on, this is your address for as long as you like. No more dirty PO boxes. Deal?"

"Deal," Kennedy said, feeling the clean whiskey buzz radiate through him.

Gil bowed slightly and headed for the door.

"Hey, Gil," Kennedy said, "will you marry me?"

Gil laughed. "Hell no, you're never home."

7

Good morning, I'm Nic Harcourt. Happy Friday. Welcome to the KCSN morning show. This morning I have a very special guest in the studio, Los Angeles–based singer-songwriter . . ."

Kennedy woke up with a start, looking for the source of the noise, and realized it was coming from the hotel clock radio. He had forgotten to unplug it the night before. After years of living in hotels, he kicked himself for making such a rookie mistake. Especially since, for once, he'd been getting some sleep.

Who uses those fucking things anymore?

He tried to cover his head with a pillow, knowing that too much physical movement would kick his light-sleeper brain into high gear, but it didn't work. He was wide-awake and he was not pleased.

Kennedy eyeballed the device, a refreshed version of the archaic red-eyed monsters of the past, with convenient connectors and a hi-fi speaker, and wondered how it would look in pieces on the Saltillo tile floor. He rolled over, fully prepared to pay for the damage he was about to inflict, and the music that started coming out of it actually slowed his roll. A woman sang with acoustic guitar accompaniment and it was haunting and beautiful. She had the sweet melodic range of a soul singer with a slight rock 'n' roll rasp that rubbed you the right way. Kennedy turned up the volume and listened intently, struck by the familiar sound but unable to place it.

She played two more songs after that and Kennedy listened while the automatic coffeemaker in the kitchenette that Gil had programmed for him kicked on. The aroma of the freshly ground beans cleared away the cobwebs. Morning sunlight was beginning to pool optimistically in places all over the room. Inspired, he fired up an app on his phone to try to identify the singer on the radio. When he saw her name appear on his screen, he did a double take. It was Love.

Sierra Narváez had been Kennedy's sister Belle's best friend in high school. They met freshman year and were instantly thick as thieves, held together by a lightning weld of common interests and a desire to subvert everything about school, youth, society, and whatever had any semblance of hypocrisy, which was just about everything in Los Angeles.

For as long as Kennedy could remember, Sierra had been an excellent guitar player and singer and aspired to be a recording artist. Her wealthy, mixed parents—Basque father, mother from St. Croix—fostered her musical aspirations from a young age by exposing her to everything from baroque chamber music to Motown to punk. Two years after Belle died, Sierra signed with a label. She had a couple of *Billboard* singles at eighteen, and seemed destined for stardom, but found herself being sucked into a world of drugs, sleazy older executives with foul intentions, and artistic imprisonment. So one day she just up and quit, changed her name to Love, and started over, building her career from the ground up, on her terms. Kennedy had very little contact with her in her twenties but heard stories from old friends about how she made a few albums on indie labels, did small-club touring, and worked as a session player.

And there she was, playing an in-studio session with Nic Harcourt, the bellwether DJ and tastemaker who'd made stars of Coldplay and Norah Jones. Hearing her voice brought back a flood of memories Kennedy hadn't conjured in many years.

"That track is off your new album, which is your first in a couple of years, right?" Nic asked.

"Yeah, I really took my time with it. I wanted every song to be well thought out and have a life of its own. I hate the notion of B-side tracks so I work on each track as if it were going to be a single."

"It shows. It's rare for me to listen to a record and not have at least one song I always skip past. But I like them all."

"Thank you. It's really nice to finally get some recognition for my work . . . from the right place, that is."

She sounded the same. Maybe a little more mature than when they were kids, but she still had the same old charmingly smart mouth.

"Let's talk about that. You got a lot of recognition when you were in your late teens. Some say you walked away from a hugely successful pop career."

"They're right. I did. But in that case success was defined as fame and fortune, the tails that wag the dog, as they say. I love music too much to have those things dictate how I make it. And that's what was happening back then. Plus, a lot of nasty old farts were constantly trying to get in my pants."

"Sounds dreadful," Nic said, laughing.

"God, it was. I had to walk away because I knew if I stayed I would wind up hating myself and hating music, which just wasn't acceptable."

"Is that why you changed your name to Love?"

"Exactly. I never wanted to forget why the hell I'm doing this."

"So, the big question is, why haven't I heard any of your post–pop emancipation work until now?"

"Probably because I spend a lot more time touring than recording. To me, playing live is the reason you become a musician. And I love the vagabond life. Playing in small clubs from Miami to . . . Marrakesh, making a lot of friends along the way, living dangerously. Makes it hard to get into the studio. I produced three albums prior to this on my own label but never released them because they weren't right. This is right."

"I couldn't agree more," Nic said. "Tell us about your gig tonight."

"Yeah, I'm really excited. I'm getting back to my roots down in Venice at The Sink, one of the places I played all the time when I was young and dumb."

"I can happily say I've been young and dumb there myself on a number of occasions," Nic said. "And I will be again tonight. What time do you go on?"

"I go on at—"

The clock radio inexplicably shut itself off.

"Son of a bitch!" Kennedy yelled.

He fumbled with it, trying to turn it back on, but when he did Love was already playing another song. Kennedy went online and looked up the show, but it was sold out. He really wanted to go and thought about contacting her, but didn't have any current information. He found her on Facebook and almost hit her up that way, but it felt weird to stalk her on social media after years of very little contact, to score a backstage pass.

Besides, he didn't have time for socializing. He had to get his head in the game and start working on analyzing the threat. Like an auto mechanic rebuilding an engine, he was going to disassemble everything he knew about airports and air travel and scrutinize each piece for flaws and weaknesses. He had no doubt that's what they had done—whoever *they* were—and the fact that intel about the threat even existed meant they were probably well into the planning stage.

Kennedy did his best thinking on the golf course, so he took the hotel car service to his private club in Pacific Palisades. It was still relatively early and the rest of the world had not yet invaded every square inch of asphalt in Los Angeles. When he arrived, a thin marine layer kept everything mercifully cool and shaded. Kennedy had not been to the club for nearly six months and was contented by its steady presence. His father and grandfather had been members. Golf was not just a pastime in his family; it was a religion. But Kennedy had been the only one with the talent to go pro.

When he got out on the course, his game came back to him, energizing his muscle memory and sharpening his senses to the nuances of the track.

Absence makes the heart grow fonder and also improves golf scores.

Being preoccupied with the Homeland memo was the perfect way to keep his intellect out of the game and let his body do what came naturally. As he played he followed his grandfather's advice and treated each shot like a game unto itself. This got him into a methodical groove, addressing every stroke without the distraction of results or thinking ahead. He finished the round at one under par and was only a few strokes off the average score for the middle of the field in a PGA tournament.

Feeling refreshed and clearheaded, he ducked into the lounge for a drink, ready to focus on the memo. He ordered a cold beer and, like with his golf game, addressed the threat in a linear fashion, making sure he didn't skip over any minuscule but important detail.

He'd learned from his Israeli instructors that most attacks fell in the *statement* category. The majority of terrorists were amateurs who often lacked the resources or intelligence to pull off something profoundly damaging, like 9/11. Instead they opted for a headline. The upside of this category was that the attacks were usually smaller in scale. The downside was that they were often successful because the attacker was willing to die to carry out the plan. Like with Japanese kamikaze pilots and suicide bombers, this approach offered a major strategic advantage because of its totally unpredictable nature.

Kennedy hadn't gotten any new intel from Wes yet, but based on the fact that this threat had grabbed the attention of several intelligence entities, it seemed like it would turn into more than a statement. Osama bin Laden didn't merely make headlines run red when he attacked the United States. To him it was more a military offensive designed to inflict extensive, even debilitating, damage on the target—not just the thousands of people on the planes and in the buildings, but also the whole country. Bin Laden knew that it would not only strike fear in the hearts of the "enemy," but it would also put America on the defensive, causing us to lash out in irrational ways that increased our vulnerability. In that way, it was guerrilla warfare, a highly effective approach for the Davids of the world looking to knock Goliath on his ass.

The only way to approach this threat was to assume it would be even bigger than 9/11. That was the nature of the beast. Whoever was planning it very likely wanted to trump all previous attacks, if not just for ego then also for impact. It was scary to think that bin Laden had weakened the United States, dividing it against itself, but that's exactly what had happened. The toll that two wars had taken on the country, along with the political carnage that made government barely able to function in any kind of constructive way, might be the camel's back—and someone might be thinking he had just the straw to break it.

"For someone who just dismantled that course, your celebration skills leave a lot to be desired."

Kennedy looked up, startled. A slim, muscular Hispanic man in his forties, dressed impeccably in all-black golf attire, was standing next to his table. The man smiled, sharp features framing perfect white teeth. He looked like an actor or politician. As if on cue, the server dropped two neat scotches on the table.

"Buy you one?" the man asked politely.

"Be my guest."

They toasted and drank. Kennedy was not pleased about the interruption, but the fact that the man had chosen the best scotch in the bar softened the blow.

"After I heard about your round, I saw you up on the club championship board. Eleven wins. Pretty impressive. Unheard of actually. Ever go pro?"

"Thought about it, but—"

"You should have. Juarez."

They shook hands.

"Thanks."

The only thing Kennedy hated more than watching golf on television was talking about it.

"What's your handicap?"

"Five," Kennedy lied.

"Bullshit," Juarez said, gently confrontational.

"I'm not looking to team up or anything. I don't really do club tourneys."

"Me neither," Juarez said. "There just aren't any real players around here anymore. Bunch of stuck-up gringos drinking beer in carts, which I can't believe they even allow. No offense."

"None taken. I'm not a fan of the gringos either."

Kennedy finished his scotch, hoping that would facilitate Juarez's exit, but the guy waved the waitress over with two more glasses before Kennedy could protest.

"*Salud*," Juarez said, raising his glass.

"Cheers," Kennedy said, raising his own.

Kennedy noticed a copper bracelet on Juarez's wrist.

"What's that, some kind of power band?" Kennedy asked.

"Side business. My kid's going to private school next year. Gringos love these things."

"Guaranteed to make you a scratch golfer," Kennedy joked.

"And improve your sex life," Juarez flipped back. "The only cool thing is, it has sports tracker tech, like Nike FuelBand. So, people know your *real* handicap and don't have to bug you about it."

"Two," Kennedy said.

"That's more like it," Juarez said.

He fished another bracelet out of his pocket and handed it to Kennedy. It was brand-new, wrapped in a clear plastic sleeve.

"I don't have any cash—"

"I'm not hustling you. Having the Ben Hogan of the club wear one is great advertising for me." He laughed.

They had another drink and shot the shit for a while. Juarez wasn't like the other morons he'd grown to hate at the club, the ones who had money and political suck but couldn't swing a club to break a window, let alone par. Juarez knew the game and didn't bore Kennedy bragging about what he had or whining about what he didn't. When they parted ways, they exchanged business cards and promised to try to play a round sometime. Kennedy hoped it wasn't bullshit, something people in LA had developed into an art. Talking to Juarez made him realize that the one thing he needed to make his life less disconnected and transient was a friend.

————

Back at the hotel, he couldn't help but wonder if he'd heard Sierra—Love—on the radio that morning for a reason. Maybe Belle had spirited into the room that night and turned on that goddamned alarm clock? That was definitely her style. And she would be pissed if he wimped out and didn't at least try to go to the show, *after I busted my ass to come back from the dead,* she would say.

Before he could talk himself out of it, he was in the hotel car service, on his way to Venice Beach.

8

his is a bad idea.

It was 9:00 P.M. and the freeway was inexplicably jammed. Kennedy had been in the car for forty-five minutes and they still had a long way to go. The whiskey buzz was starting to wear off and he was getting queasy from the driver stopping and lurching, fighting for every mile.

"Maybe we should just head back to the hotel," Kennedy said.

"At this point, it may take you twice as long to get back as it would to get to your destination, but I can turn around if you like," the driver said, eyeing Kennedy in the rearview.

"Fuck it. Let's stay the course."

"Of course. Would you like a mint?"

"A what?"

"A mint. Or a stick of gum?"

"Why?"

"Maybe you're meeting a lady tonight?"

"What makes you say that?"

"No reason, sir. How about some music?"

Kennedy stared at the parking lot of cars ahead of them on the freeway. He *was* nervous—but not in the way the driver had implied. He had to admit he'd been avoiding Belle's best friend ever since his sister died. She reminded him too much of something he could never get back. A month after Belle's funeral, Sierra had been distraught, unable to sleep or eat, battling severe depression. She had come to Kennedy, driving all the way from Santa Monica to Stanford, saying she needed to talk to someone who felt like she did.

The problem was, Kennedy had wanted to weld himself shut in his iron grief and had no desire to share feelings. When she arrived at his dorm, looking for a shoulder to cry on, he managed to put on a convincing act that he was there for her, but all of her reminiscing made him want to retreat even further into himself. After that, their communications became less frequent. She'd tried to stay in touch, but Kennedy always made excuses. Until he'd run out, and she stopped calling. And now here he was, at The Sink, wringing his hands like a freshman prom date.

The show had started by the time Kennedy arrived. It was sold out and the club was full to capacity, so the velvet-rope jockey told him to get lost. Kennedy remembered the kitchen entrance Sierra had shown him and his friends how to break into with a credit card when they were in high school. He crept around back and was blown away to see they hadn't fixed the lock after all those years. He used one of his many frequent-flier cards to slip in the door and found the last square foot of standing room.

When the pot haze cleared, he saw her on the stage. He barely recognized her at first. When she was younger, she'd always been a tomboy, an effortless star at every sport she played and quick to eschew the fashion rag trappings of teenhood. But now, with her dark bronze skin covered in exotic tattoos and platinum blond dreadlocks artfully tangled on her head like Medusa's snakes, she was an otherworldly beauty, radiating cool all over the room. Kennedy was captivated, and "Love" seemed a far more appropriate name for her now. Most of what he'd remembered about Sierra had been consumed by her stage persona. And even more fitting, her music pulled emotional strings in him to the point of breaking.

By the end of the last encore, he was at a loss as to what to do. Watching the adoring fans who knew every word to her songs made him feel like an imposter and punctuated the fact that he had thrown away what could have been a great friendship over the years. What was he going to say to her, if they could even get five minutes alone? He felt compelled to apologize for his behavior but knew that would only make things more awkward, because then he would be admitting he had avoided her on purpose. The last thing she needed coming off the high of a great show was a pedestrian walk down memory lane. He was an idiot to have thought they could pick up where they'd left off. *Too much water under the bridge*, he told himself. And Love was curious, like Belle. She would ask him a lot of questions, and the answers would expose his sad, transient existence. He opted to slip out and spare them both the agony.

He went out the same way he came in, through the back kitchen door.

"Freeze!" a voice called out behind him as he stepped into the cool night air.

9

ove was standing there in the amber glow of a naked bulb hanging over the club's garbage cans. She smiled at him, the glint in her eye a spark of knowing she had busted him cold.

"Oh hey," he said sheepishly.

"Don't oh hey me, dude. Trying to sneak out the back. I should punch you."

"I wasn't—"

"Please." She laughed. "I'm the one who showed you that door the night of the Descendents show when *you* wanted to burn a joint to get away from Charlotte what's-her-name who was hammered on the bottle of Rumple Minze she stole from her dad's liquor cabinet and kept trying to stick her tongue down your throat."

"Jesus, how do you remember all of that?"

She tossed her cigarette aside and hugged him.

"You're forgiven," she said, pulling away to get a good look at him. "Long time. Where the fuck have you been? I thought I was seeing a ghost."

"It's good to see you too . . . Love."

"How do you like the new name? Better than dumb old yuppie Sierra, right?"

"Absolutely. It might take some getting used to, but it suits you . . . and your music."

"Oh, so I might see you again this decade?"

"Yeah, of course." He wanted to crawl under a rock, and she knew it.

"You're a real piece of work, you know that? You come here unannounced, thinking you're all incognito at the back of the club—the lone tall corporate gunslinger in a sea of drug-addled kidniks—don't think for a second I didn't clock you the moment you slunk in, and then you pull this exit-stage-left shit. I'm sorry but *what the fuck* barely covers it."

"Sorry . . . It's been so long. I didn't want you to feel, I guess, obligated to talk to me after the show. You know? With all the fans . . . I know, it's stupid."

"Pretty much. Dude, it's *because* I haven't seen you in an eternity that I would want to talk to you. I mean, don't think for a minute I'm not pissed at you for shining me on all these years. But you and Belle are family. Fuck it, it's great to see you!"

She hugged him again and squeezed him so hard he couldn't breathe. Then she lit them both a cigarette.

"I don't—"

"I hate smoking alone. Just pretend."

Kennedy accepted the cigarette and tried to actually smoke it in an attempt to prove to Love that he hadn't surrendered what was left of his cool to Brooks Brothers. But the coughing fit after the first drag killed that dream.

"Thanks for playing." She laughed again.

"I never could hack those. Not even when I was trying to drink myself to death back in college."

"I need to quit so I don't end up singing through a hole in my neck with one of those electronic monster boxes."

Kennedy laughed. She always could crack him up.

"What'd you think of the show?" she asked, genuinely interested.

"I think the roaring garbage fire they call the music business is completely fucked for not making you a megastar."

"They don't like my politics."

She pulled open her thin leather vest and revealed a tattoo of Shiva holding the severed heads of Jesus and Michael Jackson just below her collar line and just above the black lace of her camisole.

"Good for you," Kennedy said, glowing red. "And for the rest of us. I haven't seen music that good for . . . ever."

"That's not saying much, is it?" she said.

"No." He laughed again. "But you don't need validation from the square business world. Look at all those adoring fans in there."

"Is that where you come from now? Planet Square?"

"Unfortunately, yes."

Love smiled but also looked concerned.

"Dude, seriously, where have you been?"

"Where haven't I been? I pretty much live on an airplane."

"That is *not* healthy."

"I know, but that's my job."

"You could quit."

"And do what?"

"I don't know, *anything*. You went to Stanford. You're a successful entrepreneur. Yes, I keep tabs on you, dumbass. You're smart. You probably have a shitload of money squirreled away because you don't have a house, a wife with credit cards, and three kids like most guys your age. And with a little work on the wardrobe, you could hop the last shuttle off Planet Square."

"Let's not get carried away." Kennedy smiled.

"Do you like it? Your job?"

"Hmm. Like it . . ."

She made a loud game show buzzer sound.

"Yes or no question. Clearly, it's a no."

"It's important. I like *that*."

"You can be important without spreading yourself so thin there's nothing but an empty jar left for you . . . and everyone else."

"Now you're speaking in lyrics," Kennedy chided.

"Maybe," she confessed with a shy grin, and lit another cigarette.

Kennedy pretended to hold a robot speaker box up to his throat.

". . . there's nothing but an empty jar left for you . . ." he sang in his best robot voice, throwing both of them into fits of laughter.

When they caught their breath, Kennedy took a long look at Love and felt like she was the type of person he needed to help him feel real again, at least once in a while.

"I'm just going to admit it," he said. "I've been a complete dick."

She held up her hand.

"Water under the bridge. You're here now. Which is awesome. And I take it you've turned over a new leaf and I can count on more of your presence in the future."

"Yes," he said firmly. "Absolutely."

"Good," she said, kissing him on the cheek unexpectedly. "Got to jump. Heading to New York tonight for a few East Coast dates. Maybe we should exchange numbers, like people who don't hate each other."

"We definitely should," Kennedy said.

She held out her hand.

"Phone please."

He entered the password and handed it to her. She entered her own number and picked up her phone when it rang. She handed his back.

"Hello, Kennedy?"

He held his phone to his ear.

"Yes, Love."

"Call me sometime, you big lug."

Belle had always called him that, and hearing it again choked him up a bit.

"Promise," he said.

She smiled and hung up.

"You better or I'll hunt you down and have your legs broken."

Love slipped back into the club through their secret entrance, leaving a smoke ring halo where she'd been standing.

10

Later that night, Kennedy restlessly paced his dark hotel suite. Seeing Love had made him feel more connected, but it had also brought up a lot of pain about Belle. Memories of the three of them kept coming, keeping him awake. And it dawned on him that the reason he'd cut Love off was not so much because she reminded him of Belle, but more because she reminded him of how *he* was before Belle died. The night before she was killed, he had treated Belle terribly. That wasn't like him. It was almost as if he'd been stuck for fourteen years in that all-business bullshit martyr role he'd played with her that night. Which was why he felt the need to work himself to death to protect total strangers.

The idea that his entire career path might be some kind of psychological grief reaction based more in repressed emotions than in logic made him feel like an idiot. He had always prided himself on making rational, fact-based decisions, and now he was questioning one of the biggest ones. And once he got into the second-guessing game, no part of his life was safe. Had he avoided relationships, both platonic and romantic, simply out of fear? The way he had isolated himself was starting to feel more and more pathetic against the foil of Love's open and truthful personality.

He was preparing to hold his nose and jump into the deep end of gloom when his mobile phone rang. Blocked number. He ignored it. Couldn't be bothered in his moment of self-flagellation. Then it rang again and he looked at the time: 3:10 A.M.

"Who the hell is this?" he answered.

"Monsieur," a man with a heavy French accent said on the other end of the line.

"I said who is this? It's three in the morning."

"My apologies. I work with Direction Générale de l'Aviation Civile in Paris and I am calling about a rather urgent matter. We would like to engage your services."

"Now?"

"As I said, the matter is urgent."

"How urgent?"

"I am unable to discuss it with you over the phone. We would like to fly you to Paris for a meeting. Our private jet is already in Los Angeles and can have you back within twenty-four hours."

"That's a bit presumptuous, don't you think?"

"You may name your fee."

"Call me back in ten minutes."

"Of course."

Kennedy hung up and considered the offer. What difference did it make if he went? It's not like he had anything better to do. And they did say he could name his price. Seemed stupid to shoo away the golden goose for no good reason. And Paris in autumn would be spectacular. This time he would stay for a few days, on their dime of course, and enjoy the city, take a little vacation courtesy of the French government. He might even have time to pop over to London and pick Wes's brain some more. And the man did say *private jet* . . . The phone rang again.

"I can fit it in," he answered.

"Very good, monsieur. We will send a car in the morn—"

"That's all right. I'll drive myself. Text me the details."

———

Kennedy took an Uber at dawn and gave his driver the directions the Frenchman sent after their phone call. He ended up at a small private terminal just off the Imperial Highway adjacent to LAX. There was no sign of anyone, and the front door was locked. Out on the apron, he saw a

Bombardier Global 8000, one of the largest private jets in the world. But it hardly looked ready for flight. The windows were covered, the wheels chocked, and there were no pilots or fuel attendants. He looked at his watch to make sure he had the right time and walked around to the gate. It was open, its heavy padlock dangling.

"Hello?" he called out.

The pilots have to be here, he thought. *Only an asshole would leave a sixty-five-million-dollar jet unattended while they went out for a Frappuccino.*

He walked through the gate, out to the apron.

"Hello? Anybody here?"

No response. No sign of anyone.

"Okay, I'm out of here," he said to himself.

"Can I help you?" a man's voice asked behind him.

Startled, Kennedy whipped around. The man was wearing a black balaclava, pointing a gun in his face.

"What the fuck—" Kennedy began.

"Passport," the man said sharply.

Kennedy handed it over. The mask looked at it, then shot him in the chest.

Kennedy panicked and looked down, but instead of a gaping bullet wound, he saw the red fletch of a tranquilizer dart jutting out just below his collarbone.

"Have a nice flight," the mask said.

Kennedy fell to his knees, his vision blurring. Four more men dressed in black, also wearing balaclavas, surrounded him and held him upright. When he lost consciousness, he fell into a lightless abyss, the voice of Belle echoing around him.

I don't want to go alone.

11

When Kennedy came to, he was disoriented, blinded by a black canvas sack wrapped around his head, and bound tightly at the wrists and ankles. He felt like he was suffocating and struggled violently to free himself. After a few minutes of bellowing obscenities and thrashing like a caged animal, he heard the sound of the engines and realized he was crammed in the baggage compartment in the tail of the Bombardier Global 8000, and they were airborne.

He drew in long, ragged breaths to calm his nerves in the claustrophobic space, but the onslaught of worst-case scenarios invading his thoughts held him right on the knife's edge of panic. He had to force himself to focus on the facts of the situation. Like a golf shot: address every angle independently and avoid the big picture at all costs. *Who the fuck were they?* No clue. Not enough information. *Why did they want him?* That was easy. He knew more about US airport security than the head of the TSA. He was a high-value target and he was a civilian—the perfect mark.

His abductors had access to one of the most expensive private jets in the world, meaning he was dealing with a well-funded group. Maybe they were the ones behind the recent threat? It made sense. If someone wanted to know every possible security weakness at all the major airports in the United States, Kennedy would be the one to beat the information out of. He could also tell them if anything had been done to safeguard airports in *response* to the threat. He'd have laughed out loud at the irony if he weren't facing torture. They were going to do all the things to him that he'd read about the CIA doing to terror suspects, things that made him sick to think about.

The internal panic voice reared its ugly head again.

I'm not trained for this. I can't even hold my fucking breath in a swimming pool for more than thirty seconds, let alone survive waterboarding.

"Shut the fuck up!" he yelled to himself inside the sweltering black hood.

He heard and felt the telltale signs that the airplane had begun its descent. The clock was ticking. He knew he was a dead man, but he had to keep his head screwed on straight in case that one chance in hell to escape presented itself.

Back to the angles. *Where were they taking him?* The airplane had a range of nearly eight thousand nautical miles. Depending on how long he'd been out, they could have taken him almost anywhere in the world. When he was losing consciousness, he was pretty sure he'd heard his abductors speaking Arabic. Having lived in Israel, he knew how it sounded. The man who shot him with the dart spoke English but had a slight French accent, which meant he might be North African. The connection to France was potentially strengthened by the type of airplane—Bombardier, a French-Canadian manufacturer.

If they were North African, they might be landing in Morocco, or more likely Algeria—somewhere they could hide him away for an indeterminate amount of time with zero cooperation from the local government if, by some miracle, someone came looking for him. This thought threw Kennedy into a very dark place. He was more than likely being taken to a hostile country to be tortured to death. When they were finished with him, they would dump his corpse like garbage, toothless and without fingertips or eyeballs, to make identification impossible. And no one was going to come looking for him. He hadn't told a soul he was going to Paris, and there were no customs records or travel documentation to track him. He was about to become the ghost Love had been talking about the night before.

The plane landed and taxied for several minutes. Kennedy listened for the sounds of other planes, but the world outside was silent. He assumed they'd taken him to a remote airstrip, which made sense, considering their cargo. He heard a door open and several pairs of strong hands dragged him onto the floor of the main cabin. He felt a hand on his neck and hoped the bag was coming off, but the hand only checked his pulse.

"Can someone please take this hood off?" he whispered hoarsely.

No reply. They weren't even talking to each other.

"Please—" he began, but a needle pricked the side of his neck and he was out.

12

Freezing, foul-smelling water thrown in his face brought Kennedy back to life, and he woke up shivering on a concrete floor that stank of bleach and old blood. They had taken the bag off his head, and his hands and feet were no longer bound. Bright fluorescent overhead lights burned into his eyes. When he could finally focus, he saw he was in a massive meat locker, surrounded by pig carcasses and sides of beef dangling from metal hooks on heavy chains. Bone saws, long knives, and cleavers big enough to fell a tree hung on the wall above a huge steel prep table.

Using what felt like his last ounce of strength, he dragged himself off the floor and got to his feet. His legs, screaming in pain with the jabs of a million pins and needles from hours of bad circulation, buckled, and he wasn't sure if his dead-fish arms could break his fall. A man grabbed him by the arm from behind, steadying him. When he walked around to face Kennedy, he wasn't wearing his balaclava, but Kennedy could tell by the eyes, deep brown and softly menacing, that it was the man who had shot him with the tranq dart at LAX. Definitely Arab, with a full beard and a scar under his eye.

"Can you hear me?" the man asked.

"Yes, I can hear you," Kennedy croaked.

"Good. Do you know your name?"

"Fuck you."

No response.

"Do you know what year it is?"

"What do you want, asshole?" Kennedy asked through gritted teeth.

The man rested the barrel of a gun on Kennedy's forehead.

"I'm not playing with darts anymore, so you should be more polite."

He walked to the door of the meat locker and knocked, signaling his men to unlock it from the outside. It sounded like they were using a padlock, which meant that the door was not going to be a viable escape route. Two more men entered, and someone outside locked them in again. Both were clean-shaven and also appeared to be Arabs. One of them was short and runty with fierce glowering eyes, and carried a military-style duffel bag. The other was heavyset, with a pockmarked face and huge burn-scarred hands.

They spoke to the man with the beard in what Kennedy thought might be Farsi, their voices intense and increasingly argumentative. During their heated exchange, Kennedy scanned every inch of the meat locker and saw no additional exits. There were large blood drains in the floor though, making it possible to smash through the tile and squeeze into a drainpipe. It wasn't a great option, especially when Kennedy thought about crawling through coagulated animal blood, but it would make it difficult for them to extract him.

A deep, mechanical sound shook the room. Elevator motor. The drains on the floor probably meant he was in the basement, so he might be able to find a way out if he could get to an upper floor. *What else?* The cold air needed to preserve the meat was likely being pumped into the room from the ceiling, as it would be too heavy to rise. He examined the ceiling for vents. There were a few, but nothing large enough to accommodate him. It was beginning to look like the blood drain was his only option when he saw a large square opening—maybe four feet by four feet—on the ceiling in the far corner of the room. *Maybe an HVAC service port?*

His mind was working overtime, analyzing every detail of the room. In the corner were stacked boxes with French words written on them, and what appeared to be a safety instruction sign, also in French, was riveted above a wall-mounted first aid kit. If he was in France, rather than North Africa, then it was possible the opening in the ceiling was put there originally as a bomb shelter escape hatch. Hundreds of old buildings in France and England had them during the endless German bombing raids of World War II. And they were often in the basement—the equivalent of a concrete-fortified bunker. If he was right about the location, and if this building were World War II era, and if it indeed was a bomb shelter door . . .

Kennedy's deductions were interrupted when he heard the heavy zipper rip open the duffel bag. The bearded one reached in and handed his heavyset associate a long serrated knife. Then he handed the runt a video camcorder. As they zip-tied his hands, Kennedy understood why the ISIS beheading victims he had seen in photographs just before their execution looked like deer in headlights. He was going to be slaughtered like one of the pigs mocking him at the end of a metal hook. The panic racing through his veins nearly made him pass out, but he bit his tongue hard, drawing blood, and the pain kept him conscious.

The heavyset man grabbed Kennedy by the hair and showed him the dirty knife.

"I will ask you questions, yes?" said the bearded man.

"Yes," Kennedy said, trying to sound strong.

"If you do not give me the answers I want, he will cut off your head like one of these pigs and your American friends will see you on CNN."

The man with the knife grabbed a hanging pig carcass and sawed its head off in a few sickening strokes. Kennedy tried not to puke.

"If you tell me what I want to know, I will shoot you in the head and you will die quickly, with honor."

"I will cooperate," Kennedy said.

The runt with the camera started arguing with the bearded man. It heated up quickly, and the bearded man backhanded him.

"He says you are a soft little woman who knows nothing and I should kill you as a political statement," the bearded man said. "I hope you have something useful to say."

"What do you want to know?"

"TSA security-pad codes for every major airport in US. Highest-level access."

Kennedy felt the blood rush out of his face. He hadn't memorized them. There were too many. And his TSA contacts usually escorted him around anyway. It must have been written all over his face because the runt started in again, pointing and shouting at Kennedy. He and the bearded man almost came to blows again. The bearded man angrily bellowed at both of his cohorts, and they all went back outside the meat locker, where they got into a violent shouting match.

Kennedy knew it was time to do or die. He brought his arms under his butt and wriggled until he could step through and get his hands in front of him. Then he raked the zip tie on a bone saw blade until it cut through and freed his hands. He grabbed one of the loose carcass hooks from a metal basket and slipped the hook tine through the latch on the door, locking it from the inside. It would hold, but not for long.

Moving quickly, he grabbed the bone saw and a long extension cord hanging near the prep table. As he ran to the back corner of the room, the men shattered the glass on the door's porthole window and opened fire, but they didn't have a clear shot through all the carcasses. Kennedy took cover and looked for a way to get up to the panel on the ceiling. One of the pig carcasses was hanging on a chain next to it. He plugged in the bone saw and secured the cord so it couldn't come unplugged, then slung the saw and extension cord over his shoulder and climbed up to the top of the carcass.

He ripped into the ceiling panel with the bone saw, cutting through the ancient plaster with ease and revealing the metal door he was hoping to find. It had a handle cut into it, so he stuffed his hand in it and pulled with all his might, but it was rusted shut. He cut the corroded hinges away with the saw and slammed the butt of it into the metal door until it broke free and fell to the floor.

As he climbed into the large metal shaft, the men outside the meat locker snapped the tine off the meat hook in the latch and rushed through the door. While Kennedy crawled through the dark, narrow passage, they sprinted across the room and climbed up after him. Kennedy was moving through the shaft as quickly as he could, cutting and bruising his elbows and knees on the rusty metal. He saw a light at the end of the tunnel when he heard one of the men coming after him in the shaft.

"Stop or I'll shoot you!" the bearded man yelled.

Kennedy pressed on, fueled by a surge of adrenaline. He reached a large duct vent with light coming through from the room on the other side. He slammed all of his body weight against the vent and fell headlong through the opening, landing hard on the floor of a commercial kitchen. While an army of kitchen staff stared in disbelief, Kennedy rose and sprinted through the swinging door and down a dark hallway. He reached a set of stairs, pounded up them, and ran down another hallway. Footsteps were coming close behind. He could hear the murmur of a crowd of people at the end of the hallway. He ran toward the sound, desperate for help. There was a swinging service door at the end of the hall. He burst through it and froze. A hundred or so well-dressed people having lunch in a posh dining room turned and stared at him in horror. In an instant, he knew where he was.

The restaurant Les Ambassadeurs at the Hôtel de Crillon in Paris.

13

Kennedy's eyes darted around the room, where he'd dined on several occasions with European clients. He was too shell-shocked to think or move. Mercifully, a woman with comforting eyes and a warm smile materialized in front of him. Her chic, understated suit gave her the air of a manager or concierge.

"Monsieur," she said with an American accent. *"Puis-je vous aider?"*

"Yes, I need to—"

"American?"

He nodded, unable to speak through the wad of cotton in his mouth.

"Me too."

She extended a manicured hand. He shook it and she led him to the lobby.

"Where are you from?" she asked.

"Los Angeles," he said, surprising himself.

Her eyes lit up.

"I'm from San Francisco."

"Oh . . . " he started awkwardly.

"You didn't tell me your name," she said.

"I know," he said, obsessively surveying the room, looking for his captors.

They stopped walking.

"Is everything all right?"

Kennedy's face flushed. The woman touched his arm. He flinched.

"Have you been a guest here before?"

"Many times," he said as the room spun slowly.

"I thought I recognized you. We have a hospitality suite. There's a phone, as well as some toiletries and light refreshments. Would you like to use it for a couple of hours?"

He was so grateful he almost burst into tears. They rode the elevator to one of the upper floors and the door opened into the foyer of an expansive suite. She led Kennedy into the sitting room, and he stopped cold.

His captors were all there, smiling at him.

"Relax and have a drink," she said pleasantly. "It's not what you think."

She sat him down in a leather club chair and poured him a glass of his favorite Japanese whiskey. Kennedy looked at the men in the room. With their normal demeanors, they looked like young professionals instead of violent thugs.

He couldn't speak.

"My name is Alia. I'm a senior operations officer in the CIA's Clandestine Service. These men are not terrorists. They're field agents."

Kennedy felt dizzy and dropped his whiskey tumbler. One of the men refilled his glass and handed it to him with a rueful smile.

"I want to apologize for the stressful nature of our evaluation," Alia said.

"Evaluation?"

"For a new intelligence-gathering program I want you to be a part of."

"I'm sorry, but you're not making any fucking sense."

"I'm recruiting you."

"Recruiting me?" he said cynically. "As what?"

"An asset."

She handed him a thick file folder with the CIA emblem and the word CLASSIFIED emblazoned across the top.

"Go ahead, read it."

He opened it. It was a highly detailed dossier on him, with photographs and surveillance documents tracking his movements over the past three years. Cold sweat filmed over his palms.

"I had to be sure I was making the right choice," Alia explained. "After

tonight, there's no doubt in my mind. What do you think? Would you consider working for us?"

"Thirty minutes ago you had me thinking I was going to be the next
ISIS sideshow in the YouTube circus. Why wouldn't I want to work for
someone like that?"

"I don't blame you for being angry," she said. "And I wouldn't have
done this if it weren't vital to national security. Would you like something
to eat? I can call—"

"Just get to the point," he said.

"That will be all for today, gentlemen," she said.

Her men filed out of the room.

"The program I want you to join is called Red Carpet, and it's the first
CIA operation of its kind ever to take place on American soil. You've read
the recent terror threat memo from Homeland Security?"

Kennedy nodded.

"The part about this being *a large-scale, coordinated attack on an indeterminate number of US airports* was taken directly from a briefing I sent
to Homeland two years ago. When I learned about this plot from our field
agents, I knew we would need a specialized asset to help us gather intel.
You."

"What could I possibly know that the CIA doesn't?"

"Your expertise in airport security is practically legendary. I'd venture
to guess you know more than the head of TSA."

"That's not saying much. And there are plenty of experts in my field."

"True, but they're mostly think-tank types. You're always in the field,
touching base with your network of clients, keeping your boots on the
ground. You're a road warrior, a million-mile flier who drinks with pilots,
knows flight attendants by name, and more important, they know *you* by
name. Even if I had a full decade to do it, I could never train the best field
agent to know what you know and move in your circles. And you have no
family ties that could be used to leverage you. You're the perfect lone wolf,
in my opinion."

"Thanks for making me feel even worse about my life."

"Your work is your life. Nothing wrong with that. It's mine too. And
if you were making a difference in that clusterfuck of DHS and TSA, you
would be a lot happier. Work with us and I can guarantee you'll make a
difference. Interested?"

"If it's anything like your test, absolutely not."

"I needed to see how you would function under extreme duress. You actually tested higher than most of the former military officers they're always sending our way. You didn't crack, kept your head, and found a way out. Quite frankly, we never expected you to actually escape. Finding that bomb shelter door was brilliant. I know seasoned field agents who would never have worked that scenario. But, as I said, the test is not the job. I just needed to know how you would react if, by some off chance, you were in a similar scenario. Since you're a civilian, we have to go with a trial-by-fire method."

"I'm flattered, but alive. What do you mean when you say *by some off chance, I were in a similar scenario*?"

"Suffice to say this will be far safer, statistically, than driving in Los Angeles. All we want you to do is provide information we don't have the resources to gather."

"Why do I have the feeling you're telling me what I want to hear?"

"I don't blame you for thinking that. It is the CIA after all. It's not like we have a stellar reputation. But the reality is that our reputation is largely fictional, thanks to books and movies. The truth is, being a spy might be one of the most boring professions on the planet. It's a hell of a lot more drudgery than danger. And we would only need you for a short assignment."

"How long?" Kennedy asked.

"Your services would be engaged for the duration of our investigation into the terror threat, which I don't anticipate will last longer than six months, and you will be paid very well for that service."

"If I wouldn't be in any danger, why put me through the stress test?"

"Because I don't just want you to be a part of this team. I want you to lead it."

"Come again?"

"I have some of our best analysts and field agents, but my leadership can only go so far," Alia said. "You have the greatest depth of knowledge relevant to this operation. The others are more utility players, but you would be the quarterback, running the field when I'm needed elsewhere. And I *will* be needed elsewhere."

Kennedy took a deep breath and sat back in his chair. Alia's offer excited him in ways nothing else had for quite some time. And, oddly enough, he'd be getting exactly what he was hoping for if he truly wanted to help stop the threat. The whole terrorist Punk'd thing she'd just put him through started to make sense in a sick way—he couldn't imagine the pressure of managing a "normal" citizen in such a critical operation. He had to admit, he had impressed himself with how he'd behaved under pressure. He remembered those applications he'd shredded after 9/11 and wondered if he might have had what it takes to be CIA after all.

"I need to think about this."

"Sleep on it. If you're still interested, you can meet the team in the morning."

She got up and retrieved a distressed-leather overnight bag from the armoire.

"Your passport, wallet, phone, a change of clothes, and some toiletries."

"Where am I staying?"

"Here." She smiled.

"Thank you."

"My pleasure," she said, walking out.

"I'll meet the team tomorrow," he called after her.

She brightened. "Are you sure?"

"Yes. That's the only way I'll be able to really tell you yes or no."

"Spoken like a true team leader. Have a nice evening."

"Thank you, I think."

After she left, Kennedy looked around at the suite, which was likely 15,000 euros a night, and felt like he was dreaming. Everything that had just happened was impossibly surreal, and his exhausted mind didn't have the energy to analyze it. The whiskey had burned through his empty stomach and gone straight to his head, sapping him of the last twitch of energy he had left. He laid down on the bed, wondering if he'd been drugged again, and passed out.

14

Kennedy woke up to the sound of someone knocking at his suite door. He looked at the bedside clock. It was a little after 9:00 P.M. He was still fatigued but no longer felt like a zombie. He got up and opened the door. A bright-eyed young woman in a suit was standing there, smiling broadly and holding two envelopes.

"Bonsoir, monsieur. Did you have a nice rest?"

"Yes, thank you."

"I am Camille, the concierge. I have made dinner and cocktail reservations for you this evening."

She handed him the envelopes.

"Thank you, Camille, but I'm kind of beat—"

She frowned ever so slightly but kept her chin up and pressed him.

"These are some of the best places in Paris and impossible to get in even if you call months in advance. Are you sure you don't want to treat yourself after your journey? It is all compliments of your colleague . . ."

Kennedy could tell he would crush Camille's little birdlike heart if he didn't comply. And soaking Alia for a massive dinner tab was the least he could do after she'd put him through hell.

"All right. I'll go. *Merci*, Camille."

She nearly burst with happiness.

"*Merci*, monsieur. Our car service will be waiting. *Bonne soirée!*"

She hopped away, and Kennedy went back into the suite to shower, change, and, in a glass of Japanese whiskey, find some courage to face the outside world. The clothes Alia had given him were a huge improvement over his own—tailored dark gray wool trousers, slim-fit black dress shirt, finished off with a buttery black leather jacket and boots. He looked like a hit man and vowed to burn his wardrobe when he got back to LA.

Dinner was exceptional. The place the zealous concierge had chosen for him was diminutive, with ten tables, and no menu. The chef prepared the meal, poured the wine, and Kennedy dutifully ate and drank until he thought he was going to burst. After dinner, the chef passed out small, hand-rolled cigarillos, and most of the guests enjoyed a smoke and a digestif on the tiny brick patio with a view of the Paris Opera House.

His second reservation was at a nameless speakeasy built into ancient catacombs beneath a cathedral in the Marais neighborhood. The drinks were works of mixology art and the clientele a collage of magazine-clipping beautiful people with brains and charm to match. When the bartender found out Kennedy was American, he introduced him to some other Americans and a few Brits gathered round the taps. They made all the Botox and bad dye job starfuckers in LA look like deranged zoo animals.

When his new friends invited him to join them on their bar crawl, he respectfully declined. He was keen to have time to himself to think more about the job and reckoned he shouldn't show up to meet Alia and her team with jet lag and a hangover. He took his drink to a quiet corner table and thought long and hard about her offer. He didn't know what they were going to ask of him, but he was fairly certain they wouldn't have put him through the three-ring terrorist-abduction circus if they didn't expect a pound of flesh.

The thing was, they were handing him exactly what he wanted on a silver platter. He would be able to pursue the would-be attackers in a meaningful way, with the CIA juggernaut at the tip of the spear. One of his stipulations for taking the job was going to be that they pay him enough to walk away from his consulting business. He had a feeling, based on Alia's apparent financial trappings, that that would not be a problem. Still, he couldn't just gloss over the fact that he was dealing with the CIA, the same people responsible for the Bay of Pigs, Watergate, and Iran-Contra. It was not an organization heralded as having the best interests of American citizens in mind. And like Operation CHAOS—a domestic spying program the CIA started in the 1950s, long before the NSA initiated it—this could easily have damaging effects on peoples' privacy and constitutional rights.

As intriguing as it was, he had to be honest with himself. Getting into bed with them was like curling up next to a pit of vipers, and he would need to take precautions to protect himself. On the other hand, the CIA's tactical approach and relative freedom to operate with impunity was one of the reasons they got things done. They tended to shoot first and let a congressional committee ask questions later.

His phone buzzed in his pocket. He'd just received an e-mail from Noah Kruz's VIP W(inner)s Circle, an invitation-only service for frequent seminar attendees. Ironically, the title of Kruz's thought for the day was "The Decisive Animal."

When people say they are making a "gut decision," they are talking about instinct. Before our brains had the ability to intellectualize everything through the neocortex, we, like our animal brothers and sisters, relied on instinct to make choices. Thinking, which should be referred to as "indecisiveness," forces us to agonize over our most basic, meaningless choices. Instinct kicks in when we are faced with life's biggest decisions because it is still our most reliable sense.

Kennedy had trusted his gut on many occasions, and it had always worked. It was when he had time to think about things, or overthink them, that he'd made the biggest mistakes in his life. There were a lot of reasons to say no to Red Carpet, but he only needed one to say yes.

15

The **6:30 A.M. wake-up call** came like a slap. A team of well-scrubbed hotel workers brought breakfast and a fresh hit man ensemble. Kennedy checked his e-mail. Before going to bed, he'd pinged Wes Bowman and inquired about Alia. Kennedy had surreptitiously snapped a picture of her with his phone when she gave it back to him, and he had e-mailed it to Wes. Wes e-mailed him back and verified she was a CIA employee. Of course, he was extremely curious why Kennedy was even asking about her, especially after their dinner in London. He wondered if Kennedy was stepping into something he wouldn't be able to clean off his shoe. Kennedy lied and said he met her on a business trip to Paris—a random encounter at the hotel bar. It wasn't a bulletproof lie, but it seemed to satisfy Wes for the time being.

After breakfast, Kennedy went out to meet his driver. It was a brisk autumn morning and the sun drew an intense saturation of color from the heroic buildings and seething river of noisy cars. A blacked-out Mercedes sedan pulled up to the curb and the driver, wearing mirrored aviators, opened the door for Kennedy.

"Passport, monsieur," he said as Kennedy slid into the backseat.

Kennedy showed him his passport and the man held the photo page under a small ultraviolet flashlight. He nodded and handed it back.

"Seat belt," he said, fastening his own.

The driver barely heard the click of Kennedy's seat belt when he punched the accelerator. He drove as if the entire French gendarmerie were in pursuit—weaving in and out of traffic, taking unexpected turns, and barreling down narrow alleys with a few inches of space between blurred metal and brick on either side. Eventually, he joined the normal flow of traffic.

"Where we are going, we are not allowed to bring any new friends," he said in a pedantic tone.

Kennedy nodded, but was doing everything in his power to keep his breakfast down. *Some fucking spy*, he thought to himself. *Carsick in a high-speed chase.*

They stopped in front of St. Eustache church and Kennedy got out.

"Go in and light two candles and cross yourself each time," the driver instructed. "And wait for the priest to show you the way." He laughed and drove off, tires squealing.

Inside the cathedral, it was deadly quiet, save for the random padding of clergy going about their solemn business. As instructed, he approached the long iron votive rack and lit two candles, crossing himself over the flames. A priest approached and bowed to him slightly, saying nothing. He motioned for Kennedy to follow him, and they walked past the whispering prayers of the altar boys to the back of the cathedral. They went through the transept and down into the entrance of the sacristy. The long, ancient hallway was dark and smelled of musty candle wax. The priest stopped at a carved wooden door, bowed again, and walked away.

Kennedy opened the door and followed the dim light down spiral stone steps.

When he reached the bottom, there was a heavy metal door with a caged lightbulb over it, like the entrance to an underground missile silo. He knocked and waved at the camera lens staring at him from the corner of the ceiling. After endless unlatching on the other side, the door swung open with an air lock hiss. Juarez, the man he'd met at the golf course, was standing in the doorway.

"Good morning. Sleep well?" Juarez said congenially, shaking his hand.

"I guess after the last forty-eight hours I shouldn't be surprised to see you."

"We're full of surprises," he said, locking the door behind them.

"Golf course was a nice touch. People always in your business out there."

"I know, right? Sorry about the frisk."

"Let me guess, tracking device?" Kennedy asked, handing Juarez the copper bracelet he'd been wearing since they met at the club.

Juarez pocketed it.

"Also helped me monitor your vitals in transit. Not bad for a rookie. Must have ice water in your veins."

Juarez led him into the operations center, a dimly lit hive of cubes and computers, with analysts working quietly.

"What do you do for Alia?" Kennedy asked.

"Counterintelligence Center Analysis Group. Otherwise known as a rat catcher. I run teams, like this one, when the company is addressing threats that may directly affect the US on domestic soil. I was actually the first to identify this particular threat, and they brought in Alia the wunderkind to plan the op, which is why you're here."

Juarez opened two heavy steel doors and they entered a conference room lined with video monitors that reminded Kennedy of a Jason Bourne movie. Seated around the conference table was the Red Carpet team. To say the people Alia had gathered for Red Carpet were an eclectic group would be an understatement. As Kennedy casually surveyed them, he could not, for the life of him, see the majority of them doing spy work of any kind, which made him feel a little less like a fish out of water. Alia strolled in and smiled warmly at Kennedy.

"Everyone," Alia said pleasantly, "this is Kennedy, our team leader. You and Juarez have already met, so let me introduce you to the rest of the team."

First to step up was a boisterous midwesterner in his thirties with a heavy beard and the build of a former offensive guard or rugby prop.

"Lambert. Nice to meet you," he said, crushing Kennedy's hand in his giant mitt.

"Lambert is a specialized skills officer," Alia said. "Before we plucked him from his high-paying job in the private sector, he was an aerospace engineer working as a global sourcing consultant for major aircraft and air traffic control equipment manufacturers. If our terrorist endeavors to exploit vulnerabilities in either of those areas, Lambert's job is to sniff him out."

"Provided the terrorist is a *him*."

All eyes turned to the corner of the room, where a young Asian woman wearing all black clothes, with closely cropped, precision-cut hair and razor-sharp features, stared back at them, mildly defiant. She was pretty but did her best to avoid being thought of as such by cultivating a non-gender-specific art school ninja look. Her presence was intense, like standing near a live electrical wire waiting to zap you senseless if you got too close.

"This is Nuri," Alia said. "She's our top computer network specialist."

"I prefer the term *hacker*," Nuri interjected. "*Computer network specialist* perpetuates the Asian nerd stereotype."

Instead of shaking his hand, she blew Kennedy a kiss.

"Why don't you tell him a little about your role here," Alia said politely.

"If you insist," Nuri said confidently.

She pulled out her iPhone and tapped the screen a few times. All the computers in the room started playing ABBA's "Dancing Queen," and a swirling disco ball appeared on their screens.

Alia folded her hands patiently and waited for her to finish. Juarez looked like he was going to go ballistic.

"Computers are stupid. Networks are even stupider," Nuri began. "My job is to own them like my bitches. But you know who is stupidest of all?"

"People?" Kennedy guessed, following her lead.

Nuri's eyes lit up. Kennedy had just scored half a Skittle with her.

"Exactly. Which is why I wrote an algorithm that feeds off the biggest human behavior databases in the world and applies the commonalities to an anthropological predictor modeling program, *which* makes it really fucking easy to predict what people will do, because they all do the same shit over and over—"

"And you apply that to network administrators—like the one that set up this network—to unzip security systems that operate like all the other fucking security systems in the world."

"I like this guy," Nuri said to Alia.

"My job is similar, but I hack humans instead of machines," Kennedy added.

"I *really* like this guy," Nuri said again, killing the music and disco balls.

"Good," Alia said, turning toward a tall, slender man in his fifties who was looking back at her with a pained expression. "I think you'll all get to like Kennedy in short order and see why we made the right choice asking him to lead this team."

The man stood and shook Kennedy's hand, bowing slightly, a gesture Kennedy could not differentiate between respect and contempt.

"Trudeau," he said drily, "weapons specialist."

"We poached Trudeau from DoD. In addition to being an adviser to three secretaries of defense, he was chief editor of *Jane's Defence Weekly* and *Jane's Intelligence Review*. He knows *everyone* in arms manufacturing. Like Lambert and Nuri, he's a specialized skills officer."

"If this were the *Enterprise*, he'd be Mr. Spock," Nuri said, waiting for Trudeau's eyes to roll nearly out of his head, which they did.

"He'll be monitoring the defense industry for anomalous transactions that might signal an allocation of deadly goods to the wrong hands," Alia continued. "I believe our terrorist, a *he* in this case, will seek out weapons only high-level military officials and contractors can access."

"Which he will get if he has the money," Trudeau said cynically.

Trudeau was the kind of person Kennedy would have pulled out of a TSA line for an additional search. He never looked anyone in the eye and, whenever he smiled, it was only to himself, as if a private joke were constantly running through his head. He spoke English perfectly but with a slight European accent, difficult to pin down. Kennedy guessed he may be Scandinavian or Swiss by birth but had been in the States most of his life. Whatever it was about Trudeau that rubbed him the wrong way, Kennedy was convinced it ran deep. The conference room doors opened and another man hurried in.

"Sorry I'm late," he said cheerfully and walked right up to Kennedy to shake his hand. "I'm Best."

"That's for sure," Nuri said, ogling him.

"Behave yourself," he said, winking and melting her silicon heart.

Best looked more like what Kennedy had pictured as a "spy." He was a little over six feet tall, square-jawed with a few days' stubble, chiseled like an MMA fighter, and sharply dressed in dark denim, heavy, scuffed black boots, and a black flight jacket.

"Thank you for joining us, Best," Alia said with a hint of annoyance that she found impossible to maintain in the blinding light of his smile.

"Let me guess," Kennedy said, "paramilitary ops."

"Give that man a blue ribbon," Best said enthusiastically, parking his ass in a chair.

"Very astute," Alia agreed.

"I read a lot of Tom Clancy novels," Kennedy joked, getting a laugh from everyone but Trudeau.

"Considering the enemy profile I think we're dealing with, I felt it necessary to make sure plenty of bite came with our bark. Best is a former Navy SEAL air operations master and he has assembled a detachment of military personnel standing by to support us. We hope we never have to use them, but it's nice to know they're at our disposal."

"For all manner of disposal," Trudeau joked, getting no laughs.

"Best and another contract agent will accompany you, Kennedy, during your assignment. Juarez and I will share those details with you later."

"Tell him about the boogeyman," Nuri said.

Alia projected a black-and-white photo on the flat screen hanging over the end of the conference table. In the photo, which was very grainy, as if it had been taken with a long lens from a distance, several men were getting out of a small motorcade of three Mercedes SUVs. It appeared all of the men were of Middle Eastern descent—except one, whose ethnicity was impossible to identify. Alia zoomed in on him. He had a shaved head with stubble on the sides and top and was of medium height, thin and wiry, almost floating in the black suit he was wearing. His face was what struck Kennedy. With hollow cheeks, thin, bloodless lips, and black sunglasses that looked like empty holes staring blankly at the world, it was a menacing skull.

"Kennedy, this charming ghoul is our prime suspect. He goes by *Lentz* and we don't know if that name is legal or assumed. And we have very little useful surveillance imagery of him, aside from this."

"I got lucky in Cairo and one of my tracker teams was able to snap this," Juarez said. "It's the only unobstructed shot of his face that we have."

"The only problem is," Alia added, "it's perfectly nondescript. Some of our analysts actually think he allowed this photo to be taken so that we would want to hang our hats on this look. But, like Juarez said, it's the best we've got."

She cycled through a few more black-and-white surveillance photos of Lentz. He was always well covered and never positioned his head in any way so that someone could get a good look at his face with long-range photography or satellite.

"It seems like he assumes he's always being watched," Kennedy said. "And I'm sure you're right about the first photo. He's giving you his face, but he has removed all identifying features—hair, beard stubble pattern, eye shape, and eye color. He has light skin, but there are Syrians whose skin is as light as a Swede's. He even has his mouth closed so you can't see his teeth, which can sometimes be helpful identifiers."

"Excellent observation," Alia said.

"Don't be impressed yet," Kennedy said. "We see this all the time at the checkpoints. People want to make themselves generic because they know there are eyes everywhere. So, they try to hide in plain sight."

"The good news is," Juarez said, "Lentz *does* leave his fingerprints on the world in how he operates. He's definitely not your cookie-cutter terror suspect, looking to get TV time for his imprisoned brothers and sisters. He doesn't support causes or regimes, and his prime motivation appears to be profit. But he has an interesting business model. He orchestrates, or helps to orchestrate, armed conflicts and unrest in destabilized regions and uses that to his advantage."

Alia switched the photo on the screen to one of a riot on the streets of Cairo.

"During the Egyptian Revolution," she said, "Lentz and his network of collaborators, many of whom were embedded in powerful seats of government, poured money into the movement so the conflict would destabilize

Egypt. In the meantime, he bought up oil tanker shipping companies to take advantage of potential delays in the Suez Canal. As it turned out, the conflict had very little effect on oil traffic through the canal, but Lentz made a few billion dollars off the oil companies by charging exorbitant shipping fees to circumnavigate Suez. Just before the conflict ended, he sold the overpriced stock of the shipping companies and walked away with even deeper pockets."

"He should have been arrested and tried under Egyptian law for inciting unrest," Juarez added, "but all of the corrupt officials whose pockets he was lining shielded him from capture. He made his money and slithered away as quietly as he came in. And anyone who opposed or even questioned what he was doing ended up like this."

The photo on the screen switched to one of a mass grave in the desert. At least twenty bodies wrapped in filthy, bloodstained sheets were stacked on top of one another.

"Hey, new guy, still want to play spy with us?" Nuri teased.

Juarez and Alia glared at her. Trudeau smiled to himself.

"Don't listen to the nerd," Best said. "The only dead body she ever saw was the parakeet she buried in her backyard."

"It's okay," Kennedy said. "I saw a lot worse when I lived in Tel Aviv."

He turned to Alia, ignoring Nuri's and Trudeau's reactions to his comment.

"How do you know he's behind the threat?" Kennedy asked her.

"Process of elimination," Alia explained. "The US has many enemies, but few have the financing and resources to pull off a large-scale attack—especially after 9/11. A foreign government could do it, but not without catastrophic retribution."

"What about Al Qaeda or ISIS?" Kennedy asked.

"We'd see them coming a mile away," Juarez added. "Too easily identified by their conspicuous ethnicities and religion, and we've pounded the shit out of their funding in the past decade. Paying young men who never made it to kindergarten to car-bomb destabilized zones like Iraq or Syria is one thing. Getting tech and personnel into the US for a large-scale attack is another."

"How do you know the scale of the attack? Better yet, how do you even know there will be an attack?" Kennedy said, digging into his devil's advocate role.

"We have reams of intel gathered from hundreds of sources—interrogations, chatter, the cousins," Juarez said.

"More important," Alia added, "we can't afford to wait around until more evidence comes into play. By then it will be too late."

16

After lunch with the team, Kennedy was feeling overwhelmed. He was used to dealing with marginally educated people who looked at him as their shining beacon of guidance, not a bizarre collection of idiosyncratic CIA officers, most of whom had some very dangerous talents. But that was exactly why they needed a "normal" person with a highly pragmatic personality to glue their disparate parts together. That alone felt like a full-time job and he was having major doubts about his ability to handle it.

And just when he was feeling most vulnerable and uncertain, Alia and Juarez briefed him privately on his assignment.

"Let me get this straight," he said, stunned. "The CIA wants to put TSA and Homeland Security under surveillance . . . and you want me to help?"

"In a nutshell," Juarez replied.

"Kennedy, this is a critical component to helping us gather more intel on the potential threat," Alia added. "The only way Lentz or any other terrorist would have the ability to carry out a large-scale attack is with operatives embedded as TSA staff. As you know, they are the last line of defense between aircraft and the world outside the security line. From what we've seen recently, TSA is our greatest vulnerability, which is why it's our highest surveillance priority."

"Homeland as well," Juarez said. "Lentz is going to need someone higher up to help his TSA operatives fly under DHS radar."

"The scary thing is, I doubt recruiting would be all that difficult," Kennedy mused. "With TSA agents especially. DHS might be a little tougher, but doable with the right amount of money. I can think of a lot of people he could flip."

"Exactly, which is why your part in this is so important," Alia said. "Your relationship with TSA and Homeland, and access to offices and equipment, is what makes you our greatest asset. We can't do this without you."

Their plan was to install surveillance equipment in twenty-five of the busiest airports in the country. Video, audio, and data-capture devices would be placed in the TSA offices at each airport. Mobile devices owned by TSA employees would be tapped as well. Additionally, they were going to install a device in one of the millimeter wave body scanners that could capture passenger images from all the other scanners in the airport. Millimeter wave also happened to be a highly efficient communication technology, used by the military for weapon and satellite guidance. The tapped machine in each airport would, essentially, be turned into an antenna that could receive data transmissions from the other body scanners, and from the carry-on and checked-luggage scanners. If anyone at the airport were to attempt to smuggle items past the security line in this manner, using their TSA badge to bypass the weapons detection alarms, it wouldn't get past the CIA.

Kennedy's job was to visit each airport, use his access to plant bugs in TSA offices, and convince the TSA chiefs that he needed to test an upgrade device in one of the millimeter wave body scanners, but in a way that didn't invite scrutiny. Basically, he had to manipulate them by exploiting their trust, which made his "asset" title even more apropos. The CIA was known for recruiting foreign assets to spy on their own governments, employers, even family.

"I know DHS, and TSA especially, have major, even dangerous, shortcomings," Kennedy said. "But that doesn't mean you should treat them like the enemy."

"Think of it more as protecting the TSA from themselves," Alia said. "You know better than anyone that if a legitimate threat fell into their laps, they would never move quickly enough, or at all, to stop it. Just think how many people would be dead if you hadn't ID'd those Somalis at JFK. You did what had to be done because TSA wouldn't. This is the same, just on a larger scale."

"And what about all the data you're going to capture without their knowledge? In addition to it being a breach of trust, which I'm aware doesn't often concern the CIA, it could also be beneficial to our enemies if that data ever fell into the wrong hands. You'll be capturing classified TSA and DHS data. If you aren't able to protect it, doesn't that defeat the purpose?"

"You think the data is in good hands now?" Juarez asked, laughing. "If the NSA can't safeguard its data, TSA and DHS sure as hell can't."

"You have a point there," Kennedy said.

"I understand your concerns," Alia said. "And I'm not going to try to tell you the risks you're pointing out are invalid. They're simply outweighed by the long list of pros that serve this operation. And keep in mind we're not working independently here. This operation has been signed off on by the director and other high-level government officials."

"You have an answer for everything, Alia. And they're all good," Kennedy said.

"Then what's the problem?"

"I guess it finally hit me what I'd be doing and I'm a little nervous about it, which makes me question everything."

"Yet, here you are," Juarez said. "Because you know none of those questions will matter if it turns out we're right and you were a part of the solution."

"What can I say? You're right. And I do want to be involved."

"Excellent," Alia said. "You're going to be a very valuable member of this team."

"There's only one potential glitch. I *rarely* have anything to do with equipment upgrades. That's always done by the vendor and usually in my absence. Not to mention Homeland constantly criticizes TSA for 'overcontracting' me. The point is, it's going to raise eyebrows if I come waltzing in out of the blue with a body scanner upgrade."

"We've thought of that," Alia said. "According to the Office of Security Capabilities' Emerging Threat policies, you, as a trusted specialized skills contractor, can apply for a grant, in collaboration with a university or lab, to develop a prototype of a device you believe will address the emerging threat. Since we have a major threat on our hands, many entities will be doing this to fill their coffers with research dollars. I already have the paperwork drawn up for this device, so all you would have to do is agree to let me submit it and our people inside DHS will expedite approval."

"Jesus, that's . . . a very elegant solution. Blameless too if DHS approves it. What about installation? That'll require a vendor mechanic licensed with Science and Tech."

"At each site visit, Best and another field agent will accompany you, working undercover as mechanics sent by the equipment manufacturer. While you run interference with TSA chiefs and staffers, they'll handle the installations and take care of security. The upgrade equipment in the scanning machines was designed to pass a spot inspection, even if an actual manufacturer rep were the inspector."

Kennedy knew he wouldn't get much flak from most of the TSA chiefs. There would be some who would take more convincing, but he could handle that. It was Homeland he worried about. They watched him like a hawk, and it was going to take a lot more than finesse to do this under their noses.

"Feeling confident?" Alia asked.

"Absolutely," Kennedy lied.

" 'Don't be careful what you wish for, because getting it is the whole point,' " Juarez said.

"Noah Kruz," Kennedy said, impressed.

"Hey, you're not the only one who drinks his Kool-Aid."

"We're going to try to deploy you as soon as possible," Alia said. "For now, I'm sending you back to LA while Juarez, Best, and I make final arrangements. Keep your bag packed."

———

The team returned to Langley and Kennedy flew home with Juarez on the same private jet that had brought him to Paris, only this time in the luxurious passenger cabin. He kicked back in a huge club chair and sipped a drink.

"I could get used to this," Kennedy said.

"I'm sure you could, but this isn't the job."

"Really? What about James Bond?"

"Double O zero? What kind of *secret agent* tells everyone his name wherever he goes? A guy like that wouldn't last five minutes in the field."

"That's where I come in. Agent Bland."

Kennedy made a gun out of his hand and blew imaginary smoke off the end of his finger. Juarez laughed and poured himself a drink.

"They don't use words like *ghost* or *spook* for nothing in this business. The Chinese have a small army of civilian assets, working undercover in the US—lots of 'normal' folks with special skills, spying for Beijing. They look about as much like spies as you, but they're damned effective and impossible to spot."

"You're taking all the fun out of this," Kennedy complained.

"Sorry. Someone has to be a reality check on this team."

"Okay, Mr. Reality Check, when Alia says there's little or no risk to this job, is she bullshitting me?" Part of Kennedy was hoping he would say no.

"Yes and no."

"Seriously?"

"We're talking about a potential large-scale attack on the most powerful country in the world, and if there's one person who can pull it off, it's Lentz. If you're part of a CIA operation created to stop this attack and put him away, do you think there might be some risk?"

"Absolutely."

"On the other hand, you don't have to worry too much because we're never going to put you in harm's way. That would be a complete waste of a valuable asset."

"Bland. James Bland."

"Bland is better than burned any day of the week. Hey, you're looking at someone who has to do all the shit they make look cool in the movies— while Alia sits in all-day meetings and plays tennis on the weekends. Trust me, there's nothing cool about the dirty work that goes with intelligence. Abductions, torture, state-sponsored murder, fucking with foreign governments, never being able to trust anyone—least of all your employer—never being able to have a normal life . . . After a while, you can't even remember whose side you're on or why the fuck you're doing any of it."

"Thanks for being honest," Kennedy said.

"Listen, man, we could have figured out a way to do the upgrades ourselves. We needed you because you know how the bad guys think. You know this world and the people running it. And if something's out of place, you're going to see it before any of us. So, keep your eyes and ears open and you just might be the reason we catch this guy."

17

What the fuck have I done?

Kennedy was lying in bed back at the Bel-Air in Los Angeles, fighting jet lag and going through Lentz's dossier. He first blipped on CIA radar after the fall of the Soviet Union and their disastrous segue into a free market economy, when the whole country was being plundered in a widespread smash and grab of resources. Analysts believed Lentz had worked in the oil business—in either the United States or Europe—because, in 1998, when the Russian economy collapsed, he purchased a massive portfolio of shares in Russian oil companies at pennies on the dollar. When the Russian economy rapidly recovered in 1999 to 2000, those shares had to have put a few billion dollars in his pocket.

In 2000, the CIA believed the new Russian president, Vladimir Putin, may have tried to have Lentz killed so that Putin and the rest of the country's newly formed oligarchy could hijack his oil shares. That was when Lentz went dark and used his fortune to pay his way off the grid. From that point on, there were even fewer Lentz sightings, with Juarez's photo being the best to date that any agency had. Ironically, this was also the time when Lentz really came into his own, engineering highly lucrative profiteering machines in places of unrest, like Iraq, Afghanistan, Libya, and Egypt.

Lentz's operations in Egypt from 2012 to 2013 coincided with the first intel reports related to the current threat. Many of his collaborators in North

Africa had been detained by the Egyptian government and handed over to the CIA for interrogation. Hundreds of hours of transcripts from these sessions revealed common and consistent threads related to a large-scale US attack. It seemed that Lentz's contempt for the United States was well known among his associates. He believed that Americans' conspicuous consumption and stranglehold on global resources caused conflicts that appeared to be region-specific but could really be traced back to US imperialism. Kennedy called Wes Bowman to see if he had been able to dig up any new intel.

————

"Before I tell you anything, I want to know more about your clandestine romance," Wes said on the phone.

At first, Kennedy didn't know what the hell he was talking about. Then he remembered the white lie he'd told Wes about meeting Alia in a Paris bar. He had to deftly get him off the subject without blowing his cover literally the first day on the job.

"If you're looking for gory details, about the sexiest thing she did was show me how she could tie a maraschino cherry stem in a knot with her tongue."

"Can't believe you didn't close the deal. She's gorgeous. You always got a lot of ass in college. You must be losing it."

Kennedy was well aware that Wes was playing to his vanity, attempting to goad him into telling more than he wanted to in order to save face with his bro.

"Losing it? I lost it years ago. I think I might be a born-again virgin."

"Why'd you want me to pull her file then? Switching to stalking?"

"You're going to laugh if I tell you."

"What, you thought if you took her out on a few dates and got her tipsy on rosé, she might share classified information that just happened to be associated with your crusade to single-handedly save the world?"

"Something like that."

The light tone of mockery in Wes's laugh meant he was buying Kennedy's Alia scenario, along with his self-deprecating amateur role.

"Laugh it up, Bowman. If you have any better ideas, I'm all ears."

"I do have some potentially useful information for you and you don't have to try to sleep with me to get it."

"Hilarious. What do you have?"

"I may have intercepted an e-mail or two from one of the assistant directors who helped author the threat memo."

"Wow, that was ballsy. How bad could they burn you for that?"

"That could land me a job as a prison bitch. Which would probably be a lateral move from this shit detail. Anyhoo, this guy is hot to trot for a TSA or DHS inside-job theory. He didn't name names but he alluded to an ability to do so several times. Which means whoever they are, they're bound to have our boys under their skin by now."

Bull's-eye, Kennedy thought to himself.

"Jesus, Wes, that's unbelievable. Could be people I work with."

"You better watch your back, man," Wes warned.

"Trust me. I am. Is there anything else to go on?" Kennedy asked.

"Are you gonna call her again? Did she give you her number?"

"Wes. Come on."

"Hey, as Hannibal Lecter says, 'quid pro quo,' now let's have it."

"I tried calling her. She gave me a fake number."

Wes lost it.

"I'm glad you find my failures with women so amusing," Kennedy said, happy that Wes was so easily convinced.

"Sorry, buddy. Okay, quid pro quo," Wes said. "My money is on DHS for the inside job. I did a little checking of my own and found out that last year the FBI was investigating some Homeland execs in a potential corruption sting. I wasn't able to find out who their suspects were, but check this shit out: the bureau agents leading the investigation are dead. Someone found them half dissolved in a bathtub full of acid at a motel in Jersey."

"That sounds professional."

"Absolutely. That's why I told you last time—you feel any heat at all and you get the hell out of the kitchen. Whoever they are, these people are not fucking around."

18

"Wow, you really know how to treat a lady," Love joked.

She and Kennedy were walking through Woodlawn Cemetery in Santa Monica in the late afternoon. Long, feathering palm tree shadows spread across the headstones in the warm fading light.

"I know, right? Thanks for meeting me out here. I haven't been for a while, and going alone seemed a little daunting," Kennedy said.

"No worries. I have a hard time coming alone too, so you're helping me get in a long-overdue visit."

They stopped at Kennedy's small family plot and sat in the grass. There was a large headstone with the names of Kennedy's mother and father. Next to it was another headstone with Belle's name, marking her empty grave.

"Voilà," Love said, pulling a bouquet of silk flowers from her carryall.

She placed them in the flower cup at the foot of Belle's stone and sat back down next to Kennedy.

"Very nice," he said.

"You hate it here, don't you?"

"Is it that obvious?"

"Painfully."

"Sorry. I like to come here to remember them but I just can't abide the whole cemetery thing."

"I'm with you. But it is peaceful. Find me another place this quiet in LA."

"How was New York?"

"Good. The album is starting to take off. Thanks to Mr. Nic Harcourt."

"I never got to tell you that's how I heard about the show. Great interview."

"You think? I thought I sounded like an indie snob."

"No, you sounded like the architect of your own destiny."

"*That* was a beautiful, yet utterly esoteric, thing to say."

"I wish I could take credit for it. I'm quoting Noah Kruz."

"The self-help guy who takes up half the shelves at airport bookstores?"

"He's more of a success guru."

"You say tomato," Love joked.

They sat for a while in silence before Love got up to tidy the stones, pulling weeds and crabgrass around them.

"Do you ever dream about Belle?" Kennedy asked.

"All the time," Love said. "We're always swimming for some reason. Boogie boarding down by Manhattan Beach Pier or doing cannonballs at my folks' pool. She was like a fish. You almost had to drag her out of the water or she'd never leave."

"Tell me about it. She made my dad buy that cheap-ass aboveground hillbilly pool. I stopped inviting friends over that summer."

"That thing was filthy after about two weeks!" Love said, laughing. "What about you? Do you dream about her?"

"Not really," he lied. "I'm a light sleeper so I don't dream much at all."

"That sucks. My dreams are more vivid than reality."

Kennedy was staring blankly at Belle's headstone.

"I'm sorry, what?" he said.

"Are you all right, dude?"

"Yeah. I'm cool. Why?"

"You're *not* cool. I can tell. I know that face. It's your golf face. Every time you had to drag ass off to one of those tournaments, you had that no-vacancy look."

"I have this big work thing coming up so I'm a little preoccupied."

"What's the big thing?" she asked, sitting down by him again.

"It's kind of like I'm going on tour, actually. I've been asked to visit twenty-five airports in about two weeks' time."

"Is that even possible?"

"Yeah, but it's going to be a bitch. And I'm really not looking forward to it."

"Shocker. Sounds awful."

"Yeah . . . You know, if something ever happened to me . . ."

"Whoa, where's that coming from?" she asked.

"Hear me out. If something ever happened to me, you're my only real next of kin. We're not blood relatives, but I don't really have anyone else who would qualify as family, you know?"

"Do you want me to pull the plug when the time comes?" She tried for a joke but couldn't hide her look of concern.

"I'm not saying that. I guess I'm kind of asking if that's okay with you. If I choke on a PBJ in my hotel room, you'll tell them where to scatter my ashes."

"Wow, you have been on the road *way* too long, my friend. Yes of course it's okay with me, but you're not going to die from a rogue sandwich or anything else. We're friends again, so I require you to be alive for that. Understood?"

Kennedy smiled and nodded.

"Good. And no matter where you say you want to be scattered, I'm just going to chuck you in the fry grease at In-N-Out. You've always loved that place and I would get a kick out of watching folks eat fries that day. Cool?"

"Sounds like a plan. Maybe we should go there now and scout it," Kennedy said.

"Graveyard soul session followed by greasy burgers and shakes. Again, you sure know how to treat a lady."

19

deposited your first payment this morning," Alia said.

It was 6:00 A.M. and she and Juarez had come to his hotel for a breakfast briefing. Alia handed him a black credit card with no writing or numbers.

"When you're holding this card, you can access your new account at our bank in Grand Cayman. The chip inside will authorize transactions by reading the heat signature emitted by the capillaries in your fingertips. The account can't be accessed via phone, Internet, or any other electronic means. You have to be there in person to withdraw funds. There are two hundred and fifty thousand dollars in there now. As long as you don't deposit any of it into any US banks, it's tax free. And there will be five more of these payments as the assignment progresses. Is that satisfactory?"

Kennedy was slightly shocked but did his best to hide it.

"That's fine. What about my expenses while I'm on assignment?"

Juarez handed him a leather briefcase.

"Cash and credit cards for travel are in the case. The cards have no limits. Also, I don't want you using your iPhone when you're working for us. Way too risky."

Juarez handed him a satellite smartphone.

"Keep this on you at all times," Juarez said sternly. "This is a closed sat network everyone in Red Carpet is on. Works like any other smartphone—

calls, data, e-mail—but it contains a GPS tracker so we know where you are at all times. Our techs set it up to receive calls, texts, and e-mails forwarded from your clients and personal contacts, so you can stay in touch with them. But only do that with this phone."

Game time apprehension was building on Kennedy's face.

"Kennedy, I want to make sure you're clear that, once we begin, there's no turning back until it's done," Alia said in her gentle yet penetrating way.

"Wow, no pressure," Kennedy half joked.

"Last chance to walk away," Alia said.

"I'm not going anywhere."

Juarez smiled, a silent shot in the arm for Agent Bland.

"Excellent." Alia sighed. "Because without you, I don't have an operation. If you're successful, you'll be a true hero. And these days, those are in short supply."

Alia briefed Kennedy on the movements of the Red Carpet team already out in the field. Lambert was touring major airline equipment manufacturers in Asia. Like Kennedy, he was going to leave a few souvenirs from the CIA behind—bugs that would enable Alia to have eyes and ears in those companies. Langley analysts had a theory that Lentz may attempt to purchase parts, sabotage them, and get them into airplanes via his airport operatives.

Trudeau was traveling around Europe and the Middle East, meeting with his contacts to see if he could flush out any leads. He had begun to focus on Eastern Europe and Russia, as they would be the places where Lentz's buyers could get a lot of firepower for his money with zero governmental interference. With every visit, he also loaded a data surveillance program Nuri had given him into any laptop or workstation he came across. This allowed her to lift transaction data and send it back to Trudeau for analysis.

Alia was ready to deploy Kennedy that afternoon and get him started planting the CIA's surveillance equipment in airports. He and Juarez would start at LAX, cover the West Coast and Southwest, and then work their way east. They went over logistics, and Kennedy helped refine the travel plan based on his more extensive knowledge of the airports and routes. When they were finished, bugging twenty-five airports in two weeks seemed doable, but there'd be little room for error.

After breakfast, Kennedy grabbed his garment bag and they went to the private terminal at LAX to meet Best and the other agent who would be installing the tech. LAX's private terminal catered to celebrities, government officials, and the über wealthy looking to avoid contamination by the unwashed masses. Alia had chosen it for the meeting because security was much tighter than at the rest of the airport, with a "paparazzi-free" environment constantly swept for listening and viewing devices, and zero exterior vantage points for long-lens peepers.

Best and Mitchell, the other field agent assisting them, were there waiting, geared up and ready to go. Mitchell was the polar opposite of Best—rough around the edges, dark and brooding. His eyes were predatory slits, and he seemed to be made of nothing but sharp-angled bones and hardened ropes of muscle. And his personality matched his look—quiet and deadly serious, showing no signs of levity or even friendliness. Both men were dressed in starched work shirts with the Hadfield Raith Worldwide logo. HRW was the top airport security equipment vendor in the country. They manufactured the millimeter wave scanners that would be getting the fake upgrade equipment.

While Best and Mitchell took care of the scanners, Kennedy's job was to plant the video, audio, and data bugs Alia needed in the airport's TSA office. Juarez showed him the surveillance tech. The devices were tiny, as small as the point of a golf tee.

"These are powered by radiant heat, like solar but without sunlight. They need a minuscule amount of juice to operate, emit no signal of their own, and they're so small you paint one white and it would blend into a bowl of rice. To tap the network, all you need to do is log on to their employee Wi-Fi with the laptop we're giving you. Nuri has an auto-send virus loaded with decoy programs to send their network security on wild-goose chases. While that's happening, our data-capture bug loads in the background."

When they finished the briefing, Alia left to catch her flight to DC. Kennedy was feeling confident about their planning, but one thing was bothering him. He was skeptical that Best and Mitchell, the two killing machines she'd sent with them, would be able to truly pass as HRW techs. He'd been around those super geeks for years and felt like attempting to fake their knowledge and expertise was a stretch. He decided to test that theory with his traveling companions.

"Guys, what do I tell my TSA chiefs is the function of this new gear?"

"New sensors to detect weapons and explosives concealed in body cavities."

"Too bad it isn't real," Kennedy said. "Show me what we're going to show them to sell this."

Mitchell handed him a tablet computer with the HRW logo. It had operational schematics and a white paper about how the "new technology" functioned.

"Impressive. Can I see the device itself?"

Juarez showed Kennedy one of the upgrade devices. It was a three-foot copper tube, three inches in diameter, with thick caps on the ends containing the connection wires and power cable. Mitchell showed Kennedy how it exactly matched a part from the millimeter wave scanning machines.

"And it won't impede scanner operation?" Kennedy asked.

"No, it's designed to work exactly like the part it's replacing," Juarez said. "The only difference is we've added our tech inside, so unless you physically take it apart, you're never going to see it."

"How the hell are we going to travel with these?"

"We won't have to. At each airport, a field agent will meet us outside the security checkpoint to give us the device," Juarez said.

Kennedy turned to Best and Mitchell.

"You guys can walk the walk with the HRW uniforms, but can you talk the talk with the actual working parts of the equipment? This whole thing will come off the rails pretty quickly if one of my more savvy TSA chiefs starts asking questions you can't answer."

"We've been training on these specific models for six months," Mitchell said with annoyance. "We probably know them better than HRW's techs."

"Even though all of this has been cleared through DHS, some of my clients are OCD and/or paranoid, so they'll definitely want to contact HRW to verify the work. How are we going to handle that?"

"All work orders have been added to the HRW maintenance logs," Best said. "If anyone calls it in, the phone center workers will verify it."

"So you've thought of everything?" Kennedy asked.

"Pretty much," Mitchell said condescendingly, shooting a look at Best.

"Even making sure Wade Connelly, HRW's chief engineer, knows about the upgrades? Wade is very hands-on, and TSA represents more revenue than all of HRW's other contracts combined. He has the ability to delay a DHS-approved upgrade for thirty days if he isn't satisfied with the specs. What's the plan with him?"

Silence. Mitchell looked at Best, hoping he had an answer. Nothing.

"I guess you hadn't thought of that. Good thing Wade is a friend of mine. Chances of him throwing a wrench in the works are slim, but it would have been more thorough to make sure he got the paperwork well in advance to avoid it. Anyway, if he calls or shows up, you should probably let me handle him."

Juarez was trying to conceal his amusement at Kennedy's sound schooling of the two smug badasses.

"Copy that," Best said amiably, somewhat impressed.

"Apologies, sir," Mitchell said, like he meant it.

————

That afternoon, their first upgrade at LAX went smoothly. Kennedy's TSA contacts were not in the office, so he quickly installed the bugs in there and Juarez verified their signal. The millimeter wave scanner upgrade was also a snap. Kennedy had chosen a machine that was being operated by some of his recent trainees. He shot the shit with them until Best and Mitchell were finished. LAX was wired and operational in less than two hours.

"Not bad, chief," Juarez said, patting Kennedy on the back as they walked to their next flight.

"Piece of cake," Kennedy said.

20

After LAX, the four of them hit the road nonstop and knocked out sixteen additional airports in Vegas, Phoenix, San Francisco, Seattle, Denver, Salt Lake City, Houston, Dallas, Atlanta, Miami, Orlando, Fort Lauderdale, Charlotte, Baltimore, DC (Dulles), and Philly. Kennedy's rapport with TSA chiefs in those airports was solid, and they encountered little or no resistance. He was getting very good at planting bugs and placed even more in other common areas used by the TSA staff. They were averaging two hours or less in each airport, which sometimes made it possible for them to hit more than one airport a day in clustered areas like Vegas–Phoenix, Miami–Orlando–Fort Lauderdale, and Baltimore-Dulles.

Kennedy's road warrior experience was paying huge dividends. With his elite status, he knew half the flight attendants and pilots in the air. If they missed a meal at an airport because they were in a town where restaurants closed at 10:00 P.M., flight attendants would always have some half-decent food they were more than willing to share—especially with a guy like Best, who might as well have been a firefighter the way the female, and male, flight attendants fawned over him. If they were lucky enough to end up on a 777, and they had no time to catch a few winks at a hotel, they were allowed to sleep in crew rest compartment bunks. But, after a long run of smooth encounters, it was time to go to JFK, home of Kennedy's nemesis, Glenn.

———

"Glenn is a man of highly predictable habits," Kennedy whispered to Mitchell and Best as they entered his office and found him sleeping on the job.

"This asshole is running the entire TSA office for JFK?" Best looked like he was considering putting a bullet in Glenn's head.

"This is a good day. Sometimes he doesn't even show up till noon," Kennedy said.

"Jesus." Mitchell scowled, also sizing up Glenn's head for a bullet.

"The good news is it's Wednesday and he's sleeping off his Tuesday-night rec league hockey bender. Probably be out for a while and when he wakes up, he'll be too bleary-eyed and starving for Chick-fil-A to care what we're doing. So, let's get cracking."

He took Mitchell and Best to Terminal 1, which serviced all international carriers. It was the farthest walk from Glenn's office and Glenn hated going there anyway because the terminal manager openly mocked him and the restaurants were too expensive. They zeroed in on one of the scanners in a closed checkpoint line and the TSA agent in charge was a woman Kennedy had trained, so she just waved and smiled.

Kennedy wanted to keep an eye on Rip Van Winkle, so he let Best and Mitchell do their thing and made his way back to Terminal 4. On his way, he stopped at Starbucks. Lizzy was working and waved him over to grab his coffee at the pickup counter.

"You're a lifesaver, Elizabeth."

"Stop calling me that. You sound like my dad. And no, I do not have dad issues."

"You seem a bit edgy today, sweetheart," Kennedy said, messing with her.

"My boss is a blond Nazi robot who keeps giving me shit about *everything*. My clothes, hair, tattoos, *counterside manner—*"

"That's an actual thing?"

"This is planet Starbucks, dude. It's like a religious cult. We worship a mermaid for chrissakes. That should tell you everything. What are you doing back so soon? Couldn't live without me? That's so sweet."

"That and tying up some loose ends before I head back home."

"Speaking of loose ends, that asshole you hate is here."

"Which one?"

"You know, that big angry ginger from Homeland Security? Always gets an Oprah chai like a little bitch."

"Shit," Kennedy said, panicked.

"What?"

"When was he here?"

"Ten minutes ago. Dude, why're you freaking out?"

Kennedy looked down the concourse for Tad Monty, *the world's biggest asshole* and the last person he wanted to see. Tad had been the most vocal when it came to minimizing Kennedy's role at JFK. He had hated Kennedy ever since he saw how much he was invoicing for every year and was always giving Kennedy's competitors advantages in hopes that they could take over some of his business.

"I need to get back to the office. Thanks, Lizzy."

Kennedy left his coffee on the bar and jogged across the concourse. When he got to Glenn's office, his worst-case scenario was unfolding. Tad Monty and two of his cronies had walked in on Glenn snoring in his own drool pool.

"Glenn!" Monty yelled.

Glenn startled violently and knocked a full cup of coffee into his crotch. When he saw Monty and his bulldogs standing there, he tried to act like nothing had happened, despite the brown wet spot on his khakis.

"Tad, Mr. Monty, I wasn't—"

"And you won't anymore, Glenn. You're fired."

"What? On what grounds?"

"Really, Glenn? You're asking me that question? If you can't see yourself for who you really are, then how the hell are you going to see a threat coming? You're a lazy imbecile and I should have done this a long time ago. Pack your shit and get out. I'll finish your shift. Turn in your key cards and badge to my associates."

While Glenn began the awkward process of packing up his pathetic desk tchotchkes and holding back crocodile tears, Kennedy tried to slip out.

"Weren't you just here?" Monty asked Kennedy, as if he could see him with the eyes in the back of his head.

"Yeah, I was training new recruits," Kennedy answered.

"And blackballing quite a few too," Tad countered.

"I just make recommendations on who I think is suited for the job."

"Right. I'm not surprised, considering who we had running the show here. So, to what do we owe the pleasure of your visit today?"

"I'm concerned about this new threat—"

"We're all concerned about it. Are you here to babysit?"

"No, I came to supervise an equipment upgrade for testing."

"Excuse me?" Tad said, glaring at Glenn.

Glenn pretended he hadn't heard the comment.

"I said I have—"

"I know what you said. I just can't believe we weren't notified."

Tad's cronies moved in next to him, leveling up the intimidation factor.

"The work order from Science and Tech was sent here five days ago and approved."

"Is that true, you idiot?" Tad barked at Glenn.

"I, uh . . ."

Glenn pretended to shuffle through soggy papers on his desk.

"Shut up and keep packing." Tad focused his twitchy rabbit eyes on Kennedy.

"Let's see it."

"What?"

"Jesus, the work order," he said impatiently.

Kennedy handed it over. Tad glanced at it and passed it to one of his men.

"Call it in."

"Is there a problem?" Kennedy tried to stay calm.

"Yeah. This is costing taxpayers a fortune and I want to make sure your buddies at Hadfield Raith aren't getting fat on the government trough with constant upgrades."

"There's no cost for the upgrade. It's only a test prototype and it's for body cavity weapon detection, the one weakness of the millimeter wave scanner," Kennedy said, choking back the vitriol he had for Tad.

"What's the catch?"

"There is no catch. It's an upgrade I've wanted to test for a long time. I even wrote the grant to get it developed—"

"Ah! There it is! *You're* getting paid. That's why you're here."

"No. I'm waiving my fee through the testing phase because I know how long it takes to get approvals on these things and I think this will correct a dangerous vulnerability."

"You expect me to believe you're some kind of Boy Scout, doing this out of the goodness of your heart? Consultants care about one thing—soaking their clients."

"I care about passengers. That's why I'm doing this."

Tad's face turned red with anger.

"You think I don't care about that?"

"I didn't say that."

"I'm denying your upgrade request. And it's time we reevaluated your role here."

"You don't have the authority to deny it, and the upgrade is pretty much finished. Glenn was sleeping so—"

"Fuck you!" Glenn said and stormed out of the room.

"Shut up, Glenn!" Monty yelled and turned to Kennedy. "I have the authority to put a stop to all work I deem dangerous or incompetent. So, let's just take a look-see at the handiwork of your techs. I have a feeling it may not be up to snuff today."

"Let me hit the head quickly and we'll go take a look," Kennedy said as pleasantly as he could.

He felt a protest bubbling up in Tad but ignored it and headed off to the bathroom. When Kennedy walked in, he could hear Glenn weeping in one of the stalls. Kennedy took a stall a few doors down and locked the door. He texted Mitchell, Best, and Juarez about the situation, flushed the toilet a couple of times, and hurried out. Glenn was standing in front of the door, staring at him with red-rimmed eyes.

"You piece of shit. This is all because of you," Glenn growled.

"Oh really, Glenn?"

Kennedy's phone buzzed. He needed to get out of there.

"Did I tell you to sleep on the fucking job?"

"It all started when you made me look like an asshole, and they've been on me ever since."

"Glenn, I saved hundreds of people's lives. That's my job. Making you look like an asshole isn't. You do a bang-up job of that all by yourself."

Glenn moved to let Kennedy pass, but Kennedy knew it wasn't over. He had visions of the guy showing up at the Hotel Bel-Air with an assault rifle.

"I'll see you around," Glenn said, reinforcing Kennedy's paranoia.

When Kennedy arrived at Terminal 1, Mitchell and Best were just finishing up the installation. They kept their cool when Monty stormed up and nearly shoved them aside to take a look at their work.

"Guys, this is Agent Tad Monty from DHS. He's conducting a spot inspection of our work today," Kennedy said in his most matter-of-fact tone.

While Mitchell and Best deftly explained the installation to Tad, he berated them, asking irrelevant questions, and the cronies sidled up to Kennedy.

"We have a few questions for you, consultant boy," one said.

"Yeah. Just to make sure all the paperwork is in order," the other chimed in.

Monty thought he was clever, trying to create a Spanish Prisoner situation by separating him from Mitchell and Best to see if their stories matched up. He walked over with a smug grin.

"You're going to fully brief my agents on every detail of this upgrade while we get someone from HRW to assist me with my inspection."

"These men *are* with Hadfield Raith," Kennedy argued.

"Management. Not the help," Tad said loud enough for Mitchell and Best to hear.

Kennedy had to think quickly. If they got someone in management from HRW to come to the airport, and they could do it by snapping their fingers, it was over. The CIA had done a decent job of creating a believable facade, but Tad Monty was about to huff and puff and blow their house down.

21

Dead man walking. **That's what** Kennedy felt like as Tad's cronies followed him back to Glenn's office. When they arrived, some of the recruits he had trained smiled and waved at him. Some of the more boisterous ones even gave him a low-key shout-out.

"You're a real celebrity around here, aren't you?" one of the goons said snidely.

"Compared to you guys, I'm Brad fucking Pitt."

Kennedy could feel his anger rising and wasn't sure how long he would be able to control it. They all sat around Glenn's desk. One of the cronies snatched Kennedy's work order from him and examined it, as if he knew what he was looking at. The other picked up the phone and called HRW, barking orders that Homeland needed a senior tech person from HRW to come to JFK as soon as possible to inspect an upgrade. The good news was that the person on the line at HRW verified that the upgrade was in the system, in keeping with what Best had told him earlier. But that was only going to hold them off so long.

Kennedy was racking his brain, trying to figure out a way to keep them from physically inspecting the gear, when Mitchell walked into the room, startling everyone.

"Need some gear," he said apologetically.

He closed the office door behind him and opened a large tool case he and Best had brought with them that day. Kennedy watched out of the corner of his eye. Mitchell was taking his time, stealing glances at Monty's men as he worked. Kennedy was relieved, figuring Juarez and his men must have schemed a way out.

"When did you first submit paperwork to DHS for your prototype grant?" one of Monty's men asked.

"A few months ago."

"And you thought it required immediate implementation?"

"Do you know how large the human colon is?" Kennedy asked.

"What are you talking about?" the man asked.

"Five feet long and three inches in diameter. Now, if I were to keister that much Semtex or C4 and detonate it on a plane, do you think I could bring it down?"

"I don't know—"

"You bet your ass I could."

Mitchell laughed out loud.

"Shut up!" Monty's crony yelled.

"But I could easily get it on a plane because these machines can't detect objects hidden in body cavities," Kennedy continued, on a roll, "which is why, since we started using them, the international heroin trade has more than doubled."

A piercing alarm went off—the kind that only sounded in the event of an attack *inside* the airport.

"Holy shit," Kennedy said.

The cronies made calls on their mobile phones, shouting at the people on the other end of the line for answers. Mitchell made a call as well. Kennedy couldn't hear what he was saying, but it was a short conversation. As soon as he hung up, Mitchell pulled a power drill with a chrome socket on the end from out of his tool case and snapped it shut. While the cronies finished their calls, he made some adjustments on the power drill. Then the cronies jumped out of their chairs and headed for the door. Mitchell moved quickly, cutting them off.

"I think we'd better stay here," Mitchell said.

"Get out of the way, idiot—"

Mitchell raised the power drill and pulled the trigger. With a pneumatic pop, a bullet ripped through the first crony's forehead and he crumpled to the floor. The other one stared at his partner in disbelief. When he finally went for his gun, he took a bullet in the mouth and keeled over onto his dead partner. Mitchell pried the slugs from the wall behind them and shoved them into his toolbox.

"Let's go," he said casually.

"You . . . Oh my God," Kennedy stammered.

Mitchell grabbed his gear and moved Kennedy to the door.

"Now."

Kennedy's mind was racing as he and Mitchell hurried out onto the concourse. He couldn't think clearly. All he wanted to do was run. He heard people screaming, and the two of them followed the sound until they saw a swarm of airport security officers and police near one of the gates. Tad Monty was there, shouting something. As soon as Kennedy got close enough, he could hear what he was saying.

"Get these people out of here!"

Then the crowd parted enough for Kennedy to see that Glenn had shot himself in the head and was lying on the floor near one of the gates with a .38 caliber revolver in his hand and a halo of blood on the carpet. A flight attendant covered in blood was screaming uncontrollably.

"Keep moving," Mitchell said, and pulled him through the gathering crowd.

They ran through the concourse. Best picked them up in a maintenance golf cart and drove them to the closest exit. Juarez was waiting for them by the curb in an ambulance. They all jumped in and sped away with the lights and siren going. Kennedy felt like he was having a nervous breakdown. He had heard the term before, and used it jokingly, but now he knew what it really meant. His heart was racing so fast, he thought it was going to explode in his throat. He could only take shallow breaths and his stomach muscles were so tight he could barely exhale. His hands and feet were tingling and starting to go numb. The worst part was the emotional blitz tearing through his coping mechanisms and going right for the throat. Juarez's voice broke his panic.

"Kennedy!"

Kennedy looked at him in the rearview.

"Give him a bag. His lips are turning blue."

"I didn't fucking sign up for this!" he bellowed into the back of Juarez's neck.

Mitchell looked at Kennedy like he might be another potential problem he'd need to take care of.

"Calm down," Juarez said sternly.

"Fuck you! Why did you kill them? They're Homeland Security agents. They might be assholes but they're on our side!"

Juarez drove down a side street and Kennedy thought he was going to be the next to take a bullet in the head.

"Those two assholes were working with Lentz," Juarez said, his voice surprisingly calm. "We've tracked them for three years, since he was in Cairo. They were part of the job."

Kennedy recalled what Wes Bowman had said about Lentz infiltrating DHS and his head began to spin even faster.

"Why didn't you tell me?" he asked.

"We didn't know they were going to show up today so it never crossed my mind."

"I can't believe this is happening," Kennedy said, mostly to himself.

Best handed him a plastic bag.

"Breathe into this. You're hyperventilating," Best said.

Kennedy did it and started to feel his feet under him again.

"Listen, man," Juarez said, "we weren't expecting this to go down either, but it did and we dealt with it. I'm sorry, but it's like I told you, this is the job. You want to bury Lentz so he can't do something that will make 9/11 seem like a drive-by shooting? You have to be willing to do what *he's* willing to do—without hesitation. Otherwise, you end up like Glenn."

"Monty," Kennedy said. "Won't he think we did it?"

"The slugs we put in those boys were a ballistic match to Glenn's gun," Mitchell said. "Juarez told me what to dial in when we were in the TSA office with Monty's men."

He showed Kennedy the power drill. It had an LCD screen on the side with a menu of gun names. The name was Smith & Wesson Model 586, 4 Inch Barrel, .38 S&W Special.

"This unit can dial in hundreds of different types of firearms. This is Glenn's gun down to the manufacturing date. Everything about the bullet impact will pass forensics. Only thing that won't is the bullet, because we can't match the specific barrel grooves."

"Which is why you took them. So, the plan was to frame Glenn?" Kennedy asked, incredulous.

"Glenn was a stroke of luck," Juarez said. "We were going to dispose of those gentlemen a different way, but Glenn decided to eat a bullet, so we took advantage of it. Disgruntled employee murder-suicide, et cetera."

Kennedy felt sick. He hated Glenn, but Jesus.

"For what it's worth, you did a great job back there," Juarez said.

"What?" Kennedy asked.

"You did a great job," Best said, slapping him on the back.

"Touch and go there for a minute, but you manned up," Mitchell said. "Kept your cool with those pricks coming down on you. Helped us get our work done. This is where I get off."

Juarez pulled over behind a black SUV that was idling.

"See you on the next," Mitchell said.

He shook hands with Juarez and Best and tried to shake hands with Kennedy but Kennedy was lost in thought, reliving the scene with Glenn lying on the floor in a pool of his own blood with the flight attendant screaming endlessly. Mitchell got out and took off in the black SUV.

"Where's he going?" Kennedy asked listlessly, just registering Mitchell's exit.

"Shangri-la," Best joked. "Or another shitty gig, whichever comes first."

Juarez drove away and looked at Kennedy in the rearview until he looked back.

"Like it or not, brother," Juarez said, as if he could read Kennedy's thoughts, "you're one of us now."

22

Two days before Kennedy was getting his come-to-Jesus at JFK, Lambert was waiting in the reception area of one of Malaysia's largest aircraft parts manufacturers. His shirt was soaked with sweat and his suit jacket was drenched with putrid rain. Prior to his final stop here in Kuala Lumpur, he had been all over Asia, visiting the aviation industry's highest-echelon companies, using the cover of a global sourcing rep from a domestic air carrier in the United States. Alia gave him a tidy expense account that greased the wheels and fast-tracked him to access the top brass at each company.

After a few five-figure bar tabs, the drunken executives, easily distracted by the professional charms of high-dollar escorts, were the perfect marks for tech theft. Key cards, mobile phones, laptops, notebooks, smart watches—all the things they relied on to run their companies—were the keys to their data kingdoms. And that's where Nuri came in. She had dispatched her minions to shadow the corporate entourages and gather the goods from sticky-fingered escorts in Tokyo, Shanghai, Taipei, Chiang Mai, and Singapore. Within a few days, she had root access to all of their internal networks. The problem was, when Lambert and a team of analysts at Langley pored over the data, they found *nothing* irregular in five years of transactions.

The Malaysian company he had gone to see that day was clean too, with the exception of an insignificant blip Lambert was reluctant to even peg as an anomaly. A third-party vendor, an avionics company that the larger Malaysian firm was preparing to acquire, was late on delivering a shipment of parts to its would-be suitor. This was common for those types of companies, run by engineers pushing to develop patented products and get them to market first in hopes of finding larger corporate buyers. Along the way, their financials were almost always a nightmare for corporate controllers to sift through in advance of mergers and acquisitions, and they had a hard time keeping up product supply for growing demand—which was why they sought acquisition in the first place.

Normally, Lambert wouldn't have given a damn about details like that, but if Lentz was savvy enough in that industry, he might know about the quirky intricacies of smaller companies and use them to his advantage. If he wanted critical aircraft parts, he would have been smart to acquire them from those firms, as they were always eager to sell to just about anyone to keep their balance sheets attractive, and they tended to dance around regulations. Even at long-shot status, this made the blip worthy of scrutiny. He and Alia decided to work a different angle and have him come in as a representative of potential investors. Alia backed it up with banking documentation showing funds in place contingent upon a review of the company's financials. This made Lambert an instant VIP, and he was able to pull all the information he needed on contracts, personnel, supply chain, and manufacturing figures.

He suffered the swampy heat to get back to the Hilton and check out the documents in his air-conditioned room with a burger and a six-man squad of Budweisers. Other than a lot of bad math, there was nothing in the company's financials that leaped out at him as suspicious. But because their productivity had been consistent over the past several quarters, it was definitely odd that they had a sudden drop in inventory on a part that had regularly been in surplus. The tech was something he'd never seen before, so he called Leo, one of his golf buddies at Boeing. Leo was a top engineer there who padded his Christmas fund with a few CIA consultant dollars from time to time. It was 10:00 P.M. in Kuala Lumpur so he was able to catch Leo as he was starting work in Chicago at 8:00 A.M.

"It's actually a neat little piece of communications gear that connects tower and autopilot systems with proprietary code transmissions based on binary—"

"Jesus, Leo, quit stroking your beard and give me the bar stool version." Lambert moaned.

"You're always so goddamned cranky when you're in Asia. Is it the sweats or the shits this time?"

"What are you, my third ex-wife? Both, as usual."

"You need to drop a few Michelins there, Tommy Boy."

"Fuck off. My kids thought you were a manatee when we were in Tampa last Christmas."

"Bullshit. They were looking at your *second* ex-wife."

"Can we talk about the thing, please? I know it's comms, but I don't have any white paper."

"The *thing*, which is its scientific name," Leo said, "allows autopilot to communicate independently with the tower using a system that can't be accessed by the cockpit and can't be intercepted or hacked by anyone other than the one with the transponder, which is the tower mainframe. Tower mainframe access is controlled like a missile silo, with several key turners needed to alter it. Bottom line is this little baby is going to make planes hijack proof. Pilot wants to use the plane as a missile, override. Some camel jockey tries to take the wheel, override."

"Camel jockey? Really, Leo?"

"Are you listening? This shit is revolutionary. Airbus developed it after that German nut job decided to plow his 320 into the French Alps."

"Why isn't it being implemented in US aircraft already?" Lambert asked.

"Pilots' union," Leo said. "They're freaking out about it."

"Thanks, Leo. Hello to the missus."

Lambert hung up and phoned Alia. As expected, she wanted him to buy up a sample ASAP. He drained his last Bud, set an early alarm, and wondered how the hell he was going to survive another day in the heat.

23

The next morning Lambert paid the avionics company a visit at its headquarters in an industrial wasteland on the outskirts of the city. He had developed a nasty cough from moving in and out of heat and air-conditioning and from the malevolent haze of the city's notoriously bad pollution. The reception area felt like a steam room, and he had to fight off cockroaches as big as his thumb trying to crawl up his pant legs. After sweltering in what he was convinced might actually be one of the lower levels of hell, he finally met with one of the company representatives. The man was very friendly, spoke English well, and nodded approvingly at Lambert's credentials.

"Is this for commercial or military use?" the man asked.

"That's classified."

"Our government does not allow us to sell to foreign military."

"I work for a major carrier in the US. The proposed use is civilian."

"Fine. Follow me." That was easy.

The man took Lambert to the production line and showed him the part and how it worked. Afterward they went to accounting to draw up the purchase order. When the man logged into his computer, Lambert captured his password with an RFID skimmer device and sent it to Langley. The analysts there were able to see the network ID and log-in as soon as the man logged out, allowing them to download the company's customer database.

As soon as they acknowledged a successful download, Lambert paid for the part and went back to his hotel. He was packing for a late flight back to DC when his room phone rang. It didn't stop, so he picked up, annoyed.

"I'm here to pick up the package," a man on the other end of the line said with an Australian or maybe a light British accent.

"Who is this?"

"Alia sent me. She doesn't want you carrying it back with you through customs. Too risky. Can I come up?"

"Give me a minute."

Lambert hung up. Alia would have told him if she were sending someone. He called her on his satellite phone.

"Guy just called me from the lobby. Said you sent him to pick up the part. I drop-shipped it to you from their office like we agreed—"

"Get out of there now," she said and hung up.

There was a knock on the door.

"Hey, it's me. Front desk let me up," the man called from the hallway, definitely a Brit.

Lambert grabbed a cigarette lighter from his pants pocket, got up on a chair, and flicked the lighter flame under the glass bubble on the fire sprinkler. The glass bubble broke and the sprinkler went off, along with the building's fire alarm system. The deafening tone started a panic on Lambert's floor. He grabbed his satellite phone and passport and jammed them in his pocket. The man was knocking hard on his hotel room door, yelling for him to open it, warning him there was a fire in the building. Lambert knocked hard on the door of the adjoining room.

"Who is it?" a voice called from the other room.

"Hotel security!" Lambert yelled back.

A frightened elderly couple opened the door. Lambert went into their room and locked the door behind him. Right after he did, he heard the door to his room being kicked in.

"You need to evacuate," he told them.

"I just need to get my purse," the wife said and went into the bedroom. She got her bag and hurried back into the room.

"Mr. Lentz sends you his regards," the husband said.

"What did you just—" Lambert began but was cut short when the wife pulled a Beretta 93R machine pistol with a barrel suppressor from her purse and emptied its twenty-round mag into his head and back at point-blank range.

24

Day 22

Kennedy poured another mini bottle of Jim Beam into a plastic cup in his room at the JFK Sheraton and ignored the incessantly vibrating Red Carpet satellite phone on the dresser. He sat in a worn vinyl chair, fully dressed, with his packed luggage on the bed. It was 4:30 A.M. and nightmarish flashes of Tad Monty's cronies, blood gushing out of their ruined heads, were playing on repeat in his mind. Kennedy had seen dead people, but even in Tel Aviv he had never seen anyone killed right in front of him, close enough to touch. The way their eyes bulged and rolled back as their bodies crumpled like marionettes clipped from strings would haunt him for the rest of his life.

"This is the job," Kennedy said out loud and drained the cup.

He went for another bottle from the minibar and stopped himself.

"But this is not me," he said. "Time to go home."

He grabbed his bags and walked out, leaving the sat phone on the dresser.

There was a 7:00 A.M. flight back to Los Angeles out of Newark, and Kennedy was going to be on it. Alia could keep her money and hero scout badges. The spectrum of potential consequences, he knew, started at grim and ended with catastrophic. There was a real chance they would kill him before they would let him walk away. He had seen damning things. And after all, he would not be missed. On the other hand, they could easily implicate him in the two TSA agents' deaths—what would probably amount to a capital murder case in federal court—so that might be enough to leverage him to keep his mouth shut. In any case, it didn't matter. Death, or even imprisonment, was far less daunting than having a front-row seat to another business-as-usual CIA snuff job.

Newark Airport was quiet when Kennedy arrived at 6:00 A.M. He had purchased first class so he could go through priority check-in. He passed the ID checkpoint without incident and cleared the millimeter wave body scanner. But the luggage-scanning agent asked him for a bag check and then took her sweet time swabbing his carry-on and briefcase for bomb materials. After she inserted the swabs into the machine for analysis, her demeanor of routine-induced boredom turned to one of suspicion. She stared for an uncomfortably long moment at the analysis screen.

"Sir, I'm going to need you to come with me for an additional luggage screening."

Kennedy knew that meant the bag had tested positive for chemical residue, which made no sense.

"Is there a problem?"

"This machine isn't giving me an accurate readout so we'll need to try another."

She signaled her supervisor, who walked over and looked at the scanner screen. Kennedy tried to relax. If he missed the flight, it would give Juarez time to track him to Newark. He just needed to stay cool and cooperate to avoid delays.

"Could you please come with me, sir?" the supervisor asked firmly.

Kennedy nodded and the supervisor led him through a door with a keypad entry, then down a long, blinding-white fluorescent hallway. Two male agents came around the corner from an adjoining hallway and greeted them. Kennedy could tell they were armed.

"Hello," one of them said in an overly friendly way.

"Hi," Kennedy replied amiably, knowing they would be looking for all the things he trained TSOs to look for—agitation, dilated pupils, heavy perspiration, nervous affect. He'd been up all night and was sweating Jim Beam, so trying to appear "normal" was taking every ounce of composure he had left.

"Thanks so much for your cooperation. If you'll come with us, we'll get this sorted out."

"May I ask what needs to be sorted out?"

"Agent Hickman's equipment is a little glitchy today, so we're going to analyze it with another machine and get you on your way," he reassured, nodding at Hickman to leave, which she did quietly.

The other male agent said nothing and took the bags as the three of them walked down the hall and into a room with what Kennedy recognized as sophisticated bomb detection scanning equipment. While the silent agent analyzed the bags, the other agent continued their friendly chat.

"Where you off to today?"

"Los Angeles."

"Great. Love it there. Business or pleasure?"

"I live there."

"Lucky you."

The other agent walked over and handed Mr. Friendly a paper. Mr. Friendly stopped being Mr. Friendly and Kennedy's heart sank. This was the room where they weeded out the false positives. At that moment, he was clearly a positive, and if Kennedy had been advising these agents, he would have told them to take him into custody.

"Will you excuse us for a moment?"

Kennedy nodded, his face feeling numb. What the fuck was happening? It was impossible that his bag had explosives residue on it. It had been in his possession the entire time they were working the airports. He never checked it, and Juarez and his team had never asked him to carry anything. Juarez and his team . . . It had to be them. They were already onto him. That was the only explanation. And if the police came to take him into custody, they would not be police officers.

They would be a CIA cleanup crew.

25

The door opened to the Draconian TSA interview room and Kennedy was surprised to see Alia walk in, carrying his luggage. A look of contempt had frozen over her usual warm smile as she sat across from him and handed him the carry-on and briefcase.

"Good-bye," she said without feeling.

"You went to all this trouble to say good-bye?"

"What trouble?"

"Bomb chemicals on my luggage?"

"I was going to send Juarez to debrief you, but I wanted to see this for myself."

"See what?"

"You turning tail. I must admit, I'm surprised."

"Turning tail?"

"Yes, isn't that what you're doing?"

"I'm quitting because I didn't sign up for—"

"I'm aware of *why* you're quitting. You've made that obvious. It's the act of quitting itself that has me puzzled."

"You said I wouldn't be in any danger."

"You aren't. And you never were."

"Are you aware of what happened at the airport?"

"Of course. I'm also aware that we handled it."

"Handled it? I'm not a killer, Alia."

"I'm sorry, did you kill someone?"

"No."

"So, you're safe and you're not a killer. Now you have no good reasons to turn your back on your team and climb out the window like some teenager protesting his parents' curfew. After all the generosity and consideration I've shown you, how could *this* have seemed like the right thing to do?"

"I was . . . afraid."

Alia sighed deeply, the corner of her mouth twitching, begging to curl itself into a condescending scowl. For the first time, she felt she had made a grave error in judgment with Kennedy. Her superiors thought using a civilian was too risky, but they had trusted her brilliance and allowed her to take a leap of faith. Now no one would be there to catch her as she fell. Kennedy was a failure, so she was a failure.

"I guess I'm just not cut out for this," Kennedy said.

"You realize that what my men did was nothing compared to what terrorists did to your own flesh and blood?" she shot back.

Kennedy flinched.

"Now do you understand my surprise at all of this?"

"Yes. I'm sorry." After the way she'd invoked Belle, Kennedy expected some small measure of understanding, but instead Alia laughed, allowing judgment to flow out of her like venom.

"You're sorry? This is a multimillion-dollar operation. You have a team in the field, risking their lives as we sit here chatting. Did you receive any of my messages about what happened to Lambert in Malaysia?"

Kennedy sat bolt upright, remembering the phone buzzing on the hotel room dresser as he drowned his sorrows.

"I'll take that as a no. My team found pieces of him in a Dumpster at the Kuala Lumpur Hilton not too long ago."

"Oh my God," Kennedy said. He felt violently ill.

"God's not going to help us, Kennedy. There's a billionaire psychopath out there committing all of his power and resources to destroying this country and spinning the rest of the world into chaos and unrest."

She moved closer to him, inches from his face.

"And 9/11 will be a tiny footnote in our last history book if he succeeds. So, you'll pardon me for reacting with contempt at the absurdity of you abandoning something so important because you felt a little queasy watching the men work—and trying to pass it off with something as meaningless as an apology. Would you have accepted an apology for Belle's death?"

Kennedy wanted to reply, to redeem himself somehow, but Alia was already walking out the door.

26

While Kennedy was back in Los Angeles, wallowing in self-pity, Nuri was in Havana, wallowing in the bureaucratic muck of the Cuban government. Thanks to Juarez, the CIA knew Lentz had a 125-acre compound on Isla de la Juventud, a small island fifty miles off the coast of Cuba. It was made-to-order for someone who wanted maximum privacy under the protection of an anti-American regime. Tourist traffic was sparse due to frequent hurricanes and the island being one of Cuba's main sources of timber and marble. And there was an airport large enough for most commercial aircraft, so Lentz could easily come and go by private jet.

The island was under Cuban rule, so all Lentz had to do was line the pockets of the right people and he had the run of the place. That was how Juarez's team found out he owned property there. A few of Lentz's Egyptian collaborators, captured in 2013, spoke of him operating out of Cuba. The CIA knew that the Cuban government kept close records of all foreign nationals living on the islands, and Juarez had acquired those records from a recent defector who had been an executive at Cuba's Central Bank. Juarez was then able to follow the money and connect the property taxes and purchase records to one of Lentz's shell corporations in Dubai.

Since discovering Lentz's presence there, the CIA had the property under constant surveillance, but Lentz made it very difficult for them to capture anything useful. In spite of this, it was the only place in the world where Lentz could be tied to a physical address, and Alia believed it was the best way to get a foothold in his operation.

Field agents had been sent before, but none of them had gotten anywhere but dead. Cubans who had known ties to Lentz, from gardeners to government officials, had the fear of God in them and kept their mouths shut. Alia needed to tap into Lentz's electronic communications—his primary mode of interfacing with the outside world—so she could track his movements and connect the dots in his network.

Her first move was to use a major US wireless phone carrier, one that had worked with the NSA to spy on American citizens, as a front to broker a meeting with Cuba's Ministry of Informatics and Communications—the country's governing body for information technology and telecommunications. Its minister was eager to learn more sophisticated methods for spying on his own citizens and controlling information flow from the outside world. So Alia sent Nuri. Her cover was a business development executive from an Internet security firm, coming to Cuba to take advantage of the newly opening border. Government officials were eager to meet her and have a technology demonstration, so they invited her to a lavish party at one of the homes of a wealthy telecom minister.

The invitation called for ultra-formal dress, so men were in tuxedos with white ties and tails and women wore gowns. Nuri wasn't fond of the exquisite Chanel number Alia sent with her, so she "modified" it to her liking and it ended up covering her about as well as a dinner napkin. And when the host tried to herd her away with the rest of the women after dessert, she defiantly joined the men on the veranda, where they'd gone to smoke cigars, drink brandy, and talk about how much American money they were going to start raking in. Nuri was drawing stares and whispers meant to intimidate her and shoo her away, but those only strengthened her resolve. She grabbed a brandy snifter, drank half of it in one gulp, and held her phone up in the air.

"Gentlemen, gather round please, while I amaze and delight you with one of my favorite parlor tricks!" She sounded like a carnival barker.

They all looked at her as if she were an escaped mental patient.

"Don't be shy. Right here on my little iPhone, I can show you every hacker attempting to jack your government servers!"

That got their attention. They huddled around her, their eyes fixed on her phone screen. She showed them a flat world map with little red dots clustered in Russia and Eastern Europe, Central America, China, and the United States. Next to the red dots were hacker usernames, like ByteME and JuliUSSleazAR.

"Who are these people?" one of the men asked.

"You really want to know?"

"Of course! But they are hackers. Don't they hide their identities?"

"They try. But I can see right through them," she bragged.

She swiped her phone screen. One by one, the true identity and geo location of each hacker was revealed, complete with last known address and mobile number.

"Better than Ashley Madison, right?" she said.

They nearly chewed off and choked on the ends of their cigars.

"The majority of these hackers are employees of the US government, working within the FBI and NSA. So much for diplomacy." Nuri laughed.

The Cubans were not amused. The minister himself joined them, and the rest of the men wilted.

"Don't you think that's funny? FBI?" she said. "After all that goody-two-shoes bullshit they've been slinging you about wanting to be your buddies?"

"No, we do not think that is funny, miss," the minister said sternly.

"Okay, fine. Irony's not your thing. *This* might make you laugh."

She swiped her screen again.

"I just uploaded their identities to a Dark Net troll community," she said.

The red dots started to disappear across the map.

"B-bye, hackers."

"What happened?" the minister asked.

"Massive denial-of-service attack on the hackers' servers. Fried down to the boards. Stick a fork in those fuckers. They're done."

"You are a frightening young woman," he said. "But I would rather have you on our side than theirs."

"That's great to hear. Because if you hire my firm, I can guarantee the US government will never gain access to your network. If they do, I will refund every penny you've spent on my service. Pro rata."

"I have a feeling that is going to be a lot of pennies," he said, laughing.

"My dad is Cuban, so you get a family discount," she said, grinning and lighting a massive cigar of her own.

Within twenty-four hours, the Cuban officials had done a full background check on Nuri and her "company" and the papers were signed. Nuri integrated her equipment and software into the Cuban government's network servers, gaining unfiltered access to all the communications of everyone using the network.

Including Lentz.

27

Kennedy had been back in Los Angeles for three days after being fired by Alia at Newark and he was still reeling from it. He felt physically ill every time he thought about the cowardice he had shown betraying the Red Carpet team, especially in light of Lambert's death. When he wasn't lying listlessly on the bed or couch, staring at the ceiling, he made feeble attempts to work and run errands, but all of it seemed meaningless in light of what he knew might be coming and how he had destroyed his chance of helping to stop it.

His phone buzzed and he checked it, hoping to hear from Love. He needed to get what had happened off his chest and she was the only person he trusted. There were no messages from her, but there were alerts about Noah Kruz's upcoming international speaking tour, and his Kruz quote-of-the-day app was blinking. He desperately needed something to drag him out of his funk, so he clicked on it and read:

There is no such thing as the word "no." Children know best because they never stop asking for what they want. Their persistence is merciless, and in the end, they always get it. If you cut this word out of your life, then you will never rest until you hear the word "yes." Do ants see anything other than the expansion of the colony? Do they "hope" someday for a bigger mound? These creatures, which barely

*have one-billionth of the neurological power of a human embryo, have
a far greater capacity for success than most full-grown human adults.*

Maybe it was time to get off his ass and get out of the hotel.

––––––

Kennedy thought he'd try to ease his mind with a round of golf, but when
he walked outside, it was pouring rain. *Perfect*, he thought as he stood
there, numb and drenched. A black sedan pulled up to the curb and the
passenger-side window rolled down. Juarez was at the wheel.

"Get in."

Kennedy's first thought was that Juarez had come to kill him. His second was that he didn't care.

"I'm here to put you out of your misery," Juarez said amiably.

Kennedy got in.

Juarez started driving. "Hey, man, I tried to get her to change her mind.
I even told her this was all her fault, that her expectations were unrealistic.
But you know these analyst types, juiced to the gills on ambition with no
patience for failure. By the way, I have no beef with you for wanting to
leave. I thought maybe my tough talk after JFK might bring you around,
but it looks like it was too little too late."

"Do you think she'd consider giving me another chance?"

"No way. She has to save face. Her protégé went AWOL after the first
operational hiccup."

"That was a *hiccup*?" Kennedy asked.

"To the brass, that's all it was. Mission accomplished, let God sort 'em
out later, et cetera. They'll tell her you couldn't stand the heat, which they'll
say they predicted, and she'll have to swallow a big fat *I told you so*. There
aren't any second chances in this game, brother. I guess you should consider yourself lucky she didn't feel the need to delete you from the balance
sheet."

"I think I might have preferred that to total exile."

"I'm glad to hear you say that."

"Why?"

"Because despite your pariah status with Alia, I think there's a way to
get you back in. If you're interested."

Kennedy perked up. "Hell yes, I'm interested."

Juarez handed him a USB drive. "Lentz has a compound on one of the Cuban islands—Isla de la Juventud. Nuri managed to get us a hack on their government network, which he uses to run his operation. All the data she captured so far is on that stick. The good news is we can track his comms all over the world and identify his collaborators—at least by location. The bad news is he's using an encryption technique our analysts can't identify."

"And you think I'm going to be able to decipher it?"

"Absolutely not. But maybe you can come up with a work-around that our team of so-called experts hasn't thought of. Unless you have something better to do."

Kennedy shoved the USB into his pocket.

"It's worth a shot," Kennedy said. "Does Alia know you're doing this?"

"Hell no. She'd kill me if she knew I was even talking to you."

28

The next day, Kennedy called some of his dad's old air force buddies, most of them engineers, to see if any of them knew anything about cryptography. Phyllis, one of their colleagues at the Space and Missile Systems Center in El Segundo, was a software engineer who collected old cipher devices as a hobby. Kennedy had coffee with her and showed her a few lines of encryption he'd copied from Nuri's Cuban data.

"Looks like gibberish," she said.

"Isn't that the point?" Kennedy said.

She laughed. "Yes, but if you've seen as much enciphered data as I have over the years, you notice patterns. There's always a pattern, whether you're dealing with old telecipher systems from World War Two, like the German Enigma, or boring old SSL code used in banking transactions. The characters in the code correspond to a key that the recipient uses to *decipher* the code. Those keys are usually some kind of number system or transposition alphabets. So, if the characters feel too randomly arranged, like these do, then you're either dealing with a super genius who has created an entirely new cipher, or it's gibberish."

She looked at the code again and started scribbling in her notebook.

"I'm just throwing a few of the more obscure keys at this code and I can't get a handle on it. Not even one word, which is rare. Cipher is a lot like computer code. It's based on previous versions of itself. I have no idea what this might be based on. Sorry I can't be of more help. What's this from anyway?"

"I work in security and my boss likes to send us these annoying problems. Thinks it keeps us on our toes. If I solve it, I win a trip to Hawaii," Kennedy lied.

She laughed again. "I think he's messing with you."

———

"I think this enciphered data is a decoy," he said to Juarez over the phone that night. "Lentz has spent a fortune successfully hiding himself from the prying eyes of the CIA. Why wouldn't he do the same thing with his data? A bullshit cipher that seemed sophisticated would present a Super Geek challenge to your analysts at Langley, and their egos would drive them to try to crack it. While they're at it, focusing resources on a dead end, Lentz is communicating another way and advancing his plan."

"Not bad," Juarez said, genuinely impressed. "The Super Geeks still haven't decoded a damn thing and, if our systems can't crack it—"

"We need to get someone close to Lentz," Kennedy said.

"Oh, we've gotten people close to Lentz . . . close range, that is. You could fit what was left of them in a Ziploc bag."

"There has to be a way."

"And I have a feeling you might find one," Juarez said.

Kennedy was not ready to give up on a second chance with Alia. He not only had to think outside the box, but he also had to live and operate there. As Juarez said, the CIA had not been able to get near Lentz. In fact, no intelligence agency had been able to pull that off. But they were probably all doing the same thing—attempting to embed an agent in the organization of a man who was essentially a hypervigilant recluse with the ability to smell a rat miles away.

The answer was not to try to get someone close to him. The answer was to recruit one of his already-close minions. He had to have a small army of them, handling logistics, resources, and financial transactions. It was like any other business. Lentz had *employees*, and there was a hierarchy governing them. Attempting to pilot fish onto someone too high up in the organization was not the right approach. The higher up the minion, the higher the pay, and the stronger the loyalty. Kennedy needed someone lower on the totem pole, but not so low they couldn't leave Lentz's back door open for him. And it needed to be someone Lentz was obliged to trust to some degree.

Kennedy knew travel, so he started there. Private would be the only way for Lentz to move freely around the world and maintain anonymity. A pilot would be someone who would have a lot of contact with him and someone he would be obliged to trust. If he were Lentz, he would engage someone and keep that person local so he could leave at a moment's notice. Kennedy contacted the Ciudad Libertad Airport in Havana. It had been Cuba's original airport before José Martí International was built, so it was large enough for big private jets and catered to a wealthy clientele. He spoke to the airport's main office, telling them he needed a large aircraft for executive travel. The flight crew needed to be experienced enough to pass muster with corporate risk management. The airport e-mailed him a list with contact information for all private pilots and aircraft they had available for service, listed in order of years of experience.

He narrowed the list to a dozen pilots with the flight hours and aircraft-type ratings to fit the profile. Juarez had Nuri pull all of their recent flight records, and only one of the pilots on the list had multiple flight logs listing Isla de la Juventud as point of origin. His name was Rico and he was a former pilot for the Venezuelan Air Force. On the surface, he seemed like an excellent candidate. He was very experienced and well trained, something Kennedy believed Lentz would look for. He was also from a country whose president despised the United States, so he may have had his own reasons, politically, to help Lentz. Finally, at thirty years old, his youth was something Lentz could use to his advantage. The average salary for young pilots even in the United States was shockingly low, so the commercial prospects in Venezuela, and most of Latin America for that matter, couldn't possibly have been able to compete with what Lentz might pay.

Juarez agreed Rico was an excellent mark, but when he mentioned it to Alia, couching it as a lead he had thought of, he had not been able to convince her to try to bring him in. She was in full ass-coverage mode and felt that recruiting one of Lentz's own people as a snitch carried too much risk. If things with Rico went sideways, Lentz would go even darker.

"Sorry, man," Juarez said, "you did some great work here but it looks like this is the end of the line."

"So, that's it? You're just going to ignore this lead and walk away?"

"I have to, brother. She's the boss. You take care."

Juarez's *Better luck next time* brush-off only galvanized Kennedy's resolve. This wasn't about getting reinstated with Red Carpet anymore. It was about saving lives, and he couldn't, in good conscience, leave this last stone unturned.

If Alia was covering her ass, it was time for Kennedy to put his on the line.

29

When you called to say you needed a favor, I figured maybe you wanted tickets to a show or a ride to the airport," Love said.

It was early evening and Kennedy had invited Love to El Carmen, a hole-in-the-wall tequila bar on the outer edge of West Hollywood. She had just come from the recording studio, so she was sporting her artfully dressed-down look—jeans, gold combat boots, and a vintage Descendents concert T-shirt. Kennedy, on the other hand, looked like he was coming off a three-day bender. He was desperate to chase down his lead in Havana and thought maybe Love could help him, so he told her about being recruited for Red Carpet and filled her in on most of what had happened. Love just listened and tried to keep her jaw from breaking on the floor.

"I know it's kind of crazy—"

"*Kind of* crazy? Dude, I can't believe you're a . . ." She looked around to see if anyone was listening and mouthed the word "spy."

"I'm not. I'm what they call an asset. They hired me because of my work and connections in airport security."

"But you got fired?"

"Yeah . . . I fucked up."

"What'd you do?"

"I'll tell you sometime. I promise. But I can't right now."

"You're kind of scaring me," she said.

"Sorry, I'm just desperate to fix this. I'm doing it for Belle. I feel like it's a chance to make good with her."

"And you want *me* to help?"

"I don't know where else to turn."

"Okay," she said, putting her hand on his. "I'll do whatever you want. We're family, remember?"

"Let me explain it to you first and you can make up your mind."

Kennedy told her about the young pilot and how they needed to get close to him in order to get close to Lentz, the man they wanted to catch. Kennedy couldn't think of a scenario where he could do it himself without raising Rico's suspicion. But Love was capable of sweet-talking the devil into going to church. Maybe she could go to Havana and get the guy on the hook.

"You want me to whore myself out for information?"

"No! Jesus. All you need to do is talk to the guy and see if you can convince him to help us. Once you get your foot in the door, the CIA can take it from there."

"You need me to be a fluffer," Love said, grinning.

"For lack of a better term, yes. But it's a mind fluff, nothing physical."

"Look at you! All protective. What does this guy look like? Not to toot my own horn, but if he's a troll and I throw the vibe all over him, he's going to be suspicious."

"He's not a troll."

Kennedy showed her Rico's picture.

"Ay, *caramba*," Love said, biting her fist.

"Okay, maybe this isn't such a great idea."

"I'm *joking*, dummy. I'll do it."

"Really?"

"Why not?" she said. "Sounds kind of fun. James Bond shit."

Kennedy gave her a hug. "Thank you. You're the best," he said.

"I know," she said. "Now give me the intel," she said, raising an eyebrow.

"You're taking this seriously, right?"

"Of course. I'm just getting into the right headspace. Sorry, I'll shut up now."

"I want to send you to Havana as soon as possible. I'll handle all the expenses, of course," Kennedy said. "And pay you very well for your time."

"Please," she said. "This is a favor, remember?"

"No, this is work, and you're getting paid whether you like it or not."

"Fine. But I don't fluff cheap," she said.

"Fair enough."

"Quick question," she said. "How do you know this guy isn't going to smoke me on the spot?"

"He's a pilot, so I doubt he spends a lot of time smoking people. But if he gets out of line at all, we'll be waiting to take him down."

"You know you're going to owe me big-time for this, right?"

"Absolutely. Whatever you want."

"If I do this, you have to promise me you're going to quit that lousy bullshit thing you call a day job and do something fun for a living."

"I promise," Kennedy said without hesitation.

"On Belle."

"Oh my God. Fine, I swear it on my dead sister, you creep."

"Good. Havana, here we come."

30

Kennedy made arrangements for he and Love to travel to Cuba via the Bahamas, and they were in Havana three days later. Without the help of the CIA, he wasn't able to get any more intel on Rico. But he knew most pilots had their favorite bars. Like cops and firefighters, they enjoyed talking shop over a few hundred beers. Kennedy spoke to a pilot friend in Miami who said that on layovers he had frequented a dive bar called Shangri-la, a half mile from Ciudad Libertad Airport. Love did her part too and found Rico on Instagram. He had posted selfies at Shangri-la, mostly on Fridays when he went there with friends to watch soccer. When Friday night rolled around, Kennedy posted up at a table in the back of the bar and waited. When Rico rolled in with his boys, Kennedy texted Love and she made her entrance.

She sat at the bar and ordered a drink while half the patrons ogled her unrepentantly. A few of them actually tried to hit on her and she shot them down in flames. In the midst of all this, she flashed Rico one look. It was quick and subtle, but it was all the invitation he needed.

"My name is Rico," he said in accented English, "and I'm going to buy you a drink."

"Knock yourself out," she said as he sat on the stool next to hers.

After a few shots and some gently provocative conversation, Rico was nice and oiled up. And like most colorfully narcissistic egomaniacs, he loved to talk about his favorite subject: himself. He went on about his time in the air force, then his move into private aviation, where he used to fly pop stars in and out of Ibiza. Since moving to Cuba, he'd been flying rich Europeans and South Americans around the world. He even bragged about having carried the occasional Bolivian marching powder payload up to the Bahamas or Key West. Love had him drooling in the palm of her hand.

"Oh my God," she exclaimed, doing her best naïve American girl impression. "What an amazing job. Do you love it?"

"It's okay . . ."

His face darkened, and he gulped down the rest of his drink. Love almost burst out laughing at the dramatic overtones. Rico was like the hunky star of a Mexican soap opera, gearing up for his big scenes. Love could tell he wanted to get something off his chest, but like most drama queens, he needed her to draw it out of him. The problem was, the bar was getting more crowded with loud soccer fans and Rico became preoccupied with the looks the other men were giving Love. She played that note like a prodigy.

"You want to get out of here?" she asked.

He nodded and left a wad of cash on the bar. They walked outside for a smoke, and when Rico got an even better look at Love under the streetlamp, the fire in his belly became an inferno.

"Where do you want to go?" she asked.

"My apartment is nearby," he said.

Love wasn't about to take one for the team. She lit another cigarette and tried to get him to open up.

"Tell me more about your job. You seemed upset in the bar."

"It's just . . . I shouldn't talk about it."

"Aw, and I thought we were making a connection."

He looked at her with stars in his eyes and touched her cheek tenderly.

"Tell me what's wrong. Maybe I can help," she cooed.

"I work for a fucking Nazi asshole," he said.

"Tell me about him. What's his name?"

Rico ranted about the "fucking Nazi asshole" he had to fly all over the world. Based on the small number of times Rico had seen him, he provided a physical description that sounded very much like what Kennedy had told her about Lentz. But Rico had never learned his name.

"Motherfucker killed my friend," he said, his eyes welling.

"Oh my God. What happened?"

"She was one of his regular girls," he said shamefully. "He goes through them like shop rags. It wasn't her thing. I know everybody says that, but she really needed the money and the *putas* know how to suck a young girl in, you know? She'd only been turned out a couple of weeks when his people picked her up. She was young and fresh, so he kept bringing her back. She made more money than she'd seen her whole life, more than even her father or grandfather ever made, so she didn't want to quit. She thought she could do it for just a while, and then buy her way to New York or Miami. But then he started asking for some really weird shit that she didn't want to do."

"What kind of weird shit?"

"She wouldn't even tell *me*. It was that bad. She just kept saying he was the devil, that no man would ever want things like that from a woman. So one night she told him to go fuck *himself*. She called me the next morning, so proud. I was proud of her too. We went out and celebrated. But after that night I didn't hear from her again. Then they found her. She was . . . I can't even say it . . ."

Rico fought back the tears. Love hugged him tightly, and he wept for several minutes. When they made it back to his apartment, Love skillfully extricated herself, telling Rico she had feelings for him and didn't want to destroy what they had by moving too quickly. So she promised to have dinner with him the next night.

"Oh, you're *good*," Kennedy told her as they debriefed later at their hotel.

"It's weird, right? I never thought in a million years I could be a *spy*."

"You're a performer, Love. And a damn good one. Plus, you're helping this guy out. This is probably the only way for him to get out of a very bad situation."

"Are you going to tell your CIA contacts about me?" she asked excitedly.

"I'm going to do better than that. I'm going to tell them to get their asses down here to watch your repeat performance tomorrow night."

31

You're one ballsy son of a bitch. I'll give you that."

The next morning, Juarez was smiling at Kennedy and Love across an outdoor café table overlooking the bay. The place was small, filthy, and loud—a local hangout for commercial fishermen and dock laborers. Juarez had chosen it because it was far from any of the city's tourist spots. Kennedy figured he might have also picked it because if he didn't like what they had to say, he could easily kill them and stuff their bodies in waste oil tanks or pay someone to haul them out for chum.

"Not as ballsy as Love," Kennedy said.

Juarez looked at Love and sized her up.

"You got that right," he said.

"What do you think?" Kennedy asked. "About tonight?"

"I think we need to prep," Juarez said. "Where did he ask you to go?"

"His place," she replied. "Shocker."

"Romantic intentions aside," Juarez began, "that's perfect. Means we don't have to do any of this in public."

"So what do I tell him?"

"Depends. How much does he know about Lentz?" Juarez asked.

"Not a lot. When I asked his boss's name, he didn't know it. I guess he mostly deals with a handler and rarely sees Lentz."

"Here's what we're gonna do. You're going to show up at Rico's place and blow his mind. He doesn't know shit about his boss? Good. Then, you tell him his boss is the head of a drug cartel family . . . and you're DEA. That'll put the fear of God in him that he needs to get out and needs your help to do it. We make you DEA so if Lentz catches wind, he'll sic his dogs on them first and we'll have time to regroup."

Kennedy could see Love was working it all over in her head.

"So, I'm asking him to be a snitch," she said. "What's in it for him?"

Juarez handed her a box of chocolates.

"Seriously?" She laughed.

"There's twenty thousand US in there. Enough to whet his appetite. Tell him there are five more stacks where that came from if he finishes the job."

"Which is?" Kennedy asked.

"Planting bugs. I want him to wire Lentz to the gills—house, cars, and private jet especially. We'll use the tech you've been installing in airports so Lentz's sweepers can't pick them up. The money will show Rico we're for real. If he bites, we'll set up a meeting tomorrow and I can prep him."

"What if he doesn't bite?" Kennedy said.

"Then Love will have to kill him and get the hell out of there."

"What?" Love yelped.

Juarez laughed. "I'm messing with you. He's not going to say no. Twenty large goes a very long way in Cuba."

"He's a man. If I do my job right, I can probably get him to pay you."

"No doubt," Juarez said.

"What if he isn't as cooperative as we would like? Or maybe even hostile?"

"Got that covered," Juarez said.

He handed Love a jewelry box. There was a silver skull ring inside with black gemstones for eyes.

"There's a bug and a GPS transmitter in there. If you feel at any time you're in danger, tap the ring three times on a hard surface and it will send out a distress signal."

Love looked at the ring anxiously.

"Don't worry, I'll be close by with Kennedy and I'll be able to get to you in five minutes."

"You all right?" Kennedy asked her.

"Yeah," she said, twisting the ring onto her finger with an air of indifference.

"We'll all recon later tonight," Juarez said. "Now you should head back to the hotel and wait there," he told Love. "Stay off the street today."

Love saluted him and took off. Kennedy got up to follow her.

"Have a seat," Juarez said. "We should have a chat."

Kennedy sat back down.

"You realize how dangerous this is, right?" Juarez asked.

"Do you want me to stop her?"

"That's not what I'm saying. I just want to make sure you're clear on what we've just asked her to do."

"Yes. And so is she. You should have seen her last night. She can handle this guy."

"I hope so. For all of our sakes."

———————

Love's dinner with Rico worked out better than expected. He had been in an especially bad mood when she came over. He told her that Lentz had killed another friend of his, a limo driver, for picking up the boss a half hour late. The man was in his sixties and Lentz's men had supposedly dragged him to death behind the limo. It was a horrific story, but Love couldn't help but think it would be good for their cause.

"Soon that will be me," Rico said gravely.

"It doesn't have to be," she said, playing off his emotions. "But we need your help to put an end to this guy. And it sounds like you might need ours."

Love told him she was DEA and delivered her snitch sales pitch. Not only was Rico eating out of her hand, but he also didn't even seem interested in pursuing her romantically anymore. He looked like a dog that had been on the business end of his master's belt for far too long. Love promised him all the things she knew he was desperate for—revenge, freedom, and a return to dignity. The money she offered sweetened the pot, but in the end, she could tell he was tired of being afraid all the time and feeling powerless to help the good people Lentz was happy to destroy. He wanted in.

Over the next two days, Juarez met with Rico and trained him on how to use the same new surveillance tech he had given Kennedy to bug airports—virtually undetectable using any known sweep tech. As a pilot, Rico was extremely gear savvy, so he learned quickly and was a natural at finding new ways to plant the devices. A week after Kennedy, Juarez, and Love left Havana, Rico had managed to bug two of Lentz's private jets and some of the cars he brought to the airport.

Not only could they record conversations, but they could also capture encrypted wireless data transmissions from mobile devices and any device communicating with his servers via his proprietary instant messaging app. The pièce de résistance was the GPS function that made it possible for Langley to track Lentz's movements around the globe.

32

I **don't know what to** say, Kennedy."

Alia had been over the moon when Juarez sent her the first data dump from Rico's taps, and she had flown to Los Angeles to celebrate with the three of them. They drank champagne on the terrace of Kennedy's hotel suite.

"You don't have to say anything," Kennedy said. "I'm just happy you're willing to take me back."

"Take you back?" She laughed. "My dear, you've fucking cracked this caper for me, in the parlance of so many hokey spy novels. Do you know how many years we've been trying to do what you did in a few days?"

"I'm glad I could be of help . . . finally."

"Humility is a fine quality, but now is not the time nor the place. You are extraordinary, and to top it all off, you've brought me a gift in your lovely friend."

"Stop, I'm turning all red," Love said, blushing.

"You're some kind of rock 'n' roll Mata Hari," Alia gushed.

"Hmm, I like the sound of that," Love said.

"How would you like to stay on the team for a while?" Alia asked, re-filling Love's glass. "Provided that's all right with our team leader."

Kennedy raised an eyebrow. He hadn't expected Alia to ask about Love joining up with them beyond Cuba.

"I think I'd like that very much," Love said, looking to Kennedy for approval.

The more he thought about putting her in harm's way, the more he had second thoughts about bringing her into the fray. He hated the idea that she might get hurt. But then he thought about how she'd handled Rico, as if she'd been doing that kind of confidence work for years. She never buckled under the pressure, and her instincts with Rico were spot-on. In fact, without her, he wouldn't have been sitting there drinking champagne, celebrating his reinstatement. And he knew damn well that Belle would've wanted him to let her be a part of the team.

"You're a natural," he said, forcing a smile. "Welcome to Red Carpet."

"Good. I have some ideas about how we can use Love's unique talents and personality," Alia said. "But our first priority is to get you back into the field."

"I wanted to talk to you about that," Kennedy said. "I have some thoughts about how to approach the equipment upgrades at the airports without raising red flags with Homeland. I have a feeling Tad Monty is going to upgrade his pain-in-the-ass status."

"That's your world, so we'll do it your way this time," Alia said.

"What's my assignment?" Love asked excitedly.

"For now, I'm going to send you out with Kennedy," Alia said. "You'll be a new hire in his consulting business, learning the ropes. While you're along for the ride, you can use your considerable skill for distraction to assist Kennedy's operation."

"What's going on with the rest of the team?" Kennedy asked.

"I have Nuri and Trudeau standing by for a briefing," Alia said.

She and Juarez opened military field laptops, and Nuri and Trudeau appeared on the screens in videoconference windows.

"There's my boy!" Nuri said to Kennedy. "Turn around. Let me look at you."

"Hi, Nuri," Kennedy said amiably.

"And is this our new recruit . . . Hey, you're hot," Nuri said to Love.

"Um, thank you," Love said. "Nice to meet you both."

"Can we get on with it?" Trudeau said, annoyed.

"Right," Nuri said. "Progress. Okay, so you know those big pink trucker pills that keep you up for hours? Well, ever since Kennedy made

Lentz his bitch, I've been taking those babies so I can keep up with the data analysis."

"How long have you been awake?" Kennedy asked.

"I lost track after what I thought was Wednesday turned out to be Sunday."

"Jesus," Alia said.

"That's what I said when I saw him five minutes ago," Nuri said. "Anyway, aside from all the piles of data gold you've heaped upon us, I found something better at the end of this rainbow a few hours ago . . . Our first cross-reference to the JFK data."

"Which is why Trudeau is here," Alia added.

"I was beginning to wonder," Trudeau said.

"It appears Lentz has been making large weapons purchases from a Russian supplier none of us has ever heard of," Alia continued.

"Oh dear." Trudeau swallowed. "Any specifics?"

"Not on the inventory. Only the location—some godforsaken place called Norilsk," Nuri added.

"I was afraid you were going to say that," Trudeau said. "The reason you haven't heard of them is because they don't exist—at least not as any kind of conventional arms dealer. They're purely black market."

"Russian mob?" Juarez asked.

"An offshoot of sorts. I don't know much about them. No one does. What I've heard is they are former Russian military, willing to supply the latest tech to anyone who can pay their exorbitant prices. A lot of people in the arms circle think they're the ones that supplied the Buk missile Russian-backed mercenaries used to shoot down the Malaysia Airlines flight over eastern Ukraine."

"They seem like the perfect bedfellows for Lentz," Alia commented.

"Indeed," Trudeau said. "Their autonomy and mob connections enable them to make quite a killing running arms. Mob launders the cash so clean that their sales are nearly untraceable. Since you've tapped Lentz's transaction at the source, I'd say that's quite a score."

"I try to be humble, but it's pretty much impossible," Nuri said.

"Yes, well you had the easy job," Trudeau snarked. "I get to go there to find out what kind of nightmare they sold Lentz and try not to get my throat cut. Now you get to watch a *real* field agent work."

"Fucking chauvinist."

"Let's not get ahead of ourselves," Juarez said. "Sending our best global arms analyst into a pit of Russian mob vipers doesn't necessarily sound like the right play."

"I tend to agree," Alia said. "We need special operators to—"

"Who could the CIA possibly send that they would not sniff out immediately, especially in a city accessible only by air with maybe ten incoming flights a day?" Trudeau asked. "They know *everyone* in the arms industry, and anyone approaching without a reputation is a dead man."

"That's exactly what you would be too," Juarez said.

Trudeau looked at Juarez and smiled sardonically.

"Money talks with them. If I approach with a sizable enough purchase, I will be drinking vodka and turning down dates with single daughters."

"Charming," Love said.

"Am I missing something?" Kennedy asked Trudeau. "You may have worked in the industry at one time, but they're going to know you're CIA now."

"Very good, Dick Tracy, you may earn your decoder pin yet," Trudeau snapped. "I will not attempt to conceal my affiliation. CIA makes illicit buys of rogue weaponry all the time."

"Perish the thought," Juarez said.

"That will be the reason I'm there—to buy some kind of untraceable evil the US government plans to use on someone they don't like while maintaining plausible deniability. Isn't it funny when the truth is so fucked-up it makes the best cover?"

"Hilarious," Kennedy said.

"Then we'll send you in for a buy," Alia said. "A type of buy they won't question. And we'll scramble some local field support to assist, so when you're in, you can go to work on whoever has the information we need. Let me know what you need for money. Juarez will handle logistics."

"Out of curiosity, how was this Russian intel connected to data collected by my airport feeds?" Kennedy asked Nuri.

"It looks like Lentz has operatives embedded in airports around the country. They've been communicating with him quite regularly about *handling the cargo* coming in from Russia."

33

Hell has frozen over.

This was Trudeau's first thought as he walked out of Alykel Airport in the Siberian city of Norilsk and waited for the car service the Russian arms dealers had promised to send. It was snowing, and heavy gray flakes swirled through the phosphorous haze. The air was thick with the putrid stench of sulfur dioxide. Breathing was like wearing a gas mask full of rotten eggs and fish guts. Soot-black snowdrifts were piled twenty feet high in places, some of them winter burial grounds for broken-down cars. It was midday and the sun was already committing suicide behind a range of dark, jagged mountains looming over the city.

A GAZ-2975 armored military vehicle, the Russian version of a Humvee, rolled slowly through the passenger pickup lane. Trudeau was the only one standing out there freezing his nuts off and coughing up a lung, so he got very nervous that they had potentially intercepted his communications with the arms dealer and were going to arrest him. If they did, he would surely end up dying in a barrel full of gasoline while they used a lit match to coerce his confession. The GAZ slowed down to a crawl, and its deep-tinted windows stared at him like a snake's eyes. Trudeau casually lit a cigarette and pretended to look at his phone. The vehicle rolled to a stop.

"Fuck this," he said under his breath and went back inside the airport.

When he got inside, he looked back and saw two Russian soldiers jogging out to the GAZ from the airport with their duffel bags. When they got in the truck, he breathed a sigh of relief. When the military vehicle left, a black Range Rover drove up and stopped in its place.

"How do you like Norilsk so far?" someone asked behind him.

Trudeau whipped around, and a man who looked like the exhumed corpse of Peter Lorre was standing there smiling at him with brown teeth. He chuckled lightly at Trudeau's startled reaction and patted him on the shoulder. When Trudeau glowered in anger, the man offered his hand.

"Smile, you'll live longer. My name is Laika, after the bitch from Sputnik Two. I'll be your gracious host today."

"Pleasure," Trudeau said, shaking Laika's bloodless, greasy hand.

"The pleasure is all mine, sir, provided you came bearing gifts."

"How do I know—"

"You don't. Our ride is waiting."

He motioned to the black Range Rover outside. Trudeau looked at it, hesitating. He had insisted Juarez not send any US paramilitary support to protect him, arguing that they would surely put the arms dealers on the defensive and either kill the deal or get him killed. Juarez had reluctantly agreed, and now Trudeau wished he hadn't. He was completely exposed, and the only local support he had was a Russian field agent he'd never met before, who was supposed to assist him with the arms dealers at their compound.

"The boss is very particular about punctuality. I've seen him castrate a man with his salad fork for arriving five minutes late for dinner."

They walked to the SUV, which was full of men who looked even scarier than Laika, with shaved heads and prison-yard builds. They were all strapped with automatic weapons, and the inside of the SUV reeked of cheap cigarettes, cologne, and body odor. They drove Trudeau to a remote compound outside the city, next to a sprawling nickel mine. The compound had been a Gulag from the late 1930s to the 1950s. The arms dealers kept the grim exteriors intact—most likely to discourage unwanted visitors—but the inside was luxurious and full of modern conveniences. Hundred-thousand-dollar sports cars were lined up on the marble foyer as big as a football field. The boss, a sawed-off fireplug of a man with a crew cut and a leather three-piece suit, greeted them.

"You were right to go back inside when the soldiers arrived at the airport."

"Why is—" Trudeau started to ask.

"Don't speak unless the boss asks you to," Laika snapped.

Trudeau nodded. The boss poured himself a pint glass of vodka and gave Trudeau the same. Trudeau waited for the boss to drink half his glass, then took a sip himself. It tasted like hair spray smelled and felt like it was scorching everything it touched, all the way to his stomach. He had to hold his breath to keep from puking.

"Do you have something for me?"

Trudeau looked at Laika, who nodded impatiently.

"Yes."

"Don't be shy."

Trudeau opened his jacket slowly and unbuttoned his shirt. He was wearing a vest that resembled body armor. The men in the room perked up and fondled their holstered weapons. Trudeau released the front of the vest from four side clips and handed it to Laika, who examined the pouches stuffed with stacks of hundreds. Trudeau removed the back of the vest and two long packets taped to his legs, also full of cash. After a few minutes of counting, Laika nodded and the boss smiled.

"Party time." Laika laughed heartily. "I'm so glad I don't have to cut you up into little pieces and feed you to the wolves."

"Me too," Trudeau said, forcing a chuckle.

Drinks were already flowing, but Trudeau insisted, before imbibing, on seeing the goods he had just purchased. Laika and his men drove him to one of the warehouses on the compound. Trudeau was photographing everything with minuscule cameras mounted on his eyeglasses, watch, and pinky ring. The photos were being automatically uploaded to a satellite, which was completely reconstructing the compound from the photo data and beaming it back to Langley. They arrived at an even larger warehouse, filled with an arsenal of modern military weapons, and Laika showed him the Buk missile launchers he had supposedly just purchased.

"Good quality," Trudeau commented, impressed.

"These are the same ones we use in the field. We don't sell surplus here."

"When will they ship?"

"They go on the truck tomorrow and tanker in two days," Laika said. "We can have them to your deployment zone within the week."

"Excellent. Now how about that drink?"

By the time they sat down to dinner, Langley had a satellite scanning infrared heat signatures of the entire compound. Trudeau politely dined on the excellent fare the chef was offering but drank moderately. Laika and the rest of the men guzzled staggering amounts of vodka. When they were all passed out or mumbling incoherently to themselves, the boss wandered off with three twenty-something escorts, one of whom was the Russian field agent assigned to support Trudeau. That was Trudeau's cue to retire to his own sleeping quarters.

———

An hour or so later, as the boss was enjoying the company of the escorts, plus a mountain of cocaine, the Russian agent rendered the other two hookers unconscious with sedative-laced champagne and dosed the boss with a fentanyl buccal tablet disguised as Viagra. The fentanyl immediately incapacitated him but didn't knock him out. He was in a state of anesthetic paralysis, his muscles unable to communicate with his nervous system. He tried to speak but only drooled on his pillow and rolled his eyes in panic. That was when Trudeau walked in carrying a black case.

"I thought I'd drop in for a nightcap," Trudeau said.

He sat on the bed next to the boss while the Russian agent opened the black case, revealing some nasty-looking torture implements.

"What she's given you is a surgical anesthetic," Trudeau said. "That's why you can't move or speak. However, I assure you that you can still feel pain."

He took a sharp steel awl and jabbed it under the boss's toenail, all the way to the cuticle. The boss's eyes rolled violently and his tongue flicked like a snake's as he tried in vain to scream.

"You see what I mean? Now, imagine what it would be like for me to cut your balls off with this."

Trudeau held a pair of rusty wire cutters in front of the boss's face.

"It would be very time-consuming, scissoring into your tender scrotum with this blunt pruning tool—which I would have to superheat in your fireplace in order to cauterize the wound while I cut. All the while you would be completely powerless to do anything. You wouldn't even be able to scream. So, tell me, are we going to be friends?"

The boss tried desperately to nod his head but only ended up rolling his eyes wildly, like a mental patient.

"I'll take that as a yes. Friends share secrets and I know you have a big one you need to get off your chest. In thirty seconds or so, you'll be able to speak. It will only be a whisper, but I'll get very close to you, like a friend, to listen. And you're going to tell me everything I want to know, yes?"

"Y-yes," the boss whispered.

"Good," Trudeau said.

The Russian CIA asset brought over the boss's laptop.

"I know you don't keep transactions on your laptop. So, I'd like you to share with us the log-in information for your Dark Net accounts. No doubt what we need is there."

The boss shook his head as much as he could. Clearly, there was a lot more at stake in giving Trudeau that kind of access.

"Are you saying no?"

"Can't do that," the boss whispered.

"Too bad. And I thought we were friends."

Trudeau clipped off the end of the boss's pinky finger. Blood spurted out. The Russian agent wrapped the wound tightly with the boss's satin robe sash to slow the bleeding. The boss looked like he was going to have an aneurism. He was trying to scream, but only a breathy whisper sound was coming out. His eyes were twitching and his tongue rolling. Trudeau threw champagne in his face to snap him out of it.

"You seem like a man who refuses to believe in the inevitability of a foregone conclusion."

Trudeau held up the bloody wire cutters.

"Is this conclusive enough for you?"

The boss nodded and gave over his Dark Net password. Trudeau logged in and simultaneously sent the access information to Langley. Things were far worse than he had ever imagined. The Russians had recently sold twenty-five Cold War–era Russian RA-115s—miniaturized tactical nuclear weapons called "suitcase nukes" because they weighed fifty to sixty pounds and could easily be transported in a suitcase or backpack. Each of them had the firepower of roughly ten kilotons of TNT. The "Little Boy" atomic bomb dropped on Hiroshima had a fifteen-kiloton blast yield.

There was an old CIA bedtime story about how the Soviets developed the Little Boys to be deployed by a network of KGB sleeper spies embedded in different cities in the United States in the late 1970s and 1980s. Based on the transaction dates and the number of weapons, it appeared Lentz might be about to make that nightmare come true.

34

A lia had anticipated that Trudeau might discover nukes, and that kind of intel came with strict protocols. She had reminded him that whatever he found was for her eyes only—she'd then be required to report it to the director, who would have to brief the president. After that, Alia would be given her marching orders and the fate of Red Carpet would be decided. Trudeau figured the Department of Defense would take over at that point, and the whole thing would be handed over to military intelligence.

The problem was, Trudeau didn't trust people like Alia and he certainly wasn't going to allow the fate of the world to rest in her hands. He had been a part of the team of weapons experts who helped to debunk the WMD claims by the Bush administration that had been the impetus for the Iraq war. He learned from that, and from many other painful experiences like it, that the suits who made the decisions at Langley might as well be lobbyists, for all the politicking they did. They were beholden to committees run by elected officials who only cared about getting reelected. And those men and women hated how difficult it was to manipulate the complex information gathered by the CIA and distill it into a message that could sound-byte the American people into agreeing to catastrophic global actions.

So Trudeau sent the intel to Juarez and Kennedy as well, letting them know he'd broken protocol to do so. If Alia was going to start tap-dancing around the truth, Juarez was the one person with the balls and authority to do what needed to be done. And if something happened to him and Juarez, which was a strong possibility, considering the danger they were going to be in after pulling the Norilsk job, at least Kennedy would have the intel. Trudeau thought that making Kennedy an asset and team leader was idiotic, but he could tell the man was an idealist, someone who cared more for the safety of total strangers than he did for himself. If everything went sideways, he felt sure that Kennedy would put his neck on the block to stop Lentz.

After all of the Dark Net files were uploaded to Langley, the Russian agent gave the boss a lethal dose of fentanyl. Next, the two of them assembled an explosive device consisting of several "romantic aids" she'd brought to the party and easily slipped past the lascivious guards. The sex toys were made of enough Semtex plastic explosive to annihilate a city block and had built-in detonators the agent controlled with her wireless phone. She activated the connection between the phone and bombs and the two of them slipped out of the compound unnoticed.

As they sped away in a mining truck the Russian agent had stolen for a cover vehicle, she detonated the charges in the boss's boudoir. The blast set off a chain reaction and the heavy ordnance at the compound exploded as well, shaking the city like a small earthquake. The subsequent fire burned the entire compound to the ground.

The Russian agent dropped Trudeau back at Alykel Airport at dawn with a duffel bag and drove the stolen truck to a vacant lot, where she torched it. In the airport terminal, Trudeau locked himself in a bathroom stall and pulled fresh clothes, a new passport, credit cards, cash, a white plastic jug, and a large, rough sponge from the duffel bag. Trudeau stripped, soaked the sponge in the liquid from the jug, and scrubbed himself with it for half an hour. It was a solvent that neutralized any of the Semtex molecules that might still be on his body. The last thing he needed, after one of the biggest "chemical explosions" in the history of Norilsk, was to fail a random test for explosive materials at the screening checkpoint.

When his skin was raw and burning, he put on his new clothes and headed back into the terminal to check in for his flight, but the woman working the ticket counter told him it was canceled due to weather. Trudeau's heart sank. In most places, a winter storm is no big deal. You get a few inches of snow; flights are held up for a few hours, one day max. In Norilsk, a winter storm pummels the city with several feet of snow, hurricane-force winds, and temperatures plunging south of negative fifty, making it possible for flights to be canceled for several days.

Trudeau was in a very dangerous position. The longer he stayed there, the more likely the Russian military would connect him to the massacred arms dealers. Even though Trudeau's travel cover as a Norwegian oil and gas exec had flawlessly gotten him through Russian customs, it wouldn't be that difficult for them to analyze recent passenger manifests from the handful of flights that had come in and treat him as a person of interest. Additionally, the Russian mob would be looking for someone to skin for destroying millions of dollars' worth of black market military stock. The airport was not safe. Going to a hotel was out of the question, as hotels meant passports, credit cards, and security cameras, all of which created a trail of digital bread crumbs. Trudeau checked to see if he could catch any of the last flights heading anywhere before the airport shut down, but there was nothing.

He had no choice but to contact Juarez for an extraction. This was also a dangerous option due to the conspicuous nature of private aircraft, but at least he would have Juarez and a support team if they had to shoot their way out. Trudeau found a quiet place and dialed Juarez on his satellite phone. It didn't even ring. Then he heard the worst thing imaginable: "Satellite signal temporarily interrupted."

Ach, putain de merde.

He kept his cool—until he saw two Russian soldiers with a dog patrolling the airport, randomly checking passports. He had to get out of there, so he went outside into the mind-numbing cold. He broke protocol and texted his support agent, hoping against hope that she could come back and get him the fuck out of there. The weather was going from bad to worse. Buses were nonexistent, but he could see the lights of a few taxicabs clustered in a parking lot on the outskirts of the airport. His only choice was to hoof it out there and hope one of them would take him to a cash-only flophouse in town to hole up until his sat service came back. Even then it could take as long as eighteen hours for Juarez to get to him once he made contact. The subzero wind reminded him he'd better find something soon or Juarez would be extracting what was left of him in the spring thaw.

35

We're going to get shot," Love said.

It was 7:00 A.M. at the Minneapolis–Saint Paul Airport, and she, Kennedy, and Best were in a rent-by-the-hour conference room in the United Club lounge, gearing up to give Kennedy's new airport-bugging scheme a test run. Love was wearing a fake explosives vest made up of composite material meant to emulate the look and density of real plastic explosives vests confiscated from Al Qaeda agents. Best had two composite pistols strapped to his legs.

They had a lot of ground to cover to finish the final airports that had been left hanging due to the Tad Monty incident—Minneapolis, O'Hare, Midway, Detroit, LaGuardia, Newark, and Boston—and very little time to do it. Alia wanted it finished in three to five days if possible, an aggressive proposition considering the distance between most of the airports and the worsening weather in the Midwest and East Coast.

But Kennedy was having a hard time focusing. The intel Trudeau had sent from Russia had changed the nature of the threat completely. The fact that Lentz had nuclear weapons in large quantities was bad enough. What made it worse was the tone of Trudeau's communication and the fact that he had asked Kennedy to keep his knowledge secret from Alia and the rest of the team. He understood Trudeau's reasoning, and was glad that he'd been entrusted with the information, but the duplicitous nature of the exchange made him uneasy. What if he found something himself that was related to the intel? How the hell was he going to communicate that to Alia so they could take action?

And the whole notion that politics might come into play at the highest levels of government made his blood run cold. That was exactly how 9/11 had happened. Politics intervened and practically rolled out a red carpet for Osama bin Laden.

"Earth to Kennedy," Love said. "You with us?"

"You're not going to get shot," Kennedy reassured her. "I'll step in before things get out of hand. Besides, they're never going to catch you anyway."

"I can't believe this is going to make it past their scanning gear," Best said.

"Not only is it going to get past the scanner, but also the explosives swab. Love's vest has bomb-making residue on it, but not from materials they can detect in their outdated system."

"This just keeps getting better and better," Love said.

"Won't they see the items on the scanner?" Best asked.

"The vest is shaped like Love's body, so it won't register as a foreign object. The position of the guns will make it very hard for even the best screener to see. These scanners are dialed way down to protect peoples' vanity, so they miss a lot."

Kennedy's new technique for getting the upgrades done was a sort of soft blackmail job on the TSA chiefs. Instead of telling them he was coming, giving them the chance to alert others and question the visit, he was going to emulate the weapons-smuggling tactics Homeland Red Teams recently used to get 95 percent of their phony contraband past TSA screening checkpoints.

Once he successfully smuggled the weapons in, and the embarrassed TSA chief was finished soiling himself, Kennedy would then generously offer to install the upgrade at no charge, thereby keeping it off the radar screen of Homeland and allowing the TSA chief to avoid getting shit from guys like Tad Monty. Alia thought the plan was brilliant.

"All set," Best said.

Kennedy inspected their work. Both setups were flawless and there were no wires or metal for the body scanner to pick up and give the agents an argument for accuracy.

MSP was one of the safer airports for him to test-market his idea. The TSA chief, a chain-smoking bureaucrat named Ralph Lee, was a friendly. He wasn't the sharpest tool in the shed, but he and Kennedy played golf once in a while, and he pretty much took whatever Kennedy said as gospel. His assistant was the one Kennedy was worried about. Janet was an insufferable busybody, constantly haranguing Kennedy about paperwork, protocols, and administrative red tape. Kennedy knew how to handle her but was not in the mood.

Best and Love queued up in the checkpoint line while Kennedy watched from the Starbucks on the other side. Love handled herself well. Having been onstage hundreds of times, she knew how to deal with nerves. She made it up to the checkpoint and looked at Kennedy. He nodded with a confident smile and she went through without incident. When she joined him at Starbucks, she looked impressed.

"I guess you are pretty good at this shit, aren't you, you big lug?"

"Let's see how Best does before we start high-fiving," Kennedy said.

Best made it past the checkpoint with flying colors as well and sat down next to them.

"I don't know if I should be happy or violently ill," he said.

"Welcome to my world," Kennedy said and called Ralph Lee.

When Ralph arrived at the Starbucks, he was his usual completely distracted self, dying to get curbside for a cigarette. Kennedy introduced Best and Love and said they'd be happy to join him. Ralph took them through a pass-code door to a loading bay outside the terminal, his unofficial smoking lounge. When Kennedy showed him the hardware Love and Best had just gotten through the checkpoint, he lit the filter end of his cigarette.

"You fucking kidding me?"

"Sorry, man," Kennedy said.

"Shit!" Ralph practically screamed. "Did Zombieland Security send you?"

"Relax," Kennedy said. "We're all friends here. They wanted me to run the Red Team test and install a prototype for a new upgrade. I'll tell them you passed."

"You're my hero, man. I've been in the penalty box since that news report came out. Do whatever you need to do. How long will it take?"

"Fifteen minutes on the outside," Kennedy said.

"Go now. Before that witch Janet gets back from her third lunch."

———

Best worked quickly, adding the upgrade in less than ten minutes, but not fast enough to avoid Janet. She shot across the terminal in her block-heeled army shoes, making a beeline for the checkpoint. Kennedy moved away from it in case she had not yet seen Best, but it was too late.

"Who's that monster?" Love asked.

"The fabled Janet."

"Shit."

"Be a dear and disappear," Kennedy said.

"Roger that," Love said, taking off.

"Well well well," Janet snarked as she walked up. "Tad Monty's bitch. You come here for another murder-suicide or just passing through?"

"Janet . . . Always a pleasure."

She eyeballed Best, who was reinstalling the access panel on the scanner. "What's he doing?"

"You've read the recent threat reports I assume?"

"I wiped my ass with them, yes."

"Arresting image. As usual, I'm the only one taking them seriously, so I'm testing a body cavity detection prototype in the millimeter wave scanners."

She immediately dialed Ralph on her mobile phone and tried to narc on Kennedy, to no avail. She hung up, obviously angry at Ralph's response.

"Janet, it's not going to—"

She got in his face. "Not going to what? Slow us down all day and create an angry mob of passengers we have to deal with after you're long gone?"

Her breath stank of sour white wine. Kennedy knew the bartender at Chili's To-Go, Janet's favorite lunch spot. Earlier that morning, he'd called Andy and told him to give Janet a two-for-one airport employee's special if she came in, which she almost always did. Janet was a notorious lush, and she had predictably taken the bait. From the smell of it, Kennedy estimated she was about four glasses in.

"I'm doing this to increase safety, which should be your concern as well, Janet."

"Get off your high horse—"

Kennedy theatrically sniffed the air between them. "Whoa. How many glasses, Janet?"

She glared at him. "Excuse me?"

He got closer to her and spoke quietly.

"How many glasses of wine did you have at lunch?"

"It's my friend's birthday," she lied.

"How many?"

"None of your fucking business."

"Maybe so, but I'm sure Ralph would consider it his business."

"Are you threatening me?"

"If Ralph realizes you're intoxicated, he is required by law to fire you. There are no second chances with TSA. Are you going to keep running your mouth so he can smell the birthday party or shag your sorry ass out of here and let me do my job?"

Kennedy had never so much as looked at her wrong in the past, and hearing him say those things shocked her into submission. She stared with her mouth open for a long, uncomfortable moment, her lips twitching to form a retort that never came.

"Tell him your kid is sick and you got called to school to pick him up."

The mention of her young son quickly snapped her out of it and she practically jogged out of the terminal.

"You're a slick motherfucker," Love said behind him.

"How long have you been there?" he asked.

"Long enough. You know I got your back."

36

Trudeau huddled next to a space heater in an abandoned apartment. He was going on almost twenty-four hours of squatting in a block of run-down flats for nickel mine workers. Luckily, the building had central heat because of the families who still lived there, but the empty unit he was able to find had two broken windows, so he'd bought the space heater, along with as much packaged food and water as he could carry, at a local store. He had gotten very lucky and was able to convince his Russian support agent that she would not get disavowed if she came back to save his ass. She had driven him there after the airport cabdrivers refused to take him and he nearly froze to death on the side of the road.

He was about to lose his mind from sleep deprivation when he finally felt his satellite phone buzz in his pocket. He pulled it out with shaking fingers and checked the screen. Sat connection was restored and the phone was downloading hundreds of text messages from Juarez, asking about his status. The last few were Juarez saying he was coming to Norilsk to retrieve him. He had secured a private plane and was going to pick Trudeau up at Valek Airport, a small airstrip nine kilometers northeast of the city. Alykel Airport was too dangerous for the extraction. Trudeau was ecstatic. Based on the time the texts were sent, Juarez would be arriving that night. Trudeau rang him.

"Are you all right?" Juarez asked.

plane. Trudeau got in back and Juarez strapped into the copilot seat.
[pi]lot started to taxi.

"[B]ogeys!" Trudeau yelled as he saw two military vehicles hauling ass
[down] the runway, lights flashing.

"[P]unch it," Juarez ordered.

[Th]e pilot hit the throttle and shot across the apron, heading for the
[runwa]y, skidding on random patches of ice. The trucks were behind them,
[rapidl]y gaining. The pilot turned onto the runway and nearly fishtailed
[into a] snowbank. When he straightened it out, he gunned the engines
[again.] The turboprops roared and the plane sped down the strip, narrowly
[missin]g another military vehicle attempting to block the runway. When
[the pla]ne hit full speed, the military trucks couldn't keep up. One of them
[lost co]ntrol on the ice. The other one was firing shots but the plane was
[out of] range. The plane took off and shook so violently from the gusting
[w]inds that the pilot was using all his strength to keep the wings level.
[Trudea]u looked back. More security vehicles were crowding the runway.

"[L]adies and gentlemen, this is your captain speaking," Juarez said,
[smil]ing. "Welcome to Get the Fuck out of Russia by the Skin of Your Ass
[Airline]s. Now sit back, relax, and enjoy your flight."

Trudeau could hear the drone of airplane engines in the background.
"Tired and freezing, but fine. What's the scenario?"

"Private plane registered as med evac for cancer patients going to Moscow for treatment," Juarez said. "Strip is a five-mile walk from your location. Better get going."

Juarez hung up before Trudeau could complain about the fact that it was arctic cold outside. Coming out of the construction site, he checked the street. Empty as a tomb. He jogged to stay warm, his lungs burning from the shock of the frigid air. He was numb all over by the time he made it to the outskirts of Valek Airport. He walked along the edge of the fence, following the map coordinates sent by Juarez and trying to make out anything that remotely resembled an airport in the driving snow, when a Russian military transport vehicle emerged from the mist, its patrol lights scanning the perimeter. Trudeau had nowhere to hide as the vehicle stopped next to him and two soldiers got out.

"Passport," one of them said sternly in Russian, pointing his assault rifle at Trudeau.

He handed them his cover passport—Norwegian businessman, oil and gas consultant. The soldiers didn't give a shit if he was Mother Teresa. They took one look at the passport and opened the back door to the military vehicle for him.

One of them motioned to the car with his rifle barrel.

Trudeau saw no way out. At least in the truck he would die warm. He got into the backseat and they shut the door, locking it from the outside. Another soldier was on the seat next to him. The soldier who had checked his passport sat in the front passenger seat and turned to address Trudeau, this time in English.

"Sir, we are detaining you for further questioning with Russian military intelligence."

"What in God's name for?" Trudeau protested.

The soldier next to him punched him hard in the face, breaking his nose. Then he slammed his rifle barrel into Trudeau's stomach, knocking the wind out of him. The soldier in the passenger seat offered him a dirty oil rag for his bloody nose.

"What is the purpose of your visit here?" the soldier asked calmly.

"I'm a businessman," Trudeau gasped. "Hired by your government. My visa is in my passport case. I demand to be taken to my embassy."

The soldier next to Trudeau backhanded him, splitting his brow. Blood poured into his eye. Then he hit him in the jaw, knocking him unconscious.

————

When Trudeau came to, his wrists and ankles were zip-tied and he could only see out of one eye. He had no idea how long he'd been out and he could no longer feel the weight of his sat phone in his pocket. He was a dead man. Soon he would be on a Russian military base, taking his last breaths in agonizing pain, not knowing if he'd said anything to compromise Red Carpet.

The dim amber lights of what was probably the nearest base hovered in the distance. He had to get out of that truck. Even if he died trying, it was going to be better than what waited for him at point B. He was getting ready to roll onto his back and start kicking the shit out of the soldier next to him when he heard a loud snapping sound, like the crack of a whip. A high-velocity sniper round zipped through the driver's-side window and decapitated the man behind the wheel. Blood, brains, and skull fragments exploded all over the dash and windshield. The vehicle spun out of control and smashed into a guardrail, nearly flipping on its side. Trudeau was thrown against the backseat and then to the floor. The soldier in the front passenger seat hit the windshield. His head shattered it and he died instantly.

The soldier next to Trudeau panicked and tried to open the back door, forgetting it was locked from the outside. He smashed the window with the butt of his rifle, but Juarez was standing there, framed by the jagged glass. Before the soldier could even think about reacting, Juarez shot him in the chest with the sniper rifle. Then Juarez shoved the rifle barrel into the open window, ready to execute any additional soldiers.

"Juarez! It's me, Trudeau!"

Juarez cut Trudeau's zip ties and dragged the corpses of the soldiers into the ditch. Then he got back in the beat-up transport vehicle and fired up the engine, flipped a U-turn, and headed toward the airport. He looked back at Trudeau, who was covered in blood and shivering.

"You hit?"

"No," he said.

The Russian military base dispatcher's voice blaste[d] speaker.

"They're checking our twenty. Keep quiet for a se[c]

Juarez grabbed the radio and spoke perfect Russ[ian] the other end of the radio. By the time he was done, t[hey] laughing about something like old pals. Juarez sign[ed] truck into the airport entrance, his eyes darting all o[ver] other military vehicles.

"Almost there. We're going to need to hustle. Their minutes from here and I'm sure they're on their way. Y[ou]

"I can make it," Trudeau said weakly.

Juarez looked at his watch. "You didn't tell those you?"

Trudeau shook his head.

"It's okay if you did. I just need to know."

"No," he answered through chattering teeth. "[I] conscious before they had a chance to ask me any q[uestions]

"Excellent."

"Fuck you," Trudeau replied.

They pulled up to the airport terminal, whic[h] a small hangar with a fuel depot. Trudeau looked had brought to fly him out of his frozen hell. It wa[s] With its odd, shark-nosed fuselage, massive roo[f] propellers reminiscent of the Spruce Goose, it di[d] confidence.

"What the fuck is that, Lindbergh's lost plane?"

Juarez laughed. "What did you expect, a trip[le] lounge? It ain't pretty, but the Sherpa can fly throu[gh] it for science missions in the Arctic."

The Russian military radio dispatcher piped u[p] ing less friendly and more insistent. Juarez repli[ed] apologetic.

"I told them we stalled on the highway. The[y] truck. That'll buy us some time."

Out on the apron, the pilot fired up the engi[nes] snow up in a huge swirling cloud. They jumped o[ut]

37

J uarez got Trudeau out of Norilsk," Alia told Kennedy over the phone
as he, Love, and Best sprinted through Detroit Airport, trying to make
a flight to LaGuardia.

"Guy's a superhero," Kennedy said in awe.

"Yeah, sometimes I think there are no limits to what that man is capable of."

"We could use him. Treads on our tires are getting pretty thin," Kennedy added.

"That was the other reason I called. You all may be retiring early."

"How's that?"

"Trudeau pulled some critical intel in Norilsk and DoD might take over."

"What's the intel?" Kennedy was hoping Alia would level with him so
he could stop pretending he didn't know about the nukes.

"It's classified for now. I'll brief you as soon as I get clearance. Suffice it
to say we know a lot more about what Lentz is planning and it's worse than
we thought."

Kennedy's heart sank. Trudeau may have been right to keep him in the
loop. For the first time, Kennedy began to see how easily Alia could distance herself, closing the curtain on him in the name of national security.

"What kind of shipment are we talking about?" he asked again.

"I can't share that with you right now, but I'll brief you when you get to Boston. Where are you now?"

"Detroit. O'Hare, Midway, and Minneapolis are done. Running to catch a flight to New York so we can handle LGA and Newark tomorrow, then on to Boston."

Kennedy and company arrived at the gate and barely made it onto the Jetway before they closed the door.

"Should we keep going according to plan?" he asked.

"Yes. Maintain status quo unless I tell you different."

"Sir, you need to switch your phone to airplane mode now," the flight attendant snapped at him, "or we can't taxi."

"Gotta go. Call you from New York."

Kennedy shut off his phone.

"What did the boss lady have to say?" Love asked.

"Not much, just wanted ideas for the office Christmas party."

"Secret Santas and everything?"

"Yep."

"Cool," Love said, unexpectedly laying her head against his shoulder and closing her eyes.

While Love and Best slept, Kennedy ordered three cups of coffee and went over Nuri's analysis of the data Rico's devices had gathered, cross-referenced with the data feeds from Kennedy's airport bugs. Specifically, he was looking for the list of IP addresses inside the airports that were communicating with Lentz using his proprietary messaging app. Most of them could be grouped with the name server Nuri had assigned to the TSA offices. But there were a few that were housed on different servers at the airport, and most of them were mobile IPs. So, whoever they were, they weren't desk jockeys—they were workers who mostly used phones or tablets to communicate on the job.

Restaurant and shop workers fell into that category, but that didn't seem like an advantageous spot to embed an operative. They were watched constantly and had no direct access to anything critical like aircraft or the tower. Kennedy cross-checked the HR records Nuri had pulled from all twenty-five target airports. With their aircraft access, baggage handlers were good candidates. But they'd been under constant video surveillance after CNN had aired hidden-camera footage of handlers pilfering checked luggage all over the country and racking up $2.5 million in stolen goods.

If he were Lentz, he would embed people in an area with high enough levels of security clearance to actually do some damage, but also with more trust and autonomy so they could almost hide their sabotage in plain sight. Outside of the pilots and flight crews themselves, there was one group that fit this description: aircraft maintenance.

Suitcase nukes . . . Avionics communications systems . . . Maintenance engineers had nearly as much access to airplanes as pilots, probably more. If Lentz could infiltrate this group, his operatives could conceal the nukes from view in the equipment stores and actually "install" them *in* the airplanes. And someone with that kind of expertise would know exactly how to conceal a device weighing from 60 to 100 pounds within the complicated systems of a 250,000-pound Boeing 737.

With a pit forming in his stomach, Kennedy remembered the avionics equipment Lambert had found in Malaysia—a communications device that could be used to control an airplane's autopilot from the ground. If Lentz were also able to install his modified version of that device into cockpits, he could override pilot control and turn a fleet of commercial jets into a fleet of long-range nuclear missiles.

38

When they were finished with LaGuardia and Newark, Kennedy, Best, and Love did their final install in Boston. Kennedy was well respected at Logan Airport, and it was one of the few places where he felt like they always listened and put his advice into action. Two of the airplanes in the 9/11 attack had come from Boston, so they were all motivated to make sure that never happened again.

Mary Cahill was the TSA chief there. With her spiky red hair and bedazzled Chico's blazers, she was a foulmouthed drill sergeant who ran a tight ship and didn't take any crap from DHS. But she was sweet on Kennedy and always put on a fresh coat of face paint when he came to visit. Because of his rapport with her, there was no need to run the fake Red Team scam to get her to allow the upgrade. She agreed without batting an eye and even fetched his team lattes to sip while they worked.

Alia had told Kennedy, Love, and Best to wait for her in a safe house she had arranged after they finished at Logan. Kennedy sent Love and Best off to the safe house but stuck around and bought Mary dinner because she threatened to beat him senseless with her pocketbook if he didn't. They hit the Legal Sea Foods in Terminal C for a couple of hours and Mary unleashed her usual tirade about how DHS was making her life miserable, how they wouldn't know a real threat if it bit them in the ass, and so forth.

As they enjoyed dessert, which for Mary was a third glass of bourbon, it occurred to Kennedy that he might as well look into his embedded maintenance operative theory while he was there. He had mentioned it to Alia right after he landed at LaGuardia but hadn't heard anything back from her yet. Why not be proactive and check to see if any of the mobile IP addresses Nuri found to be communicating with Lentz's Cuban servers via his messaging app were tied to the maintenance department servers? If he had that, he might be able to track down one of those users. Which meant he had to sweet-talk Mary into giving him access to the maintenance hangars.

"What's your beef with the wrench monkeys?" she asked.

"No beef. Just thinking that might be a good place to look for weak links in the security chain."

"Missing links more like"—she laughed—"but that's airport services and I got no jurisdiction with those zookeepers."

"Yeah, but you could open a few doors for me. To tell you the truth, I don't really want them to see me coming. Turn on the kitchen lights and the roaches tend to scatter, you know?"

"All right, you sneaky bastard. I'm game. But what's in it for me? Dinner out in the real world? Maybe Charles Street?"

She swirled her cocktail glass in front of his face.

"Bourbon that wasn't distilled on a Honduran chicken farm? Hot motel sex, provided the sheets are clean?"

"Most of the above."

"Deal. I can do without the clean sheets."

After Kennedy paid the tab, Mary gave him one of her contractor badges and her Jetway door code and sent him on his way. It was dark when Kennedy walked outside and down the stairs to the ramps. The last of the night's departures were taxiing out, and baggage handlers were dwindling to skeleton crews. Kennedy ducked into a shadowy spot under a jet bridge and dialed Nuri on his sat phone.

"Booty call?" Nuri said groggily on the phone.

"Hey, I need your help with something."

"Doesn't everyone? What's up?"

"Remember the IP we found at Logan Airport that had been in regular communication with Lentz's Cuban IPs?"

"You over there?"

"Yeah, figured we could check it out, maybe get a bead on someone."

"You might make a decent spook yet. I'm pushing an app to your sat phone called Q. It's an IP sniper, like the ones the feds use, only better, because it doesn't have any of those pesky court-ordered privacy protocols."

"Goddamned free countries. What the hell's the world coming to?"

"I know, right? Fire up the app when you get it. I've already programmed the IP in question so it will start sniffing it out right away. If the user has his special Lentz IM app open, we can deploy an API that links it to the GPS sat Langley uses to track agents and assets in the field. It's accurate to within a square meter so you buy him a cup of coffee. Cool, right?"

"Very."

"Nervous?"

"I wasn't expecting toe-to-toe contact."

"Just let Best handle it."

"Great idea if he were here."

"What? Where the hell is he? Wait, have you gone rogue?"

"Relax. He's at the safe house. I was having dinner with the TSA chief and thought, since I was here, I might as well—"

"Shit! You *have* gone rogue. I don't know if I should be impressed or send a crew to scrub you right now."

"Calm down," he whispered harshly. "And stop yelling in my ear."

"Yeah, 'cause what I should be doing is slapping you upside your head. This isn't a Netflix original series about a soccer dad spy, dummy. If you flush one of Lentz's crew you might get smoked."

"I'm not going rogue and I'm not going to get smoked. I just wanted to see if the guy is here. If I get a whiff of anything professional, I'll call it in."

"Dude, by the time *you* get a whiff, the professionals will already have a bead *on you*. I think you need to hang back and get Best over there before you do anything."

"What's that?" Kennedy said. "You're breaking up. I don't have any bars here."

"Bullshit, there's a tower less than a quarter mile—"

He hung up and texted her, saying she better not dime on him or he would tell Alia she helped him. After a string of obscene text replies, she eventually let it go. But she had sufficiently freaked Kennedy out, so he proceeded more cautiously, promising himself that if it turned out the owner of the IP address was present at the airport, he would call Best and Alia and take his licks for having attempted a solo mission.

As if the heavens agreed with Nuri, it started to rain heavily. He had gone out there without a raincoat or umbrella so he was instantly soaked. He downloaded Nuri's app and fired it up, but the interface was completely foreign to him. It was a grid with tiny flashing numbers and it reminded him of an air traffic control screen. Desperate for help, he called her back.

"You've got a lot of nerve calling me. Did you know I could kill you about thirty different ways with my bare hands?"

"I can't figure this thing out. It's completely nonintuitive."

"Yeah, to the untrained eye."

"Isn't that what *nonintuitive* means?"

"Okay, smart-ass—"

"Nuri, please. It's pissing rain. I just want to see if the guy is on shift. If he is, you can speed-rope in and kill him with your bare hands, okay?"

"There's an idea."

"Please just tell me how to use this."

"I'll do better than that. I'll mirror my app with yours so I can guide you."

"That would be amazing."

"Okay, I've got it open and I can see your signal," she said.

"Can you see his IP?"

"Checking . . . Holy shit. He, or she, *is* there."

"Really?" Kennedy whispered.

"Pretty sure, but verifying . . . Yep, definitely there."

"Jesus, where?"

Kennedy ran under the huge steel eave of the Delta maintenance hangar to get out of the rain. The mist and heavy cloud cover made the apron pitch-dark and only the occasional flash of airplane landing lights would cut through the night and briefly illuminate everything like a massive strobe light.

"Checking," Nuri said. "Signal sucks. Must be the rain. Hang on . . . Okay, got it. It looks like our bad guy's signal is coming from the apron near Terminal E, about a half a click from the Delta maintenance hangar."

Kennedy's blood ran cold.

"Are you sure?" he tried to whisper. "That's exactly where I'm standing."

"What? Yes, I'm sure." Her voice lowered. "You better get out of there."

An airplane landing light whipped across the apron as a plane taxied in and briefly illuminated a tall man dressed in a black raincoat and black baseball cap about a hundred yards away, jogging right toward Kennedy. The way he was dressed, he looked a lot more like an assassin than a maintenance worker.

"Oh shit," Kennedy said and hung up.

The airplane turned to taxi to its gate and the apron was dark again. Kennedy sprinted around the side of the Delta hangar and spotted a sea of luggage trailers stored in long rows near the service road fence. He found a place to hide among the trailers and watched for the man, hoping he was just an airport official wanting to see his credentials. But another landing light flooded the area and Kennedy got a good look as the man walked slowly toward the luggage trailers. He was holding a gun with a barrel suppressor close to his side, scanning the area with a tactical LED flashlight.

"Fuck fuck fuck," Kennedy whispered to himself.

He grabbed his sat phone and sent Nuri a 911 text. The flashlight beam blinded him and a bullet nicked the edge of the luggage trailer he was standing next to, narrowly missing his head. He ran, weaving through the labyrinth of trailers and tugs, heading for the service road fence. On the other side, there was a Dunkin' Donuts and a gas station next to one of the short-term parking lots. Bullets zipped past him, sparking off the edges of the metal trailers and bouncing with ricochet whines across the asphalt. One of them tore through his pant leg, missing his ankle by centimeters.

Kennedy could hear the man's footsteps relentlessly approaching, and the bullets kept coming. A round zipped past his ear so close he could feel its heat and he dove down under the cargo trailers and waited, his shaking hand cupped over his mouth, trying to muffle the sound of his heavy breathing. The service road fence was out. It was too high, had razor wire on the top, and was too well lit. He'd be a sitting duck up there. There was an open maintenance garage close by. It was dark inside, a good place to hide, and it had tools and equipment he might be able to use as weapons.

He heard footsteps again. The man was getting closer. How the hell was the guy finding him so quickly? He had to be tracking his sat phone, even though Kennedy wondered how he managed to lock into what was supposed to be a completely secure device. He didn't want to abandon his only connection to help but he might be able to distance himself if he ditched it. As he frantically weighed his options, he remembered something Noah Kruz had said in *The You in Universe*:

The only way to deal with aggression is with aggression. Running from someone or something perpetuates the problem because you are feeding the response the aggressor seeks. You've heard the term "feeding on the weak"? Bullies, from the playground to the penitentiary, are nourished by fear. When you meet their aggression with your own, they have nothing to eat.

It was like walking into a prison yard on the first day and beating the shit out of the biggest guy you could find. At that point, you *defined* yourself to your enemies as something other than easy prey. The guy coming after him had defined Kennedy in his head as a runner, a frightened amateur in over his head. If Kennedy wanted to live, he had to do the exact opposite of what his aggressor expected.

And there were no more places to run.

He took off his shoes and crawled out from under the luggage trailer. He threw one shoe about thirty feet and it clattered noisily across the ground. Bullets peppered the spot where it had landed and Kennedy took that opportunity to run into the maintenance garage. When he got in there, he threw the other shoe to a different spot near where the previous one had landed and bought himself a bit more time with the diversion. Then he crossed to the darkest part of the garage and hid his phone in the seat cushion of a tug parked in one of the service bays. He searched for weapons and found a heavy three-and-a-half-foot torque wrench and a fire extinguisher. The footsteps were heading toward the garage now, so he crept into a corner near his hidden phone and waited.

The man approached the door to the garage and a landing light briefly illuminated his face, an expressionless mask with black eyes. *The point of no return*, Kennedy thought. Even if he had second thoughts about killing the guy, he no longer had a choice. There was only one way out. The man crept inside quietly, holding his gun in one hand and the smartphone he was using to track Kennedy in the other. He stopped short next to the baggage tug where Kennedy's phone was hidden and checked his device. A thin slit of a grin spread across his bloodless lips, and he put the device away.

Kennedy's heart was exploding in his chest. It would be a matter of seconds before he was discovered. He had to move. The man was less than ten feet away. When the man got down on a knee to look under the tugs, Kennedy knew that would be his best chance at catching him in a position of vulnerability. He ripped the pin from the fire extinguisher—a heavy industrial dry-chemical unit for oil and gas fires—and blasted the man from behind. The assassin tried to turn and fire but the high-pressure powder mixture hit his eyes and face like a sandblaster, blinding him and knocking him down.

Kennedy ducked, anticipating the guy's instinct to fire his gun at whatever was in front of him. He emptied his mag into the back wall and was struggling to load another when Kennedy stood and swung the torque wrench as hard as he could at the man's head. The dense steel ratchet assembly struck him in the left temple and spun him around. He dropped the gun and fell hard to the floor. Blood was gushing from his head, and his feet were twitching. Then he was still. Kennedy stood there, unable to tear his eyes away from the grisly scene, unable to breathe.

39

Another flashlight beam shined in Kennedy's eyes and he looked up, dazed. There were three men dressed in military black ops garb, with helmets, goggles, and small tactical machine guns, standing at the entrance of the maintenance garage. The one shining the light on Kennedy lifted his goggles. It was Best. Kennedy started to speak, but Best signaled him to keep his mouth shut and sat him down in a dark corner on a bucket. Kennedy watched as they wrapped the dead man, the wrench, and the man's gun in sheets of nonreflective black plastic, secured with matte-black tape.

Then they covered the blood on the garage floor with powder, which congealed it into piles of mealy black lumps, like clumped cat litter. The men swept all of that into more plastic bags, and the garage was clean, like it never happened.

The entire process took less than fifteen minutes.

A refrigerated airline catering truck pulled up with its lights off and they loaded all the plastic parcels into the back. Kennedy and Best got in front and the other men in back. The driver was wearing an airport catering company uniform. Best yanked off his helmet and top pullover, revealing the same uniform underneath. He pulled Kennedy's satellite phone from his pocket and handed it back to him as they drove slowly across the apron, headed for the terminal.

"We'll drop you at the Jetway door. Mary is probably expecting you to come back through her office before you leave. I'll pick you up in another vehicle at Arrivals door seven in ten minutes. Got it?"

"Yeah."

Best shined a UV light on Kennedy's clothes.

"What's that?"

"Looking for blood."

He found a couple of spots on Kennedy's pants and sprayed them with an aerosol. They dried quickly to a crumbly powder and Best brushed them off. He looked at Kennedy's face.

"Snap out of it," Best said. "You can't go back in there with the thousand-yard stare, okay? Here, take this."

Best handed him a blue tablet.

"What is it?"

"Xanax. It'll even you out."

Kennedy swallowed the pill.

"Stop here," Best said to the driver.

They pulled up to the Jetway door Kennedy had used to access the ramps. He got out and walked up the stairs. The Xanax started kicking in and he felt like he could breathe again. The fog lifted in his head. He walked back into the terminal and looked at his watch. He'd been out there a little over an hour, not long enough for Mary to get suspicious. When he got back to her office, the place was empty. His workbag and her coat and purse were still next to her desk. Kennedy slipped the security cards she'd given him out of his pocket, wiped them for prints, and put them back in her purse.

He didn't want to leave without saying good-bye, so he called her cell. It rang in a nearby room—a loud pop music ringtone—typical Mary choice. When it went to voice mail, he called it again and followed the sound. It was coming from a room at the end of the hallway with AUTHORIZED PERSONNEL ONLY on the door.

"Mary?" he called out. "You in there?"

No reply. The door was slightly ajar. He pushed it open.

"I know I don't have clearance for this room but—"

When he opened the door, he saw it was a storage closet. He turned on the light. Mary was sitting on the floor with her back up against some storage shelves.

"Mary?"

She didn't answer. Kennedy moved closer and crouched down next to her. Her lips were blue. Her eyes were wide and staring.

She was dead.

Lentz was closing in. It was almost as if he were staring at Kennedy through Mary's lifeless eyes, telling him he hadn't seen anything yet.

40

The plane transporting Juarez and Trudeau disappeared from radar two hours ago and crashed in the Ural mountains."

It was nearly 5:00 A.M. at the Boston safe house in Beacon Hill and Alia was briefing Kennedy, Love, Nuri, and Best on their grim operational status. The sky outside was a mottled slate color, threatening any number of frigid, wet attacks. She informed them that she had just finished cleaning up the mess at Logan Airport. Her scrub crew had managed to retrieve the body of Mary, the TSA chief, before the police could find it. Now Mary was in her car at the bottom of the Charles River, just off Memorial Drive. With her blood alcohol level and a prior DUI, accidental death wouldn't be a tough sell to the local cops.

But that was the least of their concerns. An hour after Mary was wrapped up, Alia had received a call from Langley about Juarez and Trudeau, followed by satellite images of an airplane crash site, which she was showing the team as they sat around a conference table, stunned and speechless. She zoomed in on the wreckage. It was strewn across a quarter mile of rugged, snow-covered mountains.

"It fell from its cruising altitude of eighteen thousand feet in two pieces," she explained, "suggesting a midair explosion. Even if, by some miracle, they survived, temperatures are well below freezing at the crash site, with no emergency services for thousands of miles."

"I thought they left Russia days ago," Kennedy said. "Langley is just learning about their plane going down now?"

"They had laid over in a city called Surgut." She showed them remote Surgut in the Khanty-Mansi province on a sat map. "Juarez's plan was to acquire a new aircraft there to ensure they couldn't be tracked on their way back to Paris."

Kennedy could no longer keep silent about the intel Trudeau had sent him. Lentz was gunning for them, now that they knew his secret, and everyone in Red Carpet deserved to know.

"Alia," Kennedy said, "tell them about the nukes."

Alia stopped cold, staring at him in disbelief.

"What's he talking about?" Nuri asked.

"Kennedy, I know you're under a lot of strain, but I would advise you to allow me to finish this briefing."

"Trudeau found out Lentz had bought twenty-five Russian RA-115s—miniaturized nukes weighing fifty to sixty pounds—from the arms dealers," Kennedy said, ignoring her. "They're called 'suitcase nukes' because they can easily be transported in a suitcase or backpack. Each of them has the firepower of six to ten kilotons of TNT, only a few kilotons less than one of the bombs we dropped on Hiroshima."

"Why didn't we receive this intel?" Best asked.

"You know the protocols with these types of weapons," Alia said coldly. "And Trudeau clearly didn't follow them."

"Trudeau sent the intel to Juarez and me. He felt like someone other than Alia and him needed to know."

"That wasn't his call to make," Alia said.

"Why didn't you tell me?" Love asked, looking at Kennedy, fearful.

"He wasn't supposed to know," Alia said.

"And I was hoping you were going to tell the team," Kennedy retorted.

"It doesn't work that way," Alia said.

"How does World War Three work, Alia?" Best asked bitterly. "What's the fucking protocol that won't mean shit while we all burn?"

A line had been crossed. It was one thing for the others to question procedures, but Best was a soldier. He was supposed to follow orders to the bitter end. Kennedy felt like they were rapidly approaching a meltdown in Alia's leadership viability.

"If Lentz was able to do this to Trudeau and Juarez, we're dead," Love said.

"You got that right," Nuri said. "I'm just glad someone had the balls to tell us the truth." She nodded to Kennedy.

The room was quiet. Alia switched off the projector and poured herself a drink. Kennedy wanted to quit, to fold in the face of absurd odds. But he knew he couldn't. He knew he'd gone well past the point of no return. Doing anything other than stopping Lentz was nonnegotiable. He needed to be the leader he'd been asked to be.

Alia finally spoke. "As of now, I'm suspending all Red Carpet operations for twenty-four hours while I go back to DC to discuss the next steps with my superiors."

Kennedy could feel her closing herself off to the team. She had no intention of coming back to Boston. He couldn't fight her. He had to reel her in.

"Alia, this is your baby," Kennedy said calmly. "Don't go to DC. Don't let them derail us. Love is right. We're dead. But we're the only ones who know enough to move as quickly as Lentz. Handing this off is like handing someone a grenade with the pin pulled. It will just blow up in their face and Lentz wins. I appreciate your situation, but fuck Washington, fuck politics, and fuck your career. We've got nukes on the street, so it's do or die. Besides, do you really want to kowtow to a bunch of misogynist military brass who'll just tell you to stand aside and try not to cry while the men do their work?"

Alia was silent for a long moment, thinking.

"I agree with you," she said finally, surprising everyone. "And I'm sorry for keeping you all in the dark. Now that my superiors know what we know, they're going to try to take this over. In their minds, they have no choice."

"I don't know about you, Alia, but this is the kind of shit going rogue was made for," Nuri said.

Best shot her a look. Alia lit a cigarette.

"We do that, and we'll have two enemies we won't walk away from," she said.

"Fuck 'em," Best said. "I'm all in."

"Me too," Kennedy said.

"I'm with you," Love said, looking directly at Kennedy.

Nuri piped in. "Like the man said, we got bang bang on the street, boys and girls, and no one wants to be another Mark Rossini."

"Who?" Love asked.

"FBI agent who had information that could have prevented 9/11 but had his intel suppressed by the CIA's Alec Station unit to avoid embarrassing the Saudis," Kennedy said.

"And the stakes for them to suppress were *way* lower then," Nuri added.

"What do you think?" Best asked Alia.

"I think we can all agree that any action other than trying to stop Lentz is an action that will guarantee our failure and his success. We are the only chance we've got, and we can't waste any time."

"So what's our next move?" Nuri asked.

"I think we have to focus purely on taking Lentz off the board," Alia said.

"I like the sound of that," Best said.

"Good," Kennedy said. "I think I know where to start."

41

Kennedy broke his theory down for everyone. The avionics communication equipment Lambert had tracked down in Kuala Lumpur, combined with the suitcase nukes Trudeau had discovered in Norilsk, meant Lentz could turn aircraft into long-range missiles with a nuclear warhead and a sophisticated guidance system, allowing him to execute a "coordinated strike" against multiple targets in the United States—major cities, military and political targets, critical infrastructure, power plants, and anything else that would help to cripple the country. And since he would have total control of the aircraft, he could wait until it was near final approach to its target before he took the wheel, making it impossible for civil air defense to deploy fighter jets to shoot it down. The attack on Kennedy at Logan confirmed that Lentz had operatives in place to install the equipment. Provided he had not already completed his aircraft sabotage operation, their best bet would be to catch him in the act. Since he had taken out most of Red Carpet, he might not expect them to come out swinging.

"So how do we intercept—if he's still out there?" Best asked.

"The answer is in the data communications being routed through Lentz's secure servers in Cuba," Kennedy said. "We use Rico's taps and compare them with my airport taps to identify IP addresses at airports communicating with Lentz using his IM app. Presumably the owners of those IP addresses are embedded in maintenance. Then we analyze communication frequency and drop-off. It's probably safe to assume he's in frequent communication with his operatives when they are in the midst of sabotaging an airplane. After the job is done, it's probably safe to assume comms would slow or stop abruptly. If that's the case, we're too late. But if we find a comm cluster, we might be able to take him."

"Sounds like a long shot," Love said.

"Agreed, but it's all we have outside of Alia convincing the FAA to ground all flights for emergency inspections," Kennedy said.

Alia, Nuri, and Best laughed.

"What's so funny?" Love asked. "Can't you people pull that off if you have cause? All flights were grounded on 9/11."

"Yeah, *after* the Twin Towers went down," Nuri said. "Alia would be asking for the same thing, based on a theory backed by decent intel, but nowhere near signed confessions. And, no offense, Alia, but you're not exactly the darling of the company at this juncture."

"None taken," Alia said. "I think Kennedy's plan is worth exploring. I'll buy some time with Langley and call in some favors. As for the rest of you, I'm sending you to your own individual safe houses to get some rest. Get the details from Best. We can recon tonight after I know what kind of resources we have at our disposal."

"Why not stay here?" Kennedy asked.

"Too well known at Langley," Best said. "Which makes it too well known period. These other places came from my friend at the bureau. They're witness protection safe houses, so they're way off the grid."

Best handed out envelopes with keys. As they were getting ready to leave, Love sidled up to Kennedy and nudged him conspiratorially.

"I don't know about you," she whispered, "but I could use a drink."

42

"Shaken, not stirred," Love said wistfully as she sipped her second martini.

Kennedy toasted her with a glass of Jack Daniel's, the best whiskey they had in the South Boston bar Love had chosen. The place had no street sign and an alley entrance that looked like the door to a utility room. There were a handful of people tucked into dark corners, drinking and talking in hushed tones. There was an air of menace to the clientele, and they stole looks at Kennedy and Love from time to time, sizing them up.

"Proud of you, you big lug," she said, toasting him again.

"Why?"

"Without you, we wouldn't have a chance."

"We don't have a chance," he said ruefully.

"No, we have one. It's a small one. Very small. But we have it. And we wouldn't have it without you."

"Thank you for—"

She grabbed his face and kissed him hard on the lips. Kennedy was completely taken by surprise. When Love pulled away, she had tears in her eyes.

"I'm sorry," she said.

"Don't be," Kennedy said, slightly stunned.

"You're not mad at me?"

"For kissing me?"

"Yeah. I mean, I know you've been keeping me at arm's length and all, and I respect that, but it was driving me crazy."

"Me too," he said. "I won't do that anymore."

"Good," she said and kissed him again.

"Get a room," Nuri said behind them.

They turned, and she was standing there with a beer.

"Mind if I join you?"

"You don't trust the safe house either, eh?" Kennedy said.

"Hell no," Nuri said, sitting down. "Lentz put a pill in Juarez and Trudeau while they were flying over one of the most desolate stretches of nothing on the planet. I think he can find us in Boston."

"How'd *you* find us?" Love asked.

"I followed you," Nuri said. "I could tell you were scheming and I figured you might want to drown your sorrows. Just so happens, so did I."

"Very perceptive," Kennedy said.

"But you haven't figured out where you're going after this, right?" Nuri said.

"Nope," he replied.

"I have some ideas," Nuri said. "But enough business talk. Let's drink."

She looked around the bar, raising an eyebrow.

"And try not to get stabbed."

They stayed in the bar, drinking and eating until the sun went down. Nuri hacked into a local real estate site and found corporate apartments previously owned by defunct start-ups that had not yet gone on the auction block. The apartments were furnished and most likely had some leftover toilet paper and ramen noodles from businesspeople passing through. One was within walking distance in Cambridge. All they had to do was crack the key box and slip in for the night. Nuri gave them the address but told them to wait in the bar while she went there first to scout it.

After she left, Love said, "Hey, I want you to know something."

"What's that?"

"I'm still glad you asked me to help you. And I'm still glad I stayed on. I know you're protective, but this has been my choice all along and I don't regret it. Cool?"

Kennedy looked at Love across the table. Amid all the insanity that had ambushed his life when he joined Red Carpet, there was one thing that blew him away more than anything else: he loved her. He stood up, walked around the table, and kissed her.

"Cool," he said.

"We better go."

They were putting their coats on when both of their satellite phones buzzed.

43

Where have you two been?"

The last of Alia's smooth facade was gone. She practically herded them into the Beacon Hill safe house conference room.

"I've been trying to reach you. And Nuri too."

"What's wrong?" Kennedy asked, avoiding the issue of them having gone AWOL.

She switched on the local news. Three apartment buildings in different areas of the city were on fire.

"Those are all your safe houses," she said.

"Holy shit," Love said.

"I need to know where you've been and why you weren't reachable."

She pulled a gun and laid it on the table, her hand still gripping it.

"There's no need for—"

"Shut up," Alia snapped.

"We were drinking at a bar in South Boston," Kennedy said defiantly. "We didn't feel comfortable going to your safe houses. And I'm glad we trusted our instincts. Now put the gun away."

Alia left it on the table, within her reach but not theirs.

"How does Lentz know our every move, Alia?" Kennedy asked. "Is it possible someone close to us is tipping him off?"

"Where's Nuri?" Alia asked.

"We don't know," Love said.

"All of our Cuban data feeds are dead," Alia said. "Your airport feeds are still active, but all of the chatter we were hearing before—supporting a network of TSA agents working with Lentz—has ceased. And our field office in Havana received a FedEx package thirty minutes ago."

She switched the television feed to a photograph of an open FedEx box sitting on top of a pile of bloody newspapers and black plastic sheeting. Inside the box, there was a cheesecloth sack soaked with blood. She switched to the next photo and the cheesecloth had been removed. Underneath was Rico's head.

"Oh no," Love said and started crying.

Kennedy glared at Alia.

"She needs to know the truth. I'm sorry you have to see it, but I'm not in the business of sugarcoating things, especially not now."

Love fled to the bathroom. Alia watched her go, her hand remaining close to her gun.

"Where the hell is Best?" Kennedy asked.

"I don't know. I've been trying to reach him too."

"Alia, you can't protect us. You need to give us guns and all the cash you have. Now. I'm not waiting around here for the other shoe to drop."

She looked at him skeptically, then opened a locking cabinet and pulled out two Berettas in shoulder holsters with extra mags on the belt.

"You know how to shoot?"

Kennedy picked up one of the guns and held it like he was holding a snake.

"You don't know how to shoot," she said.

She showed him quickly how to load a mag, slap it into the handle, chamber a round, and operate the safety. Kennedy put the holster on.

"Money."

"Where do you think you're going to go?"

"Anywhere away from here."

"He'll find you," she said.

"He already has. Now I'm going to find him."

She handed him a couple of stacks of hundreds and he shoved them into his jacket pockets.

"Kennedy, I'm sorry."

"Me too."

He went to find Love in the bathroom at the back of the house. She was sitting on the edge of the tub with her face in her hands. A lit cigarette dangled between her fingers.

"We need to go," Kennedy said.

Love looked up and saw the gun strapped to him and the one he was offering her.

"No," she said. "I don't want that."

"I don't think you understand—"

"I understand. And we both know that's not going to save us."

"No, but it might buy us some time," he said.

"Where the hell are we going?"

"I say we stick to the plan with Nuri. Alia doesn't know where she is."

"What if Nuri is the one tipping off Lentz?"

"Then we'll retire early," Kennedy said.

Love started crying again. Kennedy put his arm around her shoulders. The front-door buzzer went off. They both looked up.

"Stay here," Kennedy said.

He tried to hand her the gun but she wouldn't take it, so he laid it in the tub next to her.

"Lock the door and stay quiet."

Kennedy left the bathroom and Love locked the door behind him.

Alia walked out of the conference room, holding a gun.

"Get out of sight," she said.

Kennedy hid in a room across the hall from the conference room so he could watch the hallway and the bathroom through a crack in the open door. He chambered a round in his Beretta and waited.

He saw Alia walk to the end of the hallway but lost sight of her when she went into the foyer. He heard the front door open and Alia speaking to someone with a male voice. They were too far away for him to understand what they were saying. He heard the front door close again. Alia said something to the man and walked out of the foyer, back into the hallway where Kennedy could see her. She turned back expectantly, as if annoyed that the man was not following her, and Kennedy heard two pneumatic pops. Bullets tore through Alia's chest and forehead.

She crumpled to the floor, dead.

Then Best emerged from the foyer holding a .22 caliber Beretta 70 with a barrel suppressor. Kennedy moved back, away from the crack in the door, and held his breath.

44

hile Kennedy stood flat against the wall, away from the door, he could hear Best stalking around the house, checking all the rooms. He had to think. He had to do something before Best got to the bathroom where Love was hiding. But if he came out and opened fire, he was a dead man. Kennedy had never shot a pistol in his life. The odds of him hitting Best at all were against him. And Best would have the second shot. He would not miss. To make matters worse, Love started whimpering in the bathroom.

"Who's there? It's Best! Come out."

Love kept whimpering. "It's Love. I'm in the bathroom. I'm hurt."

"Is anyone else here?"

"She killed Kennedy. Killed him . . ."

The whimper turned to a sob, and Kennedy knew she was doing it to distract Best so he could get a shot at him. As quietly as he could, Kennedy moved back to the crack in the door and saw Best walking slowly toward the bathroom, keeping an eagle eye on his surroundings, ready for anything.

"I'm coming," Best said. "How bad is it?"

"It's bad. Help me, please!"

When Best was a few paces from the bathroom, he opened fire, blowing holes in the door and emptying his magazine. Kennedy sprinted out from the room where he was hiding, afraid he was too late. Best heard him and turned. Kennedy aimed for the widest target, his chest, and fired three rounds. Best was blown off his feet and smashed through the bullet-riddled bathroom door.

He landed on the tile floor and tried to reach for his gun, but Kennedy pushed through what was left of the door and kicked the gun aside.

Love was perched up on the windowsill, holding on to the shower curtain rod. The bullets Best had fired hit the back wall a foot below where she was sitting. She climbed down and looked at him dying on the floor.

"Fuck you, motherfucker," she said.

"Got a cigarette?" Kennedy asked Love.

She handed him her pack and he lit one. Then he held the burning ember over Best's eyeball.

"You're going to tell me everything you know before you die or I'm going to stub this out in your eye. Then I'm going to move to your next eye, then your tongue, your lips—"

"I don't know . . . shit," Best gurgled. "He doesn't make that mistake."

"Why are you working for him?" Kennedy raged. "You think he would have given you anything other than a bullet in the head when this was done?"

"No . . . choice. No one does. My family . . ."

"Where is he now?"

Best started coughing up blood and didn't stop until he was dead.

45

I think we need to keep moving," Kennedy said, "until we have a plan."

It was dark, and he and Love were sitting in the back of a twenty-four-hour Laundromat in the Back Bay at 2:00 A.M. Both of them were exhausted and finding it difficult to think straight. Kennedy felt like there was a heavy weight on his chest, crushing the life out of him, but he didn't want Love to think he'd given up. Love looked like she had given up, no doubt plagued by the thought that Rico's death was on her. Outside, the frigid rain was starting to turn to the light, dry snowflakes that come with bitter cold.

"Is there anyone who can help us?" she asked, tears streaking down her beautiful face.

"Not that I can think of. The CIA is out. All of their agents are dead and we're alive. So, they're going to want to grill us about that first before helping us."

"Which leaves us where, exactly?"

"I don't know."

She drew in a sharp breath.

Kennedy saw the look in her eyes and almost couldn't bear it. He tried his best to retain his composure and think things through.

"Our only real option is to go to the place Nuri found in Cambridge. If she's still alive, she can get us off the street so we can eat and get some rest, try to get our heads back in the game."

"I just hope we can trust her."

"Yeah," Kennedy said, looking out the window. "I don't think we have much choice. Harvard Bridge isn't far from here. We can cross over into Cambridge and walk the rest of the way on side streets."

They walked outside. There was a strong wind coming across the river, whipping their faces with icy snowflakes. They buttoned their coats to the top and shoved their hands deep in their pockets. Kennedy gripped his gun. As they made their way across the Harvard Bridge, it occurred to him that, without real muscle, they wouldn't have a chance. He had seen the kind of killers that worked for Lentz. They needed a killer of their own.

"I think I might actually know someone who can help us," Kennedy said as they walked. "He was on my team when I started with Red Carpet. Ex–special forces type."

"But isn't he CIA?"

"He seemed like a hired gun. They only brought him in for my airport jobs. And he was the only one who wasn't there when I met the team in Paris."

"Maybe he'll take pity on us," Love said, shivering.

"It's worth a try," Kennedy said.

46

The night before, after Nuri left Kennedy and Love at the bar, she'd gone to scout the corporate apartment they were going to use to crash. She cracked the lockbox and went inside. The place was nice and there were Cokes in the fridge, so she grabbed one and turned on the TV, waiting for them to arrive. That's when she saw the story about the three burning apartments on the local news and noticed that one of them was the place where Best had tried to send her. So when she got the same 911 message Love and Kennedy had gotten from Alia, telling them to return to the safe house, she didn't trust it. No way was she walking into her own funeral.

A few hours later, she tried calling Alia from a pay phone, using a collect code so she'd know who it was. After ringing her several times with no answer, Nuri knew something was wrong. Alia *always* answered. Nuri also tried calling Love, Kennedy, and Best. Radio silence all around. Against her better judgment, she went back to the safe house where they'd all met hours earlier. The front door was standing open.

Inside, she found the bodies of Best and Alia.

When she saw Best's gun and the small entry wounds in Alia's chest and head, she knew he had killed her. And since both Alia and Best had been shot from behind, with Best's entry wounds indicating a larger-caliber bullet, it was clear someone else had killed him. In the event it might have been Kennedy or Love, she knew she had to track them down. She called both their sat phones from the safe house phone and still got no answer. Their GPS signals weren't transmitting either. But without bodies, she couldn't assume anything. They could be dead or in hiding.

What if they killed Alia and framed Best?

It was unlikely, but she'd seen shit happen on this op she never dreamed possible. Which meant *anything* was possible. And when she went to grab a gun and some ammo from the safe house stores and found guns and all the cash missing, she wasn't going to take any chances.

Before going back to the corporate apartment and potentially walking into an ambush, she called a friend for help—someone who wasn't on the company payroll, but who specialized in dirty work.

"I think you need to go in," he said without hesitation. "Try to salvage what's left of your career."

"These motherfuckers jacked my *whole* crew," she said. "And turned at least one of us. So, I'm thinking I would rather put my foot so deep in that Eurotrash motherfucker's ass, he'll be cleaning the heel of my Doc Martens with his tongue."

"I get you. And don't take this the wrong way, but you're a computer geek. You'll just get dead, and that doesn't do shit for your cause."

"Fucker. If you weren't right, I'd hang up on you."

"Be smart, Nuri. Go home. Langley can still get this guy. The right way."

47

ours later, after Nuri got off the phone with her friend, Kennedy and Love were huddled in the shadows across the street from the apartment, watching its third-floor windows for any sign of movement. The building was on a quiet residential street near a high-tech business park. There were only a few parked cars, and most of the units in the other buildings lining the block were dark. The temperature had dropped into the twenties, and Love was clinging to Kennedy for warmth.

"I don't know, Love," Kennedy whispered. "Maybe we should try to contact her first."

"How?"

"We could leave a note on the door," Kennedy suggested.

"Maybe have her meet us someplace safe? Like a police station?" Love said.

"Actually, that's a great idea. We'll leave a note, tell her to meet us at a local precinct house, then watch it from across the street to see if she shows."

"Or if the fucking grim reaper shows," Love said through chattering teeth.

"Cool," Kennedy said. "All we need is some paper."

"We suck so hard at being spies." Love giggled.

"I know," Kennedy said. "It's pathetic."

She pulled him close and kissed him.

"Do you think now's a good time to—"

"I'm just trying to stay warm," she said.

"Then come inside by the fire," said a voice behind them.

Love yelped and they both whipped around. Nuri was holding a gun on them, pensive, but not hostile.

"You guys are right," she said. "You do suck hard at being spies."

"Are you going to kill us?" Love asked, shivering uncontrollably. "Because I'm so cold I don't really care if I die anymore."

"No. But I will make you some cocoa."

Nuri led them to the apartment, where Love beelined for the gas fireplace blazing in the corner.

"How do you know you can trust us?" Kennedy asked Nuri.

"I went to the safe house," she said. "It wasn't a particularly complex crime scene. Oh, and I found this."

She plugged a USB drive into the side of the big-screen TV and turned it on.

Kennedy and Love watched while Nuri hit play. The video was a surveillance camera recording of Best murdering Alia, then getting capped by Kennedy. Love turned away, unable to watch.

"I'm sure Best intended to pull the security camera footage after he killed Alia," Nuri said, shutting the TV off. "But then again, he didn't think he was walking into the O.K. Corral, did he, Wyatt Earp?"

"So, you know you can trust us. How do we know we can trust you?" Kennedy asked.

"How do we know we can trust you?" Nuri mocked him like a little kid.

"I guess we don't have much choice," he said.

"Not really. But then again, neither do I," Nuri said.

Love laughed and gave her a hug.

"I never thought I would be so glad to see you," Love said.

"Bitch, I'm your new BFF," Nuri said, hugging her back.

———

They raided the place and ate everything that resembled food in the fridge and cupboards. By that point it was almost 5:00 A.M. and everyone was wiped out, so they turned in, Nuri in one room and Kennedy and Love in another. Love quickly fell asleep with her face buried in his chest and he followed suit, effortlessly drifting away. He had no idea how long he'd been out when a noise woke him. He opened his eyes and a gun barrel slithered out of the darkness, pointed at his face. Kennedy sat up with a start, waking Love.

"Oh my God," she said, her voice trembling.

"Where's your gun?" a man's voice asked in the shadows.

"Nightstand," Kennedy said.

"Lot of good it's doing you there," the voice said.

"Who are you?"

A floor lamp switched on. Mitchell was standing next to the bed. He was dressed in desert combat fatigues with digital camo. His usual sharp, glowering face and squinty eyes, combined with a recently sprouted patchy beard, made him look even more like he'd just been released from solitary confinement.

"Let her go—" Kennedy started.

"Put your hands on your heads," Mitchell demanded.

They put their hands on their heads and Kennedy looked at Love.

"I love—"

"Shut up," Mitchell snapped. "Now's not the time to get sentimental."

Nuri slipped in, her gun trained on Mitchell.

"Look at you, coming all this way to save us. Who's the sentimental one now?"

"Shut up," Mitchell said, putting his gun away.

"Wait, what the fuck!?" Kennedy said. "You called him? Why the hell didn't you tell us?"

"Thanks for the heart attack," Love said.

"Sorry. I didn't want to get your hopes up," she said.

"Still the same five-star pain in the ass, I see," Mitchell said to Nuri. "Get dressed, team FUBAR. We got a lot of shit to talk about."

48

Everyone got dressed and drank coffee in the kitchen as the light came up outside. The storm had lifted and mist was rising from the ground, swirling in the morning sunlight. Kennedy felt cautiously optimistic. With Nuri and Mitchell, they had what it was going to take to get a shot at Lentz.

"This is a bug hunt, pure and simple," Mitchell said, holding court. "We have to assume it's too late to do anything about Lentz's plan, which is under way. So, the best we can hope for is to kill the head and hope the body will die. If any of you disagree with that, then we got nothing else to talk about."

Everyone nodded. Mitchell looked at Kennedy specifically.

"What about you, team leader? You going to sound off or what?"

"I'm with you. And I'll be stepping over you to pull the trigger."

"Next step is to figure out what rock the bug is hiding under so we can stomp his guts out. Any ideas on how to do that?"

"He's got to be working the airports still," Kennedy said. "Otherwise he would have gone ahead with the attack by now. I think we can intercept him at one of them."

"Some of the airport data feeds are still active," Nuri said. "Lentz couldn't knock out our mobile device trackers because they're satellite-based. I'm sure we can find something in there, especially if he's working with operatives embedded in maintenance crews."

"Maintenance workers have to pass through security," Kennedy said. "Millimeter wave devices pick up the chip signal in their badges when they walk past."

"How the hell do you know that?" Nuri said.

"Sometimes the scanner antennas lock into the chip and deactivate it, so you get a bunch of pissed-off wrench monkeys yelling at TSOs."

"So, we can see from the scanner data when maintenance badges go through checkpoints and match that up with the mobile devices that are in contact with Lentz's compound in Cuba," Nuri said.

"In theory," Kennedy said.

"In theory, I have a nerd boner for you right now," Nuri said.

"Thanks?"

"I can't believe you lived this long," Mitchell said to Nuri.

"Only the good die young," Nuri said, licking her lips suggestively.

"What about the Cuban compound itself?" Mitchell asked. "I could pretty easily drop in on him Scarface-style with some mercs and a small army of local pirates."

"He hasn't been seen there in weeks," Kennedy said. "Juarez had eyes on the Isla de la Juventud airport and had sat images coming from the compound almost daily."

"Then he's probably never going back," Mitchell said. "He dusted it off like a good little villain. All right then, let's go to work on the data. He's in there somewhere."

Kennedy and Love went through reams of mobile device and millimeter wave scanner data from all twenty-five bugged airports and fed it to a series of pattern recognition algorithms Nuri had written. It was a black hole of a time suck, with each airport taking over an hour to process and analyze.

While they crunched data, Mitchell and Nuri got to work procuring mission-critical items. Money was the first priority. They had the cash Kennedy had gotten from the safe house, but it was only a few thousand dollars, not nearly enough. After her trip to Havana, Nuri had broad access to the Cuban government's financial networks so she looked for accounts they had on US soil—most likely for funding espionage operations of their own. She found several in Boston, some at well-known institutions and others at lesser known investment banks and credit unions. All told, they had close to $150 million spread out around the city in shell-corporation accounts. Nuri then captured account numbers, PIN codes, and personal data from a dozen different banks housing some of these accounts. She used that information to log in and make account signatories out of the cover identities she and Mitchell used in the field. Then the two of them went to the twelve banks and used their cover IDs to withdraw $9,500 from each account—sidestepping the banks' legal obligation to report transactions of $10,000 and higher to the feds—and bagging $114,000 in clean currency.

Mitchell stuffed a sizable cut into a suitcase and went on a tour of Boston, buying black market weaponry, mostly from the Irish gunrunners who supplied gangs and biker crews. Another chunk of money was set aside for mercs, military-trained killers with special operator backgrounds, like Mitchell's. He knew quite a few who would do just about anything if the price was right, so he put some guys on standby to assist once they pinned down Lentz's location.

On the Lentz note, Mitchell and Nuri also checked surveillance on his Cuban compound. It was a ghost town. Just to be sure, Mitchell hit up one of his contacts in Cuba and paid him to check out the place. He scoped it with infrared and didn't see any heat signatures. Nuri checked sat images and saw nothing inside the compound courtyard or perimeter of the property. Mitchell's guy cut through the perimeter fence and broke in. The place was empty.

49

After Kennedy and Love had gone through all of the data, the dining
room wall was covered with notes, photos, timelines, and other mis-
cellany. Mitchell and Nuri, fully stocked for a homegrown black ops
mission, were anxious to hear the results.

"Since Lentz hasn't been to his compound in God knows how long,"
Kennedy said, "we gave up on trying to identify mobile app users at airports attempting to contact him through his Cuban servers."

"I thought that was our best lead?" Nuri said.

"Our friend Rico, rest in peace," Love said, "was a bug-happy guy.
Most of the devices he managed to plant in Lentz's aircraft are still intact."

"When the conditions are right, we can get spotty GPS tracking data
and some cockpit chatter," Kennedy added. "The problem is there's a lag of
six to seven hours between the time that information is captured and when
it gets to us."

"That gives us no time to put a team together," Mitchell said. "We could
get data saying he's in Denver, but a lot can happen in the six or seven hours
before we get the next feed."

"Right," Kennedy said. "So, I figured if we knew his aircraft registration number, we could track him that way. Juarez knew the numbers, but
he never passed that information on to me, and I couldn't find it in any of

the Rico debriefing files. So, Love listened to every second of the cockpit chatter Rico's bugs had recorded."

"It was a bitch because of the engine noise and Rico's accent," Love added, "but we were able to piece the number together."

"I checked it against airport records at Isla de la Juventud and Havana, and the address matched Lentz's compound," Kennedy said.

"Tracking an airplane by its registration number is easy. There are a bunch of sites that normal people can use to do that," Nuri said excitedly.

"True," Kennedy said, "but those sites don't always have information on private aircraft, which is the case with Lentz's jet. We're going to need you to get into FAA flight records and piggyback on their in-flight trackers so we know where he's headed. Depending on destination, we might have enough time to get a team there."

"Hack the FAA?" Nuri asked. "All I have to do is take down one more big government agency and I'll get my Girl Scout hacker badge."

Kennedy laid a full-year calendar with notes and circled dates out on the table.

"We also worked on trying to establish a timeline for the attack," he said.

"We talked about that," Mitchell said, perturbed. "Even if we know when it's going down, we don't have the ability to stop it."

"Agreed," Kennedy said. "But any information on timeline is useful in the event that some of us don't make it and whoever is left needs to call in the cavalry."

"Sure, if we knew that we could call them in now," Mitchell countered. "But we don't have that data, so how is this anything other than guess-work?"

"Because behavior analysis is my specialty," Kennedy said. "Just hear me out. Terrorists are basically psychotic public relations whores. In addition to wanting to hit us when we're most vulnerable, they also want to do it when they'll get the most media attention for their cause."

"It's like when you're dropping an album or releasing a movie," Love said. "You have to be strategic about it to maximize the Oprah moment. The choice of 9/11 was basically branding, a tongue-in-cheek play on our emergency number, which makes the date more memorable. Trust me, no one thinks of anything else when you say September eleventh."

Kennedy said, "Since we couldn't think of any dates that have the same double meaning, like 9/11 or 10/4, we figured Lentz might be going the route of choosing a sacred cow, a time when we're happiest and, more important, most vulnerable."

"There goes Christmas," Nuri said.

"Actually, we were thinking Thanksgiving is a better option," Kennedy said. "Christmas is too religious and centers on one group. Thanksgiving is secular, so almost everyone takes part, regardless of culture."

"It's like Christmas without Jesus and expensive gifts and a looming credit card hangover," Love said. "You can fuck with Christmas, but if you fuck with Thanksgiving, you're kicking us right in our patriotic nuts."

"Yeah, but who's flying on Thanksgiving?" Best asked.

"Hardly anyone," Kennedy said, "but *the day before* Thanksgiving is the busiest travel day of the year. More planes in the air, more human cattle in the airports. If you really want to ring our bell, the day before Thanksgiving is the knockout punch."

"Every time Lentz has acted in the past," Nuri said, "it's been at the height of what Langley calls *cultural vulnerability*. Like when he helped to incite protests in Egypt during Ramadan, taking advantage of people having their minds on the holiday. He's used election riots and other forms of unrest in Myanmar to get his hooks into their natural gas reserves. I think the day before turkey day is a solid bet."

"The day before Thanksgiving is twelve days from today," Kennedy said. "If Nuri can work out the FAA hack, we might have a shot at intercepting him as he makes final preparations."

"Which brings us to our next problem," Mitchell said. "If we find him, what are we looking for? We sort of know what he looks like. We know the number of his private jet. But what we don't know is how he's moving freely around the country sabotaging commercial aircraft at busy airports. You don't do that without a cover, my friends."

Nuri turned, nodding.

"True. He's got to have a serious layer of smoke and mirrors to pull this shit off."

"Especially since it's highly likely he's traveling with the nukes," Mitchell said. "If I were him, that's how I would do it. It's old tech, so if they were handled improperly, they could be useless. And who the hell would you trust to deliver them for you?"

"Isn't that dangerous, taking them on the plane?" Love asked.

"As long as the detonators aren't attached to the bombs, they don't present any extra risk to him and his flight crew. My money's on him making deliveries."

"For that to happen, he'd need to be able to operate at each airport with very little oversight," Kennedy added. "Like a politician or foreign leader."

"Some celebrities get that kind of treatment," Love said. "If you're big enough and rich enough, you can get away with murder on private jets. Literally."

"Jesus, that's it," Kennedy said.

"What?" Mitchell asked.

"Celebrity travel. It's one of the biggest loopholes in TSA protocol because of their trusted-traveler bullshit," Kennedy explained. "If you're a big music act or touring theater show, or Johnny Depp and his Yorkies, you can preplan your trip with TSA and bypass most of the security procedures so you never get hung up in any of your tour cities, which might cost millions in revenue."

"The guy's a ghost," Mitchell said. "How would any of that be useful to him?"

"The bigger acts always bring an entourage—roadies, stylists, sound guys, video guys, lots of people and chaos he could hide behind," Kennedy said. "There's your smoke and mirrors."

"He could hide a lot more than himself too," Love added. "Rock stars and celebs end up being mules for all kinds of contraband, things that are a lot more conspicuously illegal than a bomb in a suitcase."

"So, if that's his cover, how do we break it?" Mitchell asked.

"Once I get the FAA info, we can cross-reference Lentz's stops to date with the recent tour dates of major acts currently on the road," Nuri said. "Then we can see how the stars, or starfuckers, align."

50

You guys aren't going to believe this," she said, grinning. "This is too good!"

While Nuri had worked on the FAA hack all night, everyone else crashed on whatever was soft and got a few much-needed winks. But she was like a rooster, crowing them out of their slumber. Kennedy opened his eyes to the blinding-white morning sun and recoiled like a snake being poked with a stick.

"Get up, dummy!" Nuri yelled in his face. "Santa Claus came early!"

They all assembled in the dining room, yawning and bleary-eyed, and watched Nuri dance around like a wood sprite.

"Okay, check this shit out. Got into the FAA servers by pulling some pretty brilliant moves. What else is new. Blah blah blah."

She threw down a set of papers on the table.

"That's their record of all the places Lentz's jet has been over the past year, leading up to now, of course. More on that later. Dessert first. See if you can guess *which major touring act* has dates and locations that *perfectly* coincide with Lentz's airport stops."

"The fate of the world is at stake, so yeah, let's play a fucking guessing game. Just tell us, Nuri, or I'm going to have to shoot you," Mitchell growled.

"I'll guess. Donald Trump," Kennedy said.

"This is way better." Nuri laughed and threw some more papers on the desk.

They were photographs of Noah Kruz.

"Holy shit," Love exclaimed.

"I'll be damned," Mitchell said. "I love that guy."

"You've got to be fucking kidding me," Kennedy said, looking at a shot of Noah Kruz shaking Bill Clinton's hand.

Kennedy had been to that event as a VIP. He had the same picture.

"You're sure about this?" he asked Nuri.

"I'm sure his tour matches up perfectly with Lentz's airport stops. I checked some of the local news reports, and Kruz was in some of these places within an hour of Lentz's FAA log arrival time, which could mean they were actually traveling together."

"Kennedy, what's up? You know him?" Mitchell asked.

"No. Not personally. I've just . . . been listening to his tapes, reading his books, and going to his events for years."

"Yeah, me too," Mitchell said.

"I'm even part of his VIP circle." Kennedy chuckled, trying to mask his shock and disbelief with sarcasm.

"Is that like the Mickey Mouse Club?" Nuri asked.

"It's elite status. You get it after a certain number of purchases. They give you premium ticket access, discounts on books and podcasts, meet-and-greet photo ops—"

"We might be able to use that," Mitchell said.

"How?" Kennedy asked.

"To get us close to Kruz."

"Is it like a VIP meet and greet with a band?" Love asked. "You get a photo and a T-shirt, and get to shake hands?"

"Exactly like that," Kennedy said.

"Then we can use your status to get me into the meet and greet. I can bag him and we can take him someplace quiet for a little chat," Mitchell said.

"It doesn't work that way," Kennedy said. "You have to build status over time. He hates it when people can buy their way into something instead of earning it. I would have to go to the meet and greet."

Kennedy looked like a kid who had just been told Santa Claus wasn't real.

"If Lentz is tagging along with Kruz, it's because he's got a gun to his head. This is your chance to help the self-help guru," Love said, trying to make him feel better.

It didn't work. So much of what Kruz had said or written about over the years made sense to Kennedy and actually helped him to shape his life and find success. Kruz had given him the context for truth in a world run by bullshit and lies.

If Kruz were complicit in Lentz's plan, all of that would be dead now, leaving nothing but the smoking gun of irony.

"His next appearance is in Miami at the James Knight Center," Nuri said, looking at her screen. "Day after tomorrow."

"Does your FAA data on Lentz's plane match up?" Kennedy asked.

"FAA data has Lentz's plane in Palm Beach. Kruz has an event there tonight."

"I say we roll the dice on Miami. How about you, chief?" Mitchell asked Kennedy.

Kennedy nodded.

"I'll prep my team," Mitchell said. "Nuri, get us a fucking airplane."

51

etting the team from Boston to Miami under the radar of the CIA,
Homeland Security, and Lentz was a major problem that Nuri had to
solve quickly or there wouldn't be enough time to prep before Kennedy had his Noah Kruz moment. She had to rely on bush pilots, surly
misanthropes who charged a king's ransom to drop spec ops teams into
war zones, deliver drug hauls into the United States from all over the world,
and provide no-questions-asked evac services for people who needed to
get out of hot spots in a hurry.

Kennedy and Love worked on Miami. He used his VIP code to buy
himself a $10,000 private "life sculpting" session with Kruz, while Love
focused on getting herself backstage. She'd been an opening act and special
guest for some bigger bands back in the day. The stage manager was an old
friend she'd done a lot of favors for over the years—mostly drug-related
and potentially damaging to his career—so she called in a favor of her own.
She told him she was dating Kruz and wanted him to help her surprise her
"love guru" after the show. For five hundred bucks, he told her, he would
help her out and keep his mouth shut. Once she got in, her job would be to
let Mitchell and his crew of mercs in the back door.

Kennedy briefed Mitchell and Nuri about what he knew of Kruz's
travel. When he was touring within the United States, he flew between each
city and very rarely took a bus, even if he was going a short distance within

the same state. After his Miami appearance, his tour was going to take him to the Bahamas, Puerto Rico, Jamaica, and the Dominican Republic. Kruz had a 180-foot super yacht that was once featured on *MTV Cribs*, so Kennedy figured he was probably going to use it to hit those stops and host a few of his infamous parties.

"What if we take him on the boat?" Kennedy said. "When he's isolated out in the open water?"

Kennedy showed Mitchell the vessel schematics from the manufacturer's website.

"Plenty of room belowdecks and a Zodiac on board big enough for our team to bug out if we get some heat," Mitchell observed. "Nice and private in case we need to motivate our motivational speaker to talk. You're getting pretty good at this, chief."

Nuri found Kruz's docking information and reserved a slip next to his for a rented yacht that Mitchell was going to use to stow mercs and guns until it was time to hijack Kruz. Then she got word from one of their black ops pilot contacts, a drug runner on an opium delivery tour, coming from Kandahar and stopping in Boston sometime in the next few hours on his way to Miami. They would have a direct flight, but it was a cargo plane the US military had contracted out to fly medical supplies to the army's occupying troops in Afghanistan. Because of his cargo, the pilot had carte blanche with European and US air traffic, so he took full advantage and loaded every return flight with hundreds of kilos of pure Afghan opium. He was going to make millions from the haul, but still charged them ten grand a head for the pleasure of riding three and a half hours on a dirty metal floor.

At 4:00 A.M. the next morning, Nuri got the call. The team stole an SUV from the parking garage and drove to Hanscom Field, twenty-five miles west of Boston, with all the guns and money they could carry. They arrived with twenty minutes to spare. Their pilot, a gristly Sergeant Slaughter type in his fifties wearing Saigon mirror shades and a flight suit with a decade of pit stains, demanded the cash up front and barked orders at them as they loaded in their gear. He and Mitchell nearly came to blows several times when the pilot called him a plebe and a maggot. Kennedy handed him a few more stacks to shut the fuck up and they were off.

There was a storm cell moving up the Atlantic coast, and the first hour of their trip was a living hell. There were no seat belts for them in the cargo hold, so they held on to webbing tie-down straps while the plane bucked and rolled in the soup. Kennedy was violently ill the whole flight, puking in a trash bag Sergeant Slaughter had thrown at them for airsickness, along with a few bottles of water and a bag of peanuts (his idea of a joke), before locking himself in the cockpit. The plane landed at a small municipal airfield forty-five minutes outside of Miami so Slaughter could dump the dope before flying to Homestead Air Reserve Base to resupply for another run to Kandahar.

"Um, how the fuck are we going to get to Miami from here?" Nuri asked.

They were looking out the small aft porthole window, seeing nothing but palm trees and a concrete blockhouse for a radio tower. Sergeant Slaughter opened the cockpit door and stretched, smiling like a jackass at their motley appearance.

"End of the line, ladies. Sweet swingin' Jesus it stinks in here. Gonna cost you another five hundred for me to clean that up, 'less you want me to tell the authorities about y'all."

He lit a cigarette and let the smoke ooze through his brown teeth.

"No problem," Mitchell said, handing him another stack. "Mind if we wait to go after your people pick up the goods? The fewer eyes on us the better."

"For another grand, I'd be happy to oblige."

Mitchell peeled off more bills and held them out for Sergeant Slaughter. When Slaughter reached for them, Mitchell snatched his wrist, twisted it behind his back, and slammed the man's face into the floor of the cargo hold, grinding it into the metal.

Slaughter sputtered bloody epithets through a mouth full of broken teeth and reached for his knife. Mitchell grabbed it first and shoved it into his neck at the base of his skull. Slaughter went limp.

"The drug runners are here."

Kennedy was holding a .45, looking out the porthole. He knew Mitchell wasn't just getting payback. The equation was simple. Sergeant Slaughter had to die because he would never have kept his mouth shut. The drug dealers were on their way with the only vehicle within miles of the airport. The clock was ticking and the team needed that vehicle. Which meant the drug dealers had to go too. There appeared to be six of them riding in a black Suburban, towing a horse trailer, presumably for the opium bales.

"Six including the driver," he said.

Everyone but Love grabbed weapons.

"When I start shooting," Mitchell said to Kennedy and Nuri as he slapped a mag into his .45 and jacked a round into the chamber, "you two flank the SUV and take out anyone I miss. And please try not to hit me."

Mitchell opened the rear cargo door. As it slowly lowered to the ground, the dealers got out of the SUV, bristling with weaponry. Mitchell sprinted out of the airplane and opened fire. Kennedy and Nuri followed him out. The drug dealers never had a chance to even draw their guns. Mitchell took them with scary speed and precision.

Kennedy and Mitchell dragged the bodies into the horse trailer and released the hitch while Love and Nuri loaded money and weapons into the back of the Suburban. Mitchell took the wheel and started the engine.

"Bienvenidos a Miami."

52

They made it to the city in forty-five minutes, and it was a mad dash to get everything ready. The mercs brought the rental yacht in from a different marina and tied it up on the slip next to Kruz's. They were quiet, no-bullshit men who looked just like Mitchell—leathery and battle hardened. They spent hours working with Mitchell prepping the gear, then the whole team went over every detail of the plan until it was committed to memory. By the time they were finished, it was 2:00 A.M. the day of the Kruz event. When everyone else went to their berths and collapsed, Kennedy tried to relax on deck in a chaise. It was a balmy night, with a warm breeze coming off the water that helped him shake the chill he'd gotten into his bones in Boston. Love sat next to him and passed him a bottle of red wine.

"They stock these rentals with quality hooch," she said. "I think this was bottled the year I was born."

"A good vintage," Kennedy said, toasting her.

"I figured you could use a drink after vomiting three hours straight, witnessing the gruesome, yet justified, murders of seven of the world's biggest assholes, and preparing to kidnap your life coach so you can torture him for information on his luxury yacht."

"He's not my life coach." Kennedy groaned.

"Sorry."

Love sipped her wine. Kennedy could feel her look.

"Spit it out," he said.

"What? I got nothing to spit."

"Really?" he said, remembering the kiss she had laid on him in the Southie bar.

"Really."

Kennedy smiled. "Remember when you and Belle took sailing lessons over at UCLA? She bought those preppy shoes from the L.L.Bean catalog."

"Boat shoes," Love said.

"Yeah, and that stupid Cap'n Crunch jacket."

"That was her stylish sailing jacket, you mean big brother jerk."

Love punched him in the arm.

"Don't hit me. She was the one who almost killed you."

"Oh my God, she was a disaster." Love laughed. "Lost control of the jibboom in a thirty-knot wind. Sucker knocked me into the drink. You valiantly dove in and pulled me back to the boat."

"Yep," he said, taking a swig. "Some serious hero shit."

"You were all smooth with your lifeguard training . . . but then you realized the top to my bikini had come off."

"What? I don't remember that."

"Bullshit, you practically got to second base saving my butt."

"How did I go from hero to perv so quickly?"

"I'm not saying you copped a feel. It was just funny when you saw the girls bouncing around next to your arm."

"How do you know what I saw? You were passed out."

"Not the whole time."

"Why didn't you say something?"

"Because I liked it, dummy. Jesus."

She reached for his hand. He held hers tightly.

"One thing I don't understand is how you've managed to be alone for so long."

"After Belle died . . . I couldn't see myself being some normal guy with a wife and family. All I could think about was the fact that she would never have that, so I didn't feel right having it either."

"Dude, she would have wanted you to be happy. You were the best big brother ever."

"Not when it counted. The night before she died . . . I said . . . I was horrible."

Tears rolled down his cheeks and he didn't try to hide them or play it off.

"She forgives you," Love said. "She knew you had her back. Always."

Love kissed him.

"And this? This is a good thing. I'm good with it. I spoke to Belle last night. She's good with it. How about you?"

He nodded and kissed her again.

"I'm good with it."

53

The Noah Kruz event got into full swing at 4:00 P.M. Kennedy was whisked into the venue through a private entrance with the other VIPs. There were only twenty of them and he was the only one who had purchased the one-on-one session. They waited in a posh greenroom, drinking champagne and toasting the success Noah Kruz had helped them realize. The whole scene made Kennedy's stomach turn.

An hour earlier, Love's stage manager friend had let her in through the talent entrance at the back of the venue and showed her to Kruz's Life Sculpting Suite. After he was gone, Love let Mitchell and a couple of his mercs in through the same backstage entrance, and they took up positions inside the suite. Back at the marina, Nuri and the rest of the mercs were waiting in the rental yacht. Noah Kruz's yacht pulled into its slip next to them shortly after 6:00 P.M., and his crew got to work loading cargo and preparing the boat for departure later that night.

Kennedy took his front-row seat at around the same time and, after a bombastic entrance, Noah Kruz began his ebullient presentation. Normally, Kennedy would have been rapt, hanging on every word, but that night he could barely bring himself to listen, the sound of Kruz's voice sounding hollow and inflated, like a balloon slowly releasing a roomful of hot air. And he was embarrassed by the voices of his fellow "Kruzers" droning around him. They sounded like some kind of cult parroting their leader in a shrill, robotic chorus. Kennedy slipped into an existential coma, feeling every drop of faith and enthusiasm he'd had for Kruz drain out of him. The cacophony that trumpeted the end of the show was the only thing that could slap him back to reality.

"So pick yourself up," Kruz bellowed in conclusion. "Save yourself. That's how you win. And being a winner is the best possible gift you can give to the people around you and the world. Good night!"

Standing ovation. Kruz's four beefy bodyguards fought off the crowd as he shook hands and signed autographs. Kennedy went to another tedious VIP cocktail reception back in the greenroom to wait for his one-on-one. All he wanted to do was get on with it, but he ended up having to talk to a lot of lost and damaged people who couldn't get enough of the cold cuts platter. Kruz worked the room, taking his perfunctory handshake photos and signing autographs, then breezed out.

"Hello, sir." An older man with dyed hair and eyebrows accosted Kennedy. "I'll be escorting you to your session with Mr. Kruz."

They shook hands and the man led Kennedy down the hall to the Life Sculpting Suite, where he would have Noah Kruz all to himself. When they walked in, Kruz was sitting behind a desk, waiting for Kennedy with a mildly condescending smirk on his face.

"So why do you want to save the world?" Kruz asked.

"Beg your pardon?" Kennedy said.

"It's in your personal profile," Kruz reminded him in an accusing tone.

"Right. Sorry."

Kennedy had put that in his profile years back when he wasn't completely jaded about making a difference in his work. He took the seat he was offered on the other side of Kruz's desk.

"Let's try this again," Kruz said. "Why do you want to save the world?"

Kennedy tried to think of a bullshit response but opted for the naked truth.

"Because I care about people."

Kruz pressed a button on a small electronic device on the desk. Kennedy heard an audio playback of himself saying, "Because I care about people."

"Did you hear that?"

"Yes," Kennedy said, confused.

"I don't think so," Kruz said, and played it back again.

"Because I care about people."

"The *way* you said it? How did it sound?"

"Um—"

Kruz held up his hand, stopping the "um" from going anywhere. He played the recording of Kennedy's voice again.

"It sounds like I'm full of shit," Kennedy said.

"Exactly!"

Kruz slammed his hand down on his desk so hard he knocked half of his books onto the floor. He stood up and paced around the room, cracking his knuckles. Then he got behind Kennedy and dramatically half whispered in his ear.

"How old are you?" Kruz asked.

"Thirty-three."

Kruz made a "tsk" sound.

"I would have guessed closer to forty. Your body has begun to age early. Do you know why?"

"No. Why?"

"Because you've been telling it over and over, for years, that you don't matter. The world matters. *People* matter. But not you. And you're dying a slow death. It's called chemical senescence—the mass slaughter of cells perpetrated by proteins in your blood. When you have purpose in your life, your cells continue to divide at a rate that keeps you youthful so you can carry out youthful tasks, like procreating. When was the last time you had sex?"

Kennedy looked self-consciously at Kruz's handlers.

"Months," Kennedy said.

"What, six, eight, twelve?"

"I've lost count."

A handler gave Kennedy a signed book and T-shirt, the signal that his time with the guru was almost up.

"What do you have left then?" Kruz asked.

Kennedy said nothing.

"Exactly. Nothing. Stand up."

Kennedy stood. Kruz stood in front of him, face-to-face.

"Do you want to die?"

"No."

"Louder!"

"No!"

"I believe you!" Kruz smiled proudly. "So what are you going to do about it?"

"Trust my gut," Kennedy said and put his gun in Noah Kruz's face.

54

W hat the fuck is—?" **Kruz** started to say as Kennedy fired a dart into his chest.

His security detail went for their weapons, but Mitchell and his mercs, who had already been hiding in the room, quickly took them and the rest of Kruz's handlers down with more darts. They zip-tied the wrists and ankles of his staff, duct-taped their mouths, and put Kruz into a huge commercial laundry hamper on wheels, covering him with towels and table linens. Kennedy, Mitchell, and the mercs wheeled the hamper quickly through the backstage area and back out the door they'd all come in. Love was waiting in a laundry service van the mercs had brought. They loaded the hamper into the back and took off.

———

One hour before Noah Kruz was lecturing Kennedy in the VIP room, Nuri and the mercs back at the marina had taken out Kruz's crew with tranq darts and put them belowdecks on the rental yacht. While they waited for Kennedy, Love, and Mitchell to arrive with Kruz, they prepped his yacht. Nuri modified the communications systems so it would emit false GPS data showing the boat was on its way to Nassau for Kruz's next event. This would keep the Coast Guard happy. It would also make it impossible for

Lentz to track the yacht, which he would undoubtedly be committing all his resources to do, once he realized Kruz was missing.

When Kennedy, Mitchell, and Love arrived, they moved Kruz from the laundry hamper to a berth belowdecks and were under way in a matter of minutes. Mitchell switched on a police scanner and listened for chatter. Nothing yet. Their heading was straight east toward Bimini. Mitchell wanted to avoid the southerly boat traffic to the Bahamas and the Keys and get into dark water before they got to work on Kruz.

"What if he isn't working with Lentz?" Kennedy asked.

"Then we just rolled snake eyes," Mitchell said.

"Bogus GPS signal is working great," Nuri said. "Coast Guard thinks we're on a hundred-and-eighty-degree magnetic course heading due south for Nassau, with a point-four-three-degree easterly correction for current. Engines trimmed at twenty-five knots, arrival time estimated at six-point-three-seven hours."

"Roger that," Mitchell said. "Another ten miles or so on this heading and we can have a come-to-Jesus with the guru."

———

Two hours later, when it was dark, Noah Kruz was tied to a fishing chair on the bow. The back of the chair was tethered to a cable from the boat's hydraulic deck crane. Next to the chair sat plastic buckets full of stinking chum. The deck lights were off, and Kruz was lit with military infrared floodlights. As Kennedy watched Mitchell interrogating Kruz—panicked, as Kennedy had been back in the meat locker at the Hôtel de Crillon—he was terrified they might be wrong.

"I told you, I don't know what the fuck you're talking about," Kruz said to Mitchell. "I'm a fucking motivational speaker, for chrissakes! Why would I put my career and life in jeopardy to harbor a terrorist?"

"Hoist him up," Mitchell said to the mercs.

They started up the crane, which reeled in the cable and lifted the fishing chair off the deck. The crane boom swung laterally and telescoped out so the fishing chair was hovering above open water.

"What the hell are you doing?"

"Going fishing," Mitchell said.

Mitchell dumped a chum bucket into the water below Kruz. Within seconds, it was boiling with a twisting mass of tiger, bull, and hammerhead sharks. He lowered the chair a foot. Kruz screamed.

"I'm not a professional interrogator, so you'll have to forgive my crass methods. The thing is, I don't really have the time to try to gain your trust, play good cop/bad cop, knock your pride and ego down, or whatever else is in the handbook. So, I'll just go with the naked truth. No one knows you're out here. You're going to talk to me or you're going to die," Mitchell said.

He lowered the chair another foot. Splashes from the feeding frenzy soaked the bottom of Kruz's khakis with seawater and fish blood. He screamed again.

"Screaming isn't talking," Mitchell said.

He lowered the chair another six inches.

"Stop! Stop! I said I don't know shit!"

"I know what you said," Mitchell said calmly. "But let's see if you say something different when they get hold of your feet. Oh, and so you don't bleed to death, the boys have a blowtorch to cauterize your wounds. It will be the most agonizing pain you've ever experienced, but I'm pretty sure we can keep you alive all the way up to your balls if we do this right."

"Please. This is insane," Kruz said, hanging his head in exhaustion.

Kennedy couldn't take it anymore. He was sick and tired of playing a guessing game with so many lives at stake. He remembered how Alia had been when she fired him. She didn't have time to fuck around with his feelings, and neither did they now with Kruz.

"Not as insane as trying to play tough guy and keep your mouth shut," Kennedy said as he doused Kruz with a full chum bucket.

Blood and grisly hunks of rotting fish covered him from head to toe. He vomited from the smell, dry-retching when there was nothing left to puke.

"Looks like bad cop just showed up," Mitchell said.

"Send it down," Kennedy said with authority.

"Yes, sir," Mitchell said, nodding to the mercs.

They lowered the chair to the edge of the waves. Sharks were gulping pieces of fish inches from Kruz's feet. He was whimpering something.

"What's that?" Kennedy asked.

"I just can't believe this is happening."

"Put him in the fucking water," Kennedy snarled.

"No!" Kruz yelled.

"Take it easy," Love said.

Kennedy moved the merc out of the way and grabbed the crane control. Mitchell eyeballed him tensely. Kennedy had no intention of killing their only link to Lentz, but at that moment, no one on that boat knew it. He had seen Israelis interrogate suspects, and it was all about commitment. The suspect needed to feel important, but ultimately expendable.

"I'm going to give you one last chance to tell us what we want to know, or I'm going to let the sharks take your legs and watch you bleed out."

Kennedy lowered the chair. Kruz's feet were in the water. His eyes nearly popped out of his head. A bull shark tore his shoe off, gashing his foot. Kruz screamed bloody murder. Love joined him.

"I work for Lentz! Let me up! Now!"

Kennedy raised the chair just as three sharks breached, snapping at Kruz's feet and barely missing them.

"Prove it or you're going all the way in!" Kennedy yelled.

"I'm his travel cover! He chose me because I'm not like other celebrities. I have a clean record with the FBI and DEA and my fans at TSA and Homeland gave me special status. They hired me to speak at their fucking holiday party!"

"What's he got on you?" Kennedy asked.

Kruz tried to answer him but just started sobbing, his whole body shaking.

"Bring him up," Love said to Kennedy.

55

Noah Kruz sat in a deck chair with a blanket wrapped around his shoulders. One of the mercs was dressing the wound on his foot. Once they pulled him up, he'd been more than happy to spill his guts about how Lentz coerced him into service.

"He knew things about me . . . things I was certain I had buried. And he threatened to expose them. He kept saying he was going to show people I wasn't the man I said I was. Unless I helped him. At that point, I had a shelf full of best sellers and more money than I knew what to do with. I didn't want to fuck that up."

"What was he blackmailing you with?" Love asked.

"It doesn't matter," Kennedy said. "We need to know his plans."

"He never told me what he's doing," Kruz said with conviction.

"Don't fuck with us," Mitchell said. "We can strap your ass back on that chair."

"I'm not fucking with you! Why would he risk it? He had me by the balls!"

"I've heard enough." Mitchell pulled his gun.

"Wait. Listen." Kruz was stuttering with fear. "Just because he didn't tell me anything doesn't mean I can't help you. I've been keeping notes about *everything*—where we've been, who works with him—"

"He's grasping at straws," Mitchell said. "Fucking guy played us to get him out of the water. Now we're getting the half-truth two-step."

"Noah, Lentz is planning a massive, coordinated terror attack in cities all over the country," Kennedy said, "and you've been helping him."

"What? Jesus . . ."

Kruz covered his face with his hands and started to cry again, but Kennedy slapped them away.

"We need to find him right now," Kennedy continued. "Where is he?"

A low thumping sound was heard off in the distance.

"Chopper," Mitchell whispered. "Stealth. Low acoustic signature."

"He's here," Kruz said, shaking. "He found us. He can't know I'm with you. He'll think I opened my mouth. I'm better off dead. Let me jump—"

"We can protect you," Mitchell said. "Get him down belowdecks," he said to Kennedy and Love. "Lock and load," he said to his mercs.

He barely finished speaking when a UH-60 Black Hawk helicopter appeared directly overhead without warning.

"Move now!" Mitchell yelled.

He and the mercs scrambled for their weapons. Kennedy and Love cut Kruz loose and Love took him down belowdecks. Kennedy was looking for Nuri when gunfire from the chopper rained down on the yacht. He took cover and saw her hiding under a lifeboat.

He pointed to the companionway door. She nodded and they both started crawling for it. An M84 stun grenade fell from the chopper and detonated twenty feet from them, rendering them both temporarily blind and deaf. When Kennedy was able to focus again, Nuri was gone. Black speed ropes slithered down from the chopper and commandos fell out of the sky, blasting the hell out of Mitchell and his men. They were quickly overwhelmed and Mitchell was wounded in the neck. Kennedy hauled him to his feet and helped him down the galley stairs. His wound was gushing blood and they were both soaked with it when they got to the stateroom where Love had taken Kruz. Mitchell was pale and shivering.

"Oh my God!" Love said when she saw them. "Where's Nuri?"

"I think she went over the side when the grenade exploded," Kennedy yelled, barely able to hear himself. "Get the first aid kit!"

Love grabbed it and went to work on Mitchell. She tore open two clotting sponges and jammed them into the wound.

"Can you breathe okay?" Kennedy asked him.

"Yeah," he said weakly.

Kennedy and Love covered him with a space blanket and wrapped his neck in gauze. The bleeding had slowed, but he was still shivering and fighting to stay conscious.

"He's not going to make it," Kruz said behind them.

"Bullshit, he's just in shock," Kennedy said. "Hold on, Mitchell."

"I said, he's not going to make it."

Kennedy turned and yelled, "Shut the fuck up!"

Kruz was holding Kennedy's gun. He shot Mitchell in the head.

56

Kennedy and Love stared in disbelief at Mitchell's dead body.

"Remove his sidearm and slide it on the floor to me."

Love slid Mitchell's Beretta across the tiles. Kruz expertly shucked the mag and jacked the round out of the chamber. His whole demeanor was different, cool and professional. At that moment, it became crystal clear to Kennedy why Lentz had always been so difficult to track.

It was because he'd been hiding in plain sight.

"You're Lentz," Kennedy said.

Love looked at him, incredulous.

"I prefer my new persona," Kruz said. "The old me was so clichéd, like some Eurotrash James Bond villain. It worked in the 1990s but I would rather walk a mile in Noah Kruz's shoes any day. And *he* doesn't have a target on his back." He laughed.

Kennedy did the math. Noah Kruz's first book, *(R)evolution*, was published in October of 2000, the year the CIA said Lentz went dark and dropped off the intelligence grid. Belle had given it to him as a Christmas gift. She knew Kennedy was having a hard time breaking away from the influence of their father and heard the book was changing peoples' lives. It had changed his.

"All of this was—" Kennedy started.

"A very expensive roach motel," Kruz said.

He motioned to the stairs.

"After you," he said.

Kennedy and Love walked up the stairs with Kruz's gun at their backs. On deck, Kruz's commandos were chucking the bullet-riddled bodies of Mitchell's men over the side. One of them walked over and took off his helmet.

It was Juarez.

"Hi, guys."

"Fuck. No." Love was stunned.

"I guess you're not dead," Kennedy said.

"Guess not. Although, I don't recommend skydiving at twenty thousand feet over Siberia."

"You think you're going to ride off into the sunset with this asshole?" Kennedy asked.

"Translation," Kruz said. "There's still time for you to do the right thing, Juarez."

"There is," Kennedy said.

"I've already done it," Juarez said.

"How does betraying your country and killing millions fall into that category?"

"We're just taking advantage of a business opportunity before the competition gets too steep," Kruz said. "Striking while the iron is hot, as they say."

"A business opportunity?" Love asked.

"They believe if they destabilize the US, they can sell off its resources in a global fire sale and make trillions. Another James Bond cliché," Kennedy said.

"It's no longer a belief. It's reality," Kruz said. "Many nations actually sponsored this operation, not officially of course. Some of them are even what the US State Department would call allies. And yes, their reward is a piece of the good old USA."

"There's going to be nothing left when you're finished with it," Kennedy snapped. "Then the vultures will come in and fight for the scraps, just like in Iraq."

"It's better than the alternative," Kruz said. "The US is nothing but an oligarchy, like Russia, run by wealthy brutes who want to consume everything of value in the world. Now the world will have its chance to share what Americans take for granted and put a stop to the imperialist machine run by the Bushes or the Clintons or whatever hillbilly psychopath makes it into the Oval Office next. Walmart culture is about to learn a serious lesson about the global village."

"Maybe you should explain it to them with one of your pedantic, bullshit lectures," Kennedy said bitterly.

"The ones you paid over twenty-eight thousand dollars to see?"

Kennedy looked at Love, embarrassed.

"Don't be ashamed that you were one of my biggest fans, Kennedy. I spent millions building my self-help persona, and I'm quite good at it. Case in point. You've used everything you learned from me to get where you are today. Without my books and lectures on conquering your fears, being decisive, taking risks, and knowing your true calling, you never would have found *your* true calling, which is this."

"My true calling? Everything I've *learned from you* has brought me to this moment of catastrophic failure," Kennedy said.

"That all depends on your perspective," Kruz said. "In trying to stop me, you have failed. However, without your help, there's no way I could have accomplished my objectives. So, in that way, I share this success with you."

"I never helped you," Kennedy growled.

"Actually, you were a big help. You and your friends. Running around to all those airports. So resourceful. And the way you handled TSA and DHS. Like I said, I couldn't have done this without you. Your knowledge and expertise—"

"I don't know what you're talking about!" Kennedy yelled.

Juarez laughed and shook his head.

"The millimeter wave scanner upgrades ring a bell?" Juarez said. "You installed a ten-kiloton nuclear bomb in twenty-five of the biggest airports in the US."

Kennedy could barely breathe. A wave of panic surged through his body like an electric shock.

"Kennedy," Kruz said.

His voice brought Kennedy back from the brink. Kruz was looking at him, almost prideful.

"You're *my* asset. All of this—Juarez bringing new intel about my sinister plans to the CIA, Red Carpet being formed, Alia recruiting you—was *my* operation. And you, with your considerable talents and intelligence, executed it flawlessly."

Kennedy was glad he was going to die. He was going to be responsible for the deaths of millions he swore to protect, and disgrace the memory of his dead sister. It was more than he could bear.

"When?" he heard Love say a million miles away.

"The day before Thanksgiving," Kruz said. "Biggest travel day of the year, right, Kennedy?"

He put his hand on Kennedy's shoulder.

"When does the biggest surge of passenger traffic happen on that day?" Kruz asked.

"Nine A.M. Eastern," Kennedy said listlessly.

"People want to get where they're going as soon as possible," Kruz said. "To really maximize that trough and leisure time. So the morning flights are the busiest."

"You have to stop this," Kennedy said to Juarez.

"Brother, this is my baby as much as it is his," he said.

"And he couldn't stop it, even if he wanted to," Kruz said. "It's out of our control—a stipulation of my partners. They weren't willing to place all of their trust on the shoulders of one man. Incidentally, that's why we used the millimeter wave scanners. As you may know, millimeter waves are excellent for communication. The air force uses them for missile guidance and the like. So, when the time comes, the detonators will be activated by a preprogrammed satellite signal, which will use the scanners as a receiving antenna. You remember that part of the threat memo, which was drafted by me, where it talks about *a large-scale, coordinated attack*? That means the satellite will detonate all of the bombs simultaneously, like a well-timed fireworks show, giving the federal government exactly zero response time. And nothing, not even Juarez shooting me in the head, can stop it."

"Fucking coward," Kennedy said to Juarez.

"I think it's time to say good-bye to our friends, Noah," Juarez said, ignoring Kennedy.

"A turncoat is the worst kind of traitor," Kennedy said to Kruz. "An enemy to both sides. They can't be trusted."

"You're right," Kruz said and shot Juarez in the head.

Love screamed and buried her face in Kennedy's shoulder.

"Thank you for pointing that out," Kruz said courteously. "But he was right. It is time to say good-bye."

57

Kennedy lunged at Kruz, grabbing his gun arm and wrestling him to the ground. He knocked the gun out of Kruz's hand and pointed it at his head. The commandos surrounded them.

"Get back or he's dead!"

"Let me go or they'll shoot *her*," Kruz said casually.

One of his commandos grabbed Love. She fought him, but he forced her to the ground and held her there with his knee on her chest.

"Instinct is far superior when it comes to decision making and it's very easy to deploy because you feel it without thinking," Kruz said. "What does your instinct tell you? Shoot the bad guy or save a girl who is going to die anyway?"

The helicopter came back around and hovered above them.

"Put the gun in her mouth," Kruz ordered.

"No!" Kennedy yelled, throwing the gun overboard and getting off Kruz.

Kruz stood and looked at his watch.

"Better go," he said. "I left you a consolation prize belowdecks—a beautiful new Louis Vuitton suitcase, because you're such a world traveler. Can you guess what's inside it?"

Kruz laughed. The commandos trained their guns on Kennedy and Love, who clung to each other. The chopper blade was stirring up the seas, making the yacht pitch and roll. The speed ropes dropped down. Kruz and his men grabbed them. One of the commandos was about to blow Kennedy and Love away with his assault rifle when the chopper climbed and the only rope attached to it was Kruz's. His team watched in disbelief as their ropes landed on the boat deck and the chopper flew away. They quickly forgot about Kennedy and Love and ran for the lifeboats, cursing and shoving one another out of the way.

"He put one of the nukes belowdecks," Kennedy said to Love. "We need to get off this boat. Right now."

"How?" Love asked, panicked.

Kennedy looked around and zeroed in on the fishing chair.

"Come on!"

He ripped open the scuba locker on deck, grabbed two masks, a dive tank, and two inflatable dive vests. He picked up one of the guns on deck, and he and Love jumped on the fishing chair and swung it out over the water.

"Put on your mask and vest!"

They threw on both. Kennedy had Love sit on his lap so he could hold on to her and the dive tank. A high-pitched noise started coming from belowdecks.

"That's a pulse detonator!" he yelled. "Hold on tight!"

"What the hell are we doing?" she yelled back.

Kennedy held on tightly to the chair and to Love and fired his gun at the deck crane cable lock. He missed the first three times, but the fourth hit dead center, causing it to release the cable spool. The fishing chair plunged into the black water and sank rapidly. As they descended, they took turns breathing the air from the tank. They reached the hundred-foot limit of the cable and stopped dead in the water. Kennedy pulled Love off the chair and they swam clear of it.

The suitcase nuke on the yacht detonated.

Up on the surface, the ten-kiloton blast wave blew through the boat and commandos at the speed of sound, shredding them into pieces that were instantly vaporized by a ball of fire burning at tens of millions of degrees Fahrenheit. A brilliant, swirling plume of smoke and white-hot ash shot hundreds of feet into the air and formed the shape of a mushroom before it dispersed and cascaded back down into the sea.

The explosion sent shock waves and liquid fire down into the water, but neither were powerful enough to hurt Kennedy and Love at one hundred feet below the surface. The majority of the bomb's energy was forced into the air above versus down into the densely pressurized seawater. Kennedy and Love had both been diving many times and were able to use the slow inflation of their vests to ascend without getting decompression sickness.

By the time they surfaced, there was nothing but black water below and black sky above. That far out, the water temperature was at least ten degrees lower than the balmy Florida coast. They could survive in it for a while but eventually they would succumb to hypothermia, if the sharks didn't get them first. Kennedy activated the GPS distress signal devices on their vests.

"I'm beginning to think the bomb would have been the way to go," Love joked.

"Yeah, I'm with you. Quick and painless, with cremation and burial at sea all in one shot," Kennedy said.

"Versus the slow hypothermia and/or shark mauling we're facing," Love said.

"Wow, you're a real ray of sunshine," Kennedy said. "You forgot to mention the radiation that's probably giving us brain tumors right now."

"Sorry."

Love embraced him tightly.

"May I cry on your shoulder?" she asked, crying on his shoulder.

"Just this once. But don't let it happen again."

They held their embrace for a couple of hours in the water. Their body temps made the cold more bearable, but soon they started to shiver. Kennedy fastened their vests together so they wouldn't separate if they lost consciousness. He knew they were going to die, but there was something about being there with Love that made it easier.

"You know, one good thing that came out of this is now I have someone to spend the rest of my life with," Kennedy said, kissing her.

"You're lucky it's so short that you won't have to deal with all of my annoying idiosyncrasies," she said, trying to smile.

"Like what?"

"I snore."

"Yeah, I've already experienced that," he joked.

"Stop it, I don't snore," she said. "But I do drink milk out of the carton."

"That's okay," he said. "I drink right out of the whiskey bottle."

"Well, that's legal of course," she said.

She was getting sleepy, so he shook her a bit and kissed her awake.

"I'm going to say something and it's going to sound awkward," he said.

"Shoot."

"I love you, Love."

"You're right. Awkward. I love you too, you big lug."

"Thanks for helping me pull my head out of my ass," he said.

"My pleasure."

"Someone like you could get me to do just about anything, I think."

"Oh, I'm going to have to take you up on that," she said.

She was getting drowsy again. So was he. He forced himself to keep talking.

"You know? I could use a drink. How about you?" he said.

"What'll you have?"

"Whiskey. Neat. No, 151 rum. On fire."

"Sounds delicious. Grappa for me. Served next to a roaring fire."

Love was shivering uncontrollably. Kennedy tried to hug her tighter, but he was shivering as well, and his arms felt weak and leaden. He fell asleep and woke up with a start. Love was passed out. His hands and feet were numb, and he could feel his mind slipping, draining out of him and being swallowed up in the black seawater.

He tried to shake Love awake again, but he was fading fast.

"Wake up," he whispered. "Don't want to go alone . . ."

His vision blurred. He shook his head, trying to stay awake, but a warm blackness filled his eyes and spread over his body, until he drifted off into nothingness.

58

Kennedy opened his eyes and he was back on the plane with Belle.

"You drifted off," she said.

"Yeah, sorry. What were you saying?"

"I was saying I'm proud of you."

"Bullshit," he said sarcastically. "What were you really saying?"

"It's not bullshit. You're a pretty all right brother."

"I'm proud of you too," he said, tearing up in spite of himself.

"God, you're such a crybaby." She laughed.

"I know. I'm weak, like Dad says."

"Weak, my ass."

"Hey, you're not supposed to talk like that."

"I'm on a plane. International waters. Rules don't apply. In fact, I think I'll order a drink."

"No you won't," he said. "But I might."

Belle pushed the flight attendant call button.

"Jesus, Belle."

"Told you I'm getting a cocktail."

"Cut it out. They're not going to serve you."

"They might serve *you*," she said hopefully.

Kennedy switched off the call button. Belle switched it on. Kennedy switched it off. Belle tried to switch it on and Kennedy grabbed her hand. She pulled her hand free, lunged over him, and hit the call button again. The flight attendant walked up with an annoyed sigh. They couldn't see her face, as she was backlit by the dim cabin light behind her. Kennedy stopped horsing around with Belle, instantly self-conscious about being so juvenile.

"Can I help you?" she asked.

"No, that's okay," Kennedy said, "my sister accidentally—"

"I want a drink." Belle laughed.

"No she doesn't," Kennedy said.

"Will there be anything else?" the flight attendant asked.

"No, thank you," Kennedy said.

The flight attendant leaned over him and switched off the call button. Her face was briefly illuminated. It was Love.

"Good," she said. "Because you need to wake up."

Kennedy was blinded by a bright flash of light and found himself looking into a flashlight beam a doctor was shining in his eyes. Love was standing next to him. She was pale, with dark circles under her eyes and a bandage on her forehead.

"You need to wake up . . . Ah, there he is," she said and kissed him.

59

Hey, chief. Guess you got in a little deep, eh?"

Wes Bowman stood over Kennedy, raising an eyebrow. Kennedy and Love were in a US Coast Guard base hospital in Dania Beach, Florida. They had been there for two days.

"Wes?"

"What, you were expecting the girl of your dreams? Oh wait, she's here too."

Love walked up next to Wes and smiled.

"Don't look so surprised to see me," Wes said. "You think after grilling me about this little church picnic I would just take a pass and let the vultures pick you clean?"

"I thought . . . you said you worked in IT?"

"We're all a bunch of fucking liars. That's our job. I'm actually a UK station chief. Dirty-work specialist."

"What the hell are you doing here?"

"I'm not here. I was never here. I'm on vacation in Mykonos."

"He saved our butts," Love said.

"I put a tail on you after you were in Paris. Did you ever get the feeling you were being followed? You were. By me. Tracked you to Miami. Bada-bing. Bada-boom. And that was one helluva boom. Pulled you out of the drink and here we are."

"Then you know about Kruz?"

"Yup," Wes said.

"We have to get moving. We have to stop him."

Kennedy got up and fell right to the floor. He dragged himself up under his own power but was shaky on his feet. Love held his arm.

"Take it easy," she said.

"We're going to try to stop him. Even though this is way outside my jurisdiction, and when they find out I did this they're going to crucify me—unless we can bag Kruz, in which case I'll get a medal."

"He found Nuri," Love said.

"Really? Is she okay?"

"She's in pretty bad shape," Wes said. "She had managed to get one of the lifeboats into the water during the melee on deck. Put a couple of miles between her and the bomb. Lucky for her, it blasted her with seawater, so she wasn't burned to a crisp. The lifeboat was trashed and she floated in her vest longer than you guys. When we found her, she was hypothermic, in shock, and barely breathing. Docs put her in a coma to try to stabilize her but—"

"What are her chances?" Kennedy asked.

"Not sure. I'm amazed she's lived this long."

"Which is why we have to find this motherfucker and stomp his fucking guts out," Love said through tears.

"How can you help us, Wes?"

"I have an American Express black card and a massive set of cojones. So, you tell me what needs to be done and I'll do what I do best—lie, cheat, steal, spend taxpayers' money indiscriminately, and stomp motherfuckers' guts out."

Kennedy downloaded Wes on everything: suitcase nukes installed in millimeter wave scanners at twenty-five airports. Devices set to detonate simultaneously on the day before Thanksgiving at 9:00 A.M. Eastern. Attack would be initiated by a preprogrammed satellite signal that couldn't be deactivated, not even by Kruz. The only thing they could do to stop it was to remove every single device. It had taken nearly three weeks to install them and they had seven days to yank them all out.

"Jesus, this is dicey as hell," Wes said. "Extraction is going to be a bitch, but then we have to contain the little fuckers somehow. We're talking nukes here, so we can't just toss them in the recycle bin. How am I going to scramble a containment unit in twenty-five cities by . . . now?"

"There's no time for that, Wes. They'll have to travel with us."

"You want to fly around the country in a pressurized cabin with a small arsenal of nuclear weapons? That has to be a *don't* in the TSA manual."

"They'll keep us warm at night," Kennedy said.

"Fine," Wes said. "Why not? The alternative is imminent death, so what's a few kilotons of white-hot destruction between friends? Speaking of friends, what kind of tech assistance do we need to pop these babies out?"

"I've got to do it myself," Kennedy said. "I'm the only one left who knows where to find them and what they look like."

"I'll hold the flashlight," Love said firmly.

"You can't take them out yourself and you know it," Wes said. "TSA knows you're not a qualified tech, and pulling something like that is definitely going to derail us. I'll get you an engineer with weapons experience. You can supervise."

"Fine. The bigger problem is that I'm a pariah at some of these airports by now, and Tad Monty is bound to have spread the word to the others," Kennedy added.

"Yeah, I kind of figured that, so I have a solution," Wes said. "After your tussle at JFK, Monty put in a request to the Science and Technology directorate at Homeland, asking them to pull your upgrades for further testing. The request is under review, but I can make a few calls and have them grant his wish within twenty-four hours. Paperwork would go into effect immediately, especially if the device removal is due to hazard or performance impedance."

"That's genius, but we still have to be the ones retrieving the equipment. We don't want some rookie TSO trying to handle it."

"Agreed. Since the upgrades were initiated by you through the phony grant Alia set up, Science and Tech will actually *expect* you to supervise removal."

"Is there anything you haven't figured out?" Love said to Wes.

"Yeah. Logistics are a bitch, and pretty much the only way we'll have a chance to hit all the airports in time is with a very expensive private jet and some morally flexible pilots with little regard for safety. That way we can move quickly, using private terminals at the main airports, maybe municipal airports, whatever keeps the wheels on the wagon."

"How long do you think we have until Kruz realizes we're back from the dead, cockblocking his mini Armageddon?" Love asked.

"We definitely have a head start, but he has eyes everywhere so we have to assume our advantage will be short-lived," Kennedy said.

"Agreed. And remember we have zero support from Langley. In fact, they would bag us if they knew what we were up to. The whole thing has to be stealth and low profile. Congratulations, you just graduated from asset to black ops."

"When can we start?" Love asked.

"We have roughly twenty-four hours to prep," Wes said. "Get whatever tools and supplies you need and I'll have the jet pick us up at one of the Richie Rich airports outside Fort Lauderdale. Start thinking about flight logistics. We may want to prioritize airports in the highest collateral damage zones or those close to government targets."

"I'm on it," Kennedy said.

60

Day 57

The plan with TSA Science and Tech worked, and Kennedy was cleared to remove all of the upgrades. Wes got them a former army combat engineer to travel with them to do the work and make sure the nukes didn't accidentally detonate. Once they had all the bombs in their hot little hands, they would turn them over to DoD for containment and their hero status might keep them out of prison for breaking a phone book of federal laws. Kennedy worked logistics with two pilots who looked like they'd been dragged out of a bar in Tijuana after a five-day bender. He charted a course for them to hit the West Coast and Southwest first, then move through the middle of the country and finish in the East behind a nasty weather system coming down from Canada.

"Monty is tracking the Science and Tech thing," Wes said to Kennedy and Love on the day they took off. "He's been probing the Department of Justice to bring charges against you."

"For what?" Kennedy asked, incredulous.

"It doesn't matter. He's blowing smoke. The problem is, he's high up in the food chain at DHS, so they can't ignore him."

"What can we do about it now?" Love asked.

"Nada," Wes said. "I'm just keeping you in the loop. While you're on the road, I'll keep my eye on him and let you know if you're about to step in it. If Justice starts paying attention to him, we might have a problem. Have a nice trip."

———

The pilots turned out to be top-notch, and once they got cleaned up, they were excellent at snowing airport staff into thinking they were a couple of buttoned-up good old boys from Texas. Flight manifests said they were hauling a rock star, Love, on tour. When people saw her, they had no problem believing it. The key with the private jet was speed. They could hit three to four, sometimes five, airports in a twenty-four-hour stretch without breaking a sweat. It was easy to see why the wealthy chose private. Without all the airport-delay bullshit, it was almost like driving.

On top of that, TSA paperwork Wes conjured for them made their work a breeze. TSA chiefs actually avoided Kennedy when he arrived to pull the upgrades. They were either afraid of associating with him because of Tad Monty or they were embarrassed for him and didn't want to deal with the awkwardness of Kennedy being clipped by the biggest asshole at DHS. Even the weather was cooperating, making their first four days of travel all over the West Coast, Pacific Northwest, Southwest, and Midwest smooth sailing.

But Love had been right when she said it all seemed too good to be true. By the time they got to Detroit, Tad Monty was waiting.

"You got about five minutes to get the fuck out of this airport or I'm calling the police and having you removed."

"You can't do that," Kennedy said, standing toe-to-toe with him.

Monty backed off slightly at Kennedy's bravado. Even Love raised an eyebrow.

"Bullshit, I can't. Watch me."

Kennedy waited and didn't move. He kept his eyes on Monty the whole time.

"I have an order from TSA Science and Tech to remove these upgrades. Based on your request. If you attempt to impede me in any way, I can have *you* arrested."

Love walked up.

"Everything all right?" she asked.

"Who the fuck is this bitch?" Monty snarled.

"Can I talk to you in private, Tad?" Kennedy asked.

"Let's go."

Love was giving him a *What the fuck* look as they walked away. The engineer was closing the panel on the scanner machine.

"Finished here," he said. "Where's he going?"

"TSA paperwork," Love said. "Shouldn't be long."

As Kennedy and Tad walked toward the office, Kennedy stopped and used the keypad to one of the employee locker rooms the airport manager had allowed him to use from time to time to sleep or shower.

"Hey, where do you think you're going?" Monty said.

As Kennedy slipped inside the locker room, which was one of the few places in the airport without security cameras, he looked around to make sure the place was empty. When Monty knocked, Kennedy let him in.

"You want to tell me how you got access to this—"

Kennedy locked the bolt on the door and punched him square in the face. Monty fell back hard against the wall, dazed, and felt the blood running out of his nose. He took a swing at Kennedy, but missed, and Kennedy kicked him in the nuts. Monty doubled over, dry-heaving and cursing under his breath. He stood up straight again and looked at Kennedy, furious.

"I'm going to fucking kill you—"

He took another swing and Kennedy hit him with a right cross to the jaw, knocking him to the floor. Monty struggled to get up but Kennedy put a foot on his chest and pushed him back down.

"Down, boy. You don't want to fuck with me right now," Kennedy warned.

"Have you lost your mind?" Monty asked, fear flashing in his beady eyes.

"Maybe. You see, Tad, you've ended my career. And remember what happened when you ended Glenn's career?"

"Are you threatening me?"

"Yes. And if you show up at any more airports where I'm trying to do what's left of my job, I'll kill you. No one ever saw this little exchange between us. It's not on any of our security cameras. And no one is going to believe someone like me did this to someone like you. At least for long enough for me to come to your house in Long Island—with the beautiful pond and boathouse—yes, I know where you live—and cut your throat in your sleep. I trained with the Israelis, motherfucker. And believe me, they taught me a lot more than how to pick a scumbag out of a crowd. So, you have to ask yourself if it's worth it. I'm already out. You did your job."

He pressed on Monty's chest with his foot, causing Monty to cough and wheeze.

"But if you push me, I've got nothing else to lose. No house. No family. No kids. All the things *you* have . . ."

Kennedy took his foot off Monty's chest and walked to the door. Tad was just lying there, buying all the bullshit Kennedy had just shoveled into his face. He was genuinely afraid for his life, which almost made Kennedy laugh out loud.

"I'm glad we finally understand each other."

61

Wes Bowman was pleased with the progress of Kennedy and company. Tad Monty seemed to drop off the radar screen in Detroit, which he was hoping would clear the way for them to finish the East Coast without incident. Wes had been sending spotters to some of the airports as a security measure. Both he and Kennedy knew that, no matter how much wool they pulled over the TSA's eyes, sooner or later Kruz was going to get wise to their actions and move to stop them. The spotters were there to pick up tails and dispose of them. The first signs of Kennedy and Co. being followed came in Detroit. Spotters didn't bag anyone, but they had seen four men covering them in rotations.

When the team was at LaGuardia, Wes flew in. Kennedy and Love were with the engineer, working on the scanner, and the spotters clocked the same men they'd seen in Detroit. Wes called Kennedy and told him to bring Love and the engineer and meet him outside on the Departures curb when they were finished.

"What's up? What are you doing here?" Kennedy asked.

"Just finish up and get out here."

They walked outside and found Wes having a cigarette in the smoking area.

"You finish?" he asked.

The engineer patted the Pelican case that contained the nuke.

"All right, listen up," Wes said. "Kruz's people are here, so follow me and do exactly as I say. Understood?"

They nodded and he led them into the parking garage, where he stripped the door lock on a BMW sedan and they got inside. Wes made Kennedy get behind the wheel, with Love in the passenger seat and him and the engineer in back.

"Valet key," Wes said.

Love opened the glove compartment and handed the valet key to Kennedy.

"Where are they?" Love whispered.

Three men with guns walked into the garage and spread out. Wes pointed them out and pulled his gun. The engineer pulled his as well.

"Start the car," Wes said.

Kennedy started it. As soon as he did, one of the men stepped out in front of the car fifty feet away and pointed his gun at them.

"Punch it!" Wes said. "Love, get down!"

Kennedy hit the accelerator and sped right at the man as he fired three rounds into the windshield. One of them hit the engineer in the head, killing him. Wes secured the bomb case on the floor and hung out the window, firing back at the man. He shot him in the shoulder and spun him around before Kennedy hit him at full speed with the car and threw him like a rag doll through the windshield of another car.

Kennedy raced through the garage and got on the exit ramp. One of the men fired at them from behind, blowing a hole in the back window. The bullet ripped through Kennedy's headrest and narrowly missed him as it lodged in the dash. Wes shot back and hit the man in the chest and forehead.

They rounded the corner and were spiraling down the exit ramp when another man jumped from the ledge on the next floor up, and onto the roof of the car. He smashed Love's side window and tried to get his gun into the car to shoot, but Kennedy swerved hard and the man lost his grip. Trying to catch himself, he dropped his gun into Love's window. She picked it up and fired it through the roof, blowing him off the top of the car. Kennedy saw him in the rearview as he smashed into a concrete pillar and rolled down the exit ramp.

Kennedy floored it out of the parking garage and drove them to the cargo terminal where the pilots were waiting with the plane. He stopped the car and everyone tried to catch their breath. Love was freaking out. She couldn't stomach the sight of the dead engineer, so she got out and jogged back to the plane.

"I'll take care of this," Wes said, covering the body with his coat.

"Can you get me someone else?" Kennedy asked.

"Not enough time. You have two days to knock out the last two airports. Think you can do it yourself?"

"I have to. Whatever it takes."

62

After LaGuardia, there were two airports left to disarm—Charlotte and Atlanta.

Because of the heat Kruz had on them, the pilots changed destination headings and altered their course several times on their way to Charlotte, not committing to an airfield until an hour before landing. They chose the Gastonia Municipal Airport twenty miles from Charlotte Douglas, and took a taxi in. Love was looking worse for the wear. Killing Kruz's thug at LaGuardia was clearly weighing heavily on her, but she didn't want to talk about it. Kennedy tried to convince her to sit Charlotte out and get some rest until he got back, but she refused to leave his side.

When they got to the airport, Kennedy went right to the scanner and pulled the bomb. He didn't want to take any chances, so he put Love in a cab, and she took the device back to the plane. While he was closing up the scanner panel, Dot, Charlotte's TSA chief, walked up. She was in her sixties and looked like a Norman Rockwell grandmother, with roller-sculpted hair and a wise face. She smiled at Kennedy and touched his hand in a neighborly way. She was a friend, but he could tell she was miffed.

"You're a good man to come visit me like this," Dot said. "But I sure would have appreciated a call first."

"Sorry, Dot. Trying to get all these done before the holiday."

"Yeah, I heard about that. Seemed like a good fix to me. But, I guess you win some, you lose some."

"Don't I know it," Kennedy said, anxious to get the hell out of there.

Her mobile phone rang.

"Excuse me a minute," she said and picked up. "This is Dot."

While she had her phone call, Kennedy called Love to check on her. She didn't answer. Dot finished her call and walked back over.

"Buy you a cup of coffee? You look like you could use it," she said.

Kennedy looked at his watch.

"Actually, Dot, I don't know if I have time. Got another plane to catch."

"Okay, I'll walk you to your gate," she said.

They walked down the concourse, but Dot turned and started walking in the opposite direction of the gates.

"I hate to have to break it to you, Dot, but we're going the wrong way."

"Come on, I want to show you something. You're going to love this. It won't take but a minute."

"All right. I guess I can spare at least one minute," Kennedy said, feeling the pressure to get out of there mounting.

She punched in her keypad code and opened a door that led to an elevated platform overlooking the apron and airplane ramps. The engine noise was deafening. Dot moved closer to him and smiled. Kennedy felt uncomfortable.

"Tell you a secret?" she asked.

"Uh, sure?"

She leaned in and whispered, "FBI just called me back in the office. Airport is surrounded with federal agents. They're looking for you."

"What—" Kennedy started.

"Just shut up and listen," Dot said, still congenially. "There's only one way out of here. Catawba River's about a mile past the airport fence. Can you swim?"

"Dot, what the hell—"

"I said, can you swim?"

"Yes."

"All right. Now, before you go, I need to ask you a question. And the way you answer that question is real important. Understood?"

Kennedy nodded.

"Why are they after you?"

She looked at him long and hard. He knew if he didn't answer truthfully, she would never believe any bullshit. Dot had a lot of talent for the job, and Kennedy had trained her and her people very well. If she didn't like his answer, he'd never even make it down the platform steps. So he told her the truth, and she could see he wasn't lying.

"Is Charlotte Douglas Airport safe?" she asked.

"It is now," he said.

"Good. I thank you for that. Better run along now. And good luck."

"Thanks," he said and took off down the stairs.

As Kennedy was sprinting across the apron, Love and the pilots were already in FBI custody. When he got near the airport fence, police cars and government SUVs sped after him at about ninety miles per hour and closing fast. By the time he got to the fence and started climbing, they were a hundred yards off his tail and he could hear them on their bullhorn shouting for him to stop. The top of the fence had a short coil of barbed wire. Kennedy threw his coat over it and flipped over the top. He tore up his arm and legs on the wire tines and landed hard on the other side.

The police got out of their truck and ran after him, guns drawn, still shouting at him to stop. Kennedy ran into some tall bushes for cover and kept running, his lungs burning. The cops opened fire. Bullets zipped through the underbrush and exploded in the dirt around his feet. He zigzagged through the dense growth, branches clawing at his arms and legs, shredding his clothes. When he reached the river, he was so exhausted he could barely stand. He looked back and saw the police truck barreling toward him on a dirt road a mile down to his left. More bullets peppered the undergrowth and skipped across the water. He dove headfirst into the river, which was moving swiftly and cold as ice. More bullets exploded across the surface, so he swam deeper and let the current carry him for as long as he could hold his breath. He was about to black out so he surfaced, gasping for air, and found himself in a wooded area dotted with trailer homes, rotting boathouses, and abandoned cars.

The cops were nowhere in sight, but he wasn't going to wait for them. When the current slowed, he struggled to swim ashore. He hauled himself up on the bank and sat against a tree, trying to catch his breath and control the violent shivering. He felt his pockets. His wallet and phone were gone, but he still had a wad of soaking-wet cash, maybe $300. He looked at his watch. It was nearly 5:00 P.M. The next day was the day before Thanksgiving. In sixteen hours, 9:00 A.M. Eastern Time, Kruz's device would detonate at the Atlanta airport, which was 250 miles away. He had no team and no resources. And now he was a fugitive.

63

"Six feet tall. One hundred eighty pounds. Black hair. Blue eyes . . ."

Kennedy heard the newscast blaring from a TV inside a double-wide parked in the trees near the river. He moved closer, craning to see the television. His TSA contractor badge photo filled the screen. The news couldn't have been worse. Love and the pilots were in custody, being treated as enemy combatants by Homeland Security, accused of attempting to bomb the Charlotte airport. Kennedy was being billed as the ringleader, a terrorist taking revenge on the US government because his sister was killed on 9/11.

If it weren't so dire, he would have been impressed by the spin. Like the slick best-selling guru he'd embodied for years, Kruz was in control of the narrative. If Kennedy got caught before Atlanta was vaporized, he would be blamed. He was knowledgeable enough to pull it off and his fingerprints were all over everything. The news version of Love was that she was a political agitator who shared Kennedy's hatred of America, something she had originally learned from her socialist parents.

The motive, knowledge, physical evidence, eyewitness testimony from a respected member of DHS (Tad Monty), and damning video evidence would be irrefutable in a press-driven kangaroo court. The news even cited the threat memo, saying Homeland could now close their investigation after having heroically countered this heinous act of terror. Kennedy checked his watch. He didn't have time to think about any of that anymore. He needed to be on the road to Atlanta within the hour.

He moved through the woods along the river, looking for a drivable vehicle, but most of the cars he saw were either up on blocks or hollowed-out, rusting shells that had been picked over for parts. He saw an aluminum storage garage large enough for an RV or a boat. There was no house attached, so he crept around the perimeter of it and found a garage door on one end with an entry door on the side. The entry door was bolted, but the garage door had not closed all the way, leaving about an eight-inch gap. Kennedy looked through the gap. There was a newish-looking pickup, and a small fishing boat on a trailer.

Kennedy ran back to one of the abandoned sedans he'd seen in the woods and looked in the trunk. He dug through wet garbage and a sizable rat's nest and found a rusty tire jack, which he used to jack up the garage door just high enough to crawl inside. The truck was an F-150 in excellent condition with a nearly full tank of gas. He was looking for the keys when it occurred to him he had no idea how he was going to disarm the scanner at Atlanta Hartsfield once he got there. He was a fugitive, with his photo splashed all over the six o'clock news. TSA would have seen his picture by then, and most of them knew him anyway, along with a lot of airport employees. He was racking his brain when the owner of the garage came storming in with a pistol in his hand.

"Where the fuck are you, asshole!" he yelled at the top of his lungs.

Kennedy lay down on the front seat before the man could see him, and waited. When he walked up to the driver's-side door, Kennedy kicked it open, smashing it in the man's face and knocking the gun out of his hand. The man fell to the floor of the garage and Kennedy jumped out, looking for the gun. It was under the boat and Kennedy was trying to grab it when the man kicked him in the ribs and he fell ass over teakettle into a fishing canoe. The man jumped on him, punching and kicking, but Kennedy shifted his weight and rolled the canoe to one side, pitching them both out. The man, who was extremely overweight, was out of breath and sweating profusely from the heat in the garage. As he struggled to get up off the floor, his hands white-knuckling a boat oar he intended to use as a weapon, Kennedy kicked the oar into his face, knocking him out cold. He searched the man's pockets and found the keys to the truck. He jumped in and was about to drive away, when he saw something on the far wall of the storage garage that gave him an idea about how he could pull off Atlanta.

64

We're all going to die.

It's 8:00 A.M. and this is the one thought screaming over and over in Kennedy's head as he attempts to estimate the seemingly infinite number of holiday travelers standing between him and his destiny: the TSA checkpoint. He forces the fog to lift temporarily from his mind so he can assess the situation. If his observations are even marginally correct, at the rate the line is moving, it will take seventy-two minutes for him to get to the front.

He has to get there in forty-five.

It will take at least ten minutes to pull the nuke from the scanning machine, leaving a gaunt five-minute cushion before it's set to detonate at 9:00 A.M. Zero room for error.

Kennedy has reached a new, almost hallucinatory, level of exhaustion. After jacking the pickup truck in Charlotte, he drove all the way to Atlanta, using as many back roads as possible to avoid state troopers. Whenever he saw a police car behind him, he pulled off to a side road and went miles out of his way to get back on track. By the time he got to the airport, it was 7:00 A.M. and the place was already jam-packed.

He's wearing a filthy raincoat and baseball cap he took from the pickup's owner to cover his even filthier fugitive-on-the-run clothes.

He shakes off the withering fatigue and checks his watch.

Forty minutes.

The line has slowed to accommodate a train of Rascal-driving heifers crippled by Doritos and Mountain Dew. The snake of travel amateurs, engorged with humanity, seems to have ground to a halt. He needs a next move. As he contemplates it, obsessively scanning his surroundings, his blood runs cold. Noah Kruz is standing fifty heads behind him. He's disguised flawlessly in an Atlanta Police Department uniform.

"Fuck," Kennedy says out loud.

Weary parents schlepping kids, strollers, and hand luggage scowl at him. Kennedy's heart beats faster and sweat soaks his clothing. *They're all going to die,* he thinks, remembering the yacht. *In an instant, they will be nothing but gray dust settling on an iron-black crater, a new American monument to the beginning of the end.*

Kennedy checks his six again. Kruz is working his way through the crowd with his hand on his sidearm, coming for him. Kennedy's mind is racing.

He knows time is running out. He has to arrest me and get us to a minimum safe distance before detonation. I have to move. Now.

He unbuttons the filthy raincoat and moves out of line, walking quickly toward the TSA checkpoint. While he walks, he allows his coat to fall open. That's when he hears the first scream, which rises quickly to full-panic pitch and incites many more, spreading like wildfire. Those who aren't cowering in fear are pointing and shouting at him, trying to get the attention of the authorities.

Kennedy throws off the overcoat, exposing the vest underneath.

Throngs of people gawk in disbelief. Realizing he only has seconds to make it to the TSA checkpoint before he gets a bullet in the head, he breaks into a full sprint. This action ignites blind chaos in the crowd. Kennedy looks back. Kruz cuts through the stumbling masses like a blade and draws the inky blur of a semiautomatic pistol from his holster. He stops, assumes the measured stance of a marksman, and takes aim.

"Put your fucking guns away!" Kennedy bellows for all to hear. "This vest is wired with enough dynamite to kill everyone in a one-hundred-yard radius!"

He holds up his hand, clutching a metal apparatus slithering with wires.

"This is a dead man's switch! You kill me, we all die!"

The police keep their guns trained on him, shaking with fear and uncertainty, speaking furiously into their radios. Passengers freeze in their tracks, crying, whimpering, and shielding their tearful children. Kennedy sees Kruz coming and points at him.

"Somebody wants to be a hero! Stand down!"

Kruz opens fire. Bullets hum and spit past Kennedy's head and ricochet off the walls. The screams are deafening. Kennedy takes cover behind one of the metal bag conveyors. More bullets ricochet and shatter a glass restaurant wall in the concourse. Cops charge after Kruz, yelling for him to stop, but he opens fire on them too, wounding several and sending others diving for cover. People stampede helter-skelter, blinded by terror. Kennedy looks at his watch again.

Ten minutes.

Having swept the police out of his way, Kruz comes at Kennedy unhindered. The SWAT team advances on them, automatic weapons shouldered. Kennedy runs right at a cop, who tries to shrink back into the crowd but ends up falling at Kennedy's feet.

"Don't kill me!" the cop screeches.

"Give me your fucking gun!"

The cop hands him his Beretta and Kennedy opens up on Kruz. He hits him in the thigh and Kruz falls under the stampeding passengers. Kennedy beelines for the body scanner and pulls the tools he took from the man's garage out of his pocket. He needs both hands, so he rips the "dead man's switch" from his hand and drops it on the ground, revealing that it's just a metal lure box wrapped in thick, multicolored big-game fishing line that looks like wires. The "explosives vest"—thirty marine distress flares strapped to his body with duct tape—is loosening from the sweat on his shirt.

He looks at his watch.

Two minutes.

Kennedy is shaking as he pops off the maintenance panel and locates the device. He finds the bomb casing and has to remove the mounting screws with a manual screwdriver, which feels like it takes an eternity. The last screw falls out and he's about to pull the connector wires and power cable when Kruz tackles him from behind. They roll across the ground, kicking and punching. Kruz grabs him by the collar and shoves his gun under Kennedy's chin.

"Sometimes we need a two-thousand-pound oak to fall on our head for us to see the forest for the trees," Kruz says.

"And sometimes the forest needs to burn."

Kennedy rips one of the signal flares from the duct tape on his chest, pulls the safety cap, and ignites the flare in Kruz's face. The bright red flame, burning at over 1,600 degrees Fahrenheit, incinerates his face and engulfs his head and shoulders in flames. While he writhes on the floor, the high-pitched sound of the bomb's pulse detonator starts to cycle up.

Thirty seconds.

Kennedy sprints back to the scanning machine. The detonator pitch is reaching an earsplitting level. SWAT officers are racing to intercept him. One of them stands in his way and Kennedy flattens him with a forearm shiver. The momentum of the hit carries Kennedy into the scanner. With seconds to spare, he wraps his hands around the bomb and yanks it with all his strength, tearing out the connector wires and power cables. He falls to the floor, hugging the bomb close to his chest like a small child.

He closes his eyes and smiles as the high-pitched whine of the detonator quickly cycles down and goes quiet again. When he opens them, he's surrounded by SWAT officers pointing assault rifles at him.

"Back the fuck up!" Wes Bowman yells behind them. "That's a ten-kiloton nuke he's holding and I'm pretty sure you don't want your trigger finger to slip!"

SWAT parts like the Red Sea, revealing Wes holding his CIA badge. He's flanked by two men wearing full-nuclear hazmat space suits. A federal bomb squad containment vehicle is pulling up behind them. The bomb squad astronauts gently take the device from Kennedy. Wes helps him up off the floor and slaps handcuffs on him.

"Department of Justice has instructed me to take this man into custody!"

Wes's men load Kennedy into an airport golf cart, and they drive him away.

"Well, what the hell are you all looking at?" Bowman yells at the cops and SWAT. "Get these people out of here! What part of ten-kiloton nuke did you not understand? Oh, and you might want to bag up that smoldering corpse! It's Thanksgiving for chrissakes!"

EPILOGUE

ARLINGTON NATIONAL CEMETERY—THREE MONTHS LATER

Kennedy and Love are sitting in silence next to a new headstone. The sun breaks through the cloud cover and the freshly cut white marble shines, brilliant and ethereal. Love is playing guitar and humming softly.

"I miss her," Kennedy says.

"Yeah. Me too. Just once, I'd like to hear her smart-aleck, wisecracking mouth again, you know? One more time."

"Even if she was annoying me," Kennedy says.

"And she would too," Love says. "But you could never get that mad at her."

"No, because she would make you laugh before you got pissed off."

"I know, right?"

Kennedy takes a deep breath of the crisp winter air.

"It's nice out here," Love says. "I think she would like it."

"Especially being surrounded by all these war heroes."

"We'd never hear the end of that." Love laughs.

"She'd probably make us salute her," Kennedy says, catching her laugh.

Love stops playing and salutes the stone. Kennedy does as well.

"She deserves it," Kennedy says.

"Yeah," Love says, standing. "Shall we?"

"We shall," Kennedy says and stands up with her.

They stand there and take one last look as the sun begins to fade, casting a pale light that makes everything look frozen in time. Love kisses Kennedy lightly on the lips and they hold each other for a long moment, reluctant to let go.

When they part, Kennedy looks at his watch.

"It's getting late. Don't want to miss our flight."

Kennedy gently pats the top of the headstone and Love straightens the flowers they brought before they walk back across the frozen ground to the cemetery entrance. As they pass through the huge iron gates, a black Range Rover with tinted windows pulls up, and they get in.

Wes Bowman is at the wheel.

"Nice visit?" he asks.

"Very nice," Kennedy says.

The back passenger door opens and Nuri jumps into the car, wringing her hands.

"Holy shit it's cold out there!" she says, holding her fingers over the heat vent. "Of course they put the Asian war heroes way the hell out in the BFE section. Grandpa sends his love by the way."

Wes starts driving them down the long access road.

"Hey, how does Belle's stone look?" Nuri asks.

"Beautiful," Love says.

"It's perfect," Kennedy adds.

He turns to Wes.

"Hey, thanks again for getting my little sis a marker out here. I'm sure that required a few mountains be moved. Means a lot."

"No sweat. I figured she could teach all those old war dogs a thing or two about courage. Plus, it's not every day I get to do something that's actually beneficial to the world while working for the CIA. Speaking of which . . ."

Bowman hits a button on the steering wheel and the nav map in the dash changes to a videoconferencing screen. A CIA emblem appears, accompanied by a smooth, artificial female voice.

"Identification," the voice says evenly.

"Bowman."

"Kennedy."

"Nuri."

"Love."

"Identification verified. Hold please."

The face of a CIA analyst—a handsome young Brit in a perfectly tailored suit—appears on-screen.

"Hello, Heathrow," Kennedy says.

"Afternoon, sir."

"What's our operation status?"

"Unfortunately," Heathrow begins, "we've just received a bit of a curveball. Loading map."

A map of the United Arab Emirates fills the screen.

"Your target has changed locations for the meeting with his Iranian and Russian financiers. It appears he was getting skittish about security in Dubai, so he set the meeting in Muscat, at his cousin's compound."

The screen changes to a map of Oman, the Emirates' neighboring country, zooms into an area outside the capital of Muscat, then switches to a sat image of a massive compound with posh homes and a fleet of luxury cars.

"How sure are we about this?" Wes asks.

"Sat images confirm, along with reports from the cousins we have dug in with his entourage."

"Our assets there are solid," Love says.

"Agreed. What does that do to our schedule?" Kennedy asks.

"I spoke to logistics," Heathrow continues. "Since the meeting is still taking place at the same time, but now over four hundred kilometers farther from the original site, it makes our ability to get you to the new site on time very uncertain."

"Numbers," Wes says.

"Target never meets with anyone for more than thirty minutes," Kennedy answers for Heathrow. "Our margin for error just went from narrow to zero."

"Doing the actual math," Nuri adds, "from this point on, we would have to either make up time or be perfectly on schedule with every travel connection, from the three flights we're now going to have to take to get there, right down to whatever nightmarish ground transportation they have in that backwater of a country Oman. Probably Uber camel."

"Exactly," Heathrow says. "Which is why logistics recommends you scrub the operation and wait for a new window to intercept the target."

"It took us four weeks to get this window, and this meeting could very well be the last step in getting Iran the tech it needs for long-range nukes," Kennedy says. "We can't afford to wait for another window."

"Agent Bowman, you'll have to make the call on this one," Heathrow says drily. "Logistics filed their recommendation with operational brass here, so only the senior agent in charge can supersede."

Wes looks to Kennedy.

"What do you think, team leader?"

Kennedy looks at Love, who gives him a roguish grin. Nuri looks at the car screen and makes the "jagoff" motion with her fist. Kennedy looks back at Wes, smiling confidently.

"Let's see," he begins. "Seven thousand–plus miles in three legs through twenty-eight different climate zones in less than twenty-four sleepless, malnourished hours, with ground travel unknowns, hostile host country, questionable tactical support, a revolving door of intel, the Russian military, and bloodthirsty Iranian government officials with suitcases full of cash, all to black-bag a target who is, arguably, the deadliest arms dealer in the world. Does that about sum it up?"

"In a nutshell," Bowman says.

"Piece of cake."

ACKNOWLEDGMENTS

Thank you to my family—Amanda, Skoogy, Kenners Bear, Jo Mama, Mary B, and Ky—for the love, patience, and support that kept me going through the long hours consumed by this book. Thank you to my Simon & Schuster team—Sarah Knight, Brit Hvide, Marysue Rucci, Jonathan Karp, Erin Reback, Dana Trocker, Kaitlin Olson, Flag Tonuzi, and Tamara Arellano—for another fine collaboration. Thank you to my hardworking representatives—Hannah Brown Gordon, Brad Mendelsohn, and Jeff Frankel—for keeping the dream alive on paper and celluloid. Thank you to all those who generously provided their time and expertise in my research process—Tom Blank; Mingzhong Wu, PhD; Michael Wells Jr.; Jenny Fischer; Mallory Sinclair; Ted Frericks; and Gregory Ford Pike. Thank you to my guardian angels—Kenneth, Tina, Kara, Margaret, and Gilbert Kuhn; Warren and Bernie Witham; Nana DuWors; Big Bri Mahoney; and Nixon—for reminding me of the beauty and terror of impermanence, how it has shaped me, and how it has informed the motivations of my protagonist. *Ubi concordia, ibi victoria.*

Turn the page for more from Shane Kuhn in

THE INTERN'S HANDBOOK

1

IT'S THE HARD-KNOCK LIFE

If you're reading this, you're a new employee at Human Resources, Inc. Congratulations. And condolences. At the very least, you're embarking on a career that you will never be able to describe as dull. You'll go to interesting places. You'll meet unique and stimulating people from all walks of life. And kill them. You'll make a lot of money, but that will mean nothing to you after the first job. Assassination, no matter how easy it looks in the movies, is the most difficult, stressful, and lonely profession on the planet. From this point on, whenever you hear someone bitch about his job, it will take every fiber of your being to keep from laughing in his face. This work isn't for everyone. Most of you are going to find that out the hard way because you'll be dead by the end of the month. And that's still just the training phase.

If you're having second thoughts, that's a natural reaction. The idea of killing people for a living is what second thoughts were made for. In response to all of your questions regarding whether or not you'll feel bad, lose your nerve, live in constant fear, or even want to kill *yourself*, I can provide one simple answer: yes. All of your worst nightmares will come true in ways you never imagined. And either you'll get over it, or you'll be gargling buckshot. Either way, you're covered.

When you reach your darkest hour—which will arrive daily—take comfort in the fact that you never really had much of a choice in the matter. Like me, you're gutter spawn, a Dumpster baby with a broken beer bottle for a pacifier. We've been described as "disenfranchised." Our diagnosis was "failure to thrive." We were tossed from county homes to foster homes to psych wards to juvenile detention centers—wards of the state with pink-slip parents and a permanent spot in line behind the eight ball. Little Orphan Annie would have been our homegirl. So, what were you going to do with your life, starve on minimum wage, greeting herds of human cattle at Wal-Mart? Sell your ass to Japanese businessmen? Peddle meth to middle school kids? I think not. For the first time, you're going to be able to take advantage of being a disadvantaged youth because everyone knows that orphans make the best assassins. Try humming "It's the Hard-Knock Life" while you empty a fifteen-round Beretta mag into Daddy Warbucks's limousine and you'll see just how sweet revenge can be.

If you're reading this, you are a born killer and the people that recruited you know that. You have all the qualifications. First off, you've never been loved, so you feel no empathy for loss. To experience loss, you have to have had something to lose in the first place. Since love is the most important thing you can ever feel, and you've never felt it, then you are bereft of just about every emotion except anger.

And let's talk about anger. Have you ever heard of Intermittent Explosive Disorder? Even if you haven't heard of it, you've experienced it. It's that blinding, uncontrollable rage that turns you into a violent, sometimes homicidal, maniac. Maybe you beat your foster brother half to death for drinking the last Pepsi. Or maybe you fully unleashed it on your juvie cell mate and granted him an early release in a body bag. All the social workers, corrections counselors, and psych doctors, with their nicotine-stained fingers and permanent caffeine twitch, have classified you as dangerously antisocial with a footnote about how you have nothing constructive to offer society. But at Human Resources, Inc., everything that made you a pariah will now make you a professional.

Now let's talk about brains. You've been kicked, thrown, and dragged out of every school you ever attended. But if you're reading this, you are of genius level intelligence, even though you probably beat the shit out of every bumper sticker honor student in your town. How else would you have survived? Only someone with wits beyond her years can stay alive when the whole world thinks she'd be better off dead. You're at the top of the evolutionary food chain, adapting to things in ways that would have made Charles Darwin soil his Harris tweeds.

———

Finally, you may have noticed you have some extraordinary physical abilities. I'm not talking about superpowers, for those of you whose only male role models came from a comic book rack. If you had been raised by something other than wolves, you might have played football or basketball or earned your black belt in something. You would have excelled because you are stronger, faster, and more agile than the average person. Your reflexes are like lightning and your field of vision captures everything down to the finest detail. Incidentally, that's why you avoid crowds. Simultaneously concentrating on every movement made by hundreds of people is not only overwhelming, but it also makes you hate humanity even more than you did before. Bottom line: you did not choose this career, it chose you.

This is your handbook. *The Intern's Handbook*. It's not a part of your new-hire welcome packet. In fact, if they catch you reading it, you will be dead before you can turn the page and your faceless, fingerless corpse will be divided into six trash bags and dissolved in a vat of sulfuric acid in some nameless New Jersey chemical plant. So, please be discreet, because there's a good chance this handbook will save your life.

My name is John Lago. Of course, that's not my given name because my biological parents were too busy disappearing from my short life to sign my birth certificate, which said "Male Baby X." My foster parents called me whatever they managed to blurt out between backhands and booze. So when I was old enough to scrape up a hundred bucks, I paid a guy to forge me a new birth certificate and make a man out of me.

Why John Lago? I could have chosen anything and it's not every day that you get the opportunity to name yourself. It all started with my love of classic cinema. The only friend I ever had growing up was Quinn, the projectionist at the local porn theater. When the place closed for the night and all the pervs slithered home, Quinn would spool up some amazing films from his extensive collection. I grew up on Stanley Kubrick and Akira Kurosawa. I knew who Clint Eastwood was before I knew who was president. For me, film is the great escape (which is also an amazing movie), and I recommend you cultivate an appreciation for it because you're going to need something other than hideous, soul-eating nightmares to occupy your mind. Monsters like us can learn to be human beings from watching movies. All of the experiences we never had are covered in film, and they can be our emotional cave paintings, guiding our path among the ranks of normal society. So your assignment, should you choose to accept it, is to try watching something other than epic fails and donkey porn on YouTube. Just avoid assassin movies, because they'll give you all kinds of bad ideas.

Back to my self-inflicted, Hollywood-inspired moniker. My surname is born out of the greatest era in American cinema—the 1970s. "Lago" is the name of the doomed western town in Clint Eastwood's *High Plains Drifter*, a film that is, without question, the story of my life. I chose "John" because, even though I'm guaranteed eternal damnation, I'm a big fan of John the Baptist. He prepared the unwashed masses for the coming of the Messiah, is given props in the Qur'an for his Purity of Life, and unlike Jesus, he never asked God for a get-out-of-jail-free card before Herod served his head up on a silver platter. I learned all of this by watching Chuck Heston bring the fucking brimstone when he played headless John in the biblical epic *The Greatest Story Ever Told.*

As for the rest of the meat puppets in this tragic parable, some of the names have been changed to protect the guilty. I didn't manage to stay aboveground and out of a supermax hellhole by broadcasting the identities of my contacts at HR, Inc. or my targets. And I'm not going to start now. In keeping with the theme, their names have been pulled from the venerable celluloid of classic and contemporary cinema. If you can figure out what films they come from, you'll get extra credit.

I've been an employee of HR, Inc. since I was twelve years old. I'm now twenty-four, soon to be twenty-five. I have "completed the cycle," as they say. When I started here, my recruiting class consisted of twenty-seven smart-ass punk motherfuckers with two feet in the grave, including myself. There are three of us left. So you might say I know a few things. Or in what is undoubtedly your parlance—that of a *modern-day* smart-ass punk motherfucker with two feet in the grave—"Dude's got mad skills, yo." Hip-hop, you have fucked the king's English for life. Good on you.

If you're anything like I was at your age, you're probably convinced you're going to live forever. I have news for you, brothers and sisters. The shortest distance between truth and bullshit is six feet straight down. It doesn't matter if you believe me or not because there's no greater reality check than a 230 grain .45 caliber hollow point hitting your forehead at 844 feet per second.

So swallow your pride and *read this book.* I don't have to write it. I'm doing you a favor. In fact, I'm risking my neck for you, and I've never even met your sorry asses. The thing is, no one ever gave me the heads-up on anything when I started this gig. Of course, I had my training. But I never got the inside scoop. In most businesses, you learn the ropes from those with more experience. Not this one. Bob, our intrepid leader, wouldn't talk dirty to his wife unless she was on a need-to-know basis. In my opinion, Bob's tight-ass approach to secrecy is the reason why many of my classmates now have tree roots growing out of their eye sockets. He calls himself a "big picture guy." This is a Business 3.0 way of saying he doesn't give a shit about anything but the bottom line, least of all you. There are more where you came from, and when you whack one mole in this business another invariably pops up. Protecting the interests of his "clients"—the bloated, scotch-guzzling frat boys of the nouveau American aristocracy—is his first and only priority. Everyone else is expendable.

You are my priority. If I can save some of you—the most pathetic human punching bags next to the orphans in India that swim in rivers of human excrement—then maybe I'll only end up in the seventh circle of hell instead of the eighth. And if you live through all of this, maybe you can make some kind of name for yourself, shrug off the filthy rug you've been swept under, and create a legacy that transcends trailer parks, drunken beatings, and fucking for food. We will probably never meet. However, in our own twisted way, we are the family that none of us ever had and we have to stick together. It might not be much, but this little handbook is the only proof you've got that someone has *your* back.

Despite the fact that absolutely no one ever had my back, I'm rapidly approaching the ripe old age of twenty-five, a milestone that very few of you will ever cross. While most young professionals are just getting their careers started at twenty-five, that is the mandatory retirement age at HR, Inc. According to Bob, it is the cutoff point at which people begin to question anyone who would be willing to work for free. And I quote: "Even if people believe you are still an intern at twenty-five, you will call attention to yourself as a loser who is way behind in his or her career path. And calling attention to yourself is a death sentence."

The whole philosophy behind HR, Inc. is that an intern is the perfect cover for an assassin. Again, quoting Bob:

"Interns are invisible. You can tell an executive your name a hundred times and that executive will never remember it because they have no respect for someone at the bottom of the barrel, working for free. The rapport they have with their private urinal far exceeds the rapport they will ever have with you. The irony is that all you really have to be is an excellent employee with a strong work ethic and they will heap important duties on you with total abandon. The duties that their lazy, entitled admins and junior execs wouldn't do without guns to their heads are actually critical day-to-day tasks that keep a business running. They also open the doors to proprietary data, personal information, and secure executive areas. The more of these duties you voluntarily accept, the more you will get, simultaneously acquiring the keys to the kingdom: TRUST AND ACCESS. Ultimately, your target will trust you with his life and that is when you will take it."

As much as I hate to stroke Bob's ego, the concept is fucking genius. But why, you may ask, do we go to so much trouble just to whack someone? *La Femme Nikita* can pop a guy with a sniper rifle from a hotel window while she runs a hot bath. Couldn't we park ourselves on a rooftop with an L115A3 long range sniper rifle and shoot our targets like fish in a barrel? A British commando in Afghanistan took out two Taliban soldiers from over eight thousand feet with that baby. That's like drilling someone in Battery Park while you're eating dim sum in Chinatown.

There are many reasons why we don't do things like they do in the movies or on the battlefield. First off, even a Navy SEAL sniper is going to miss once in a while, and they're the best in the world. Bullets and physics are a real bitch, and *we* can't afford to miss. Second, when high-profile mucky mucks start getting splattered all over the streets of the biggest city in America with military-issue weaponry, that's called a *pattern*. Patterns are one of the FBI's favorite pastimes. Mix that with politics and you've got so much heat you can't whack a pigeon without getting black-bagged and taken to Guantanamo Bay for the all-inclusive interrogation and torture package. It's ironic, but this work requires the utmost finesse. That's what separates the professionals from the shirtless hillbilly dipshits you see on *Cops*.

If one can provide a high-quality product for a reasonable price, there's a huge market for assassinations. As long as you avoid patterns and make it seem like your target's enemies are the hitters, you can — yes I'm going to say it — *get away with murder and make a killing.*

The key to success in this business is quality personnel. That would be you. Here at HR, Inc. we are trained very well. It takes years to perfect this so-called craft, which is why they recruit us when we're young. But excellent training does not guarantee success or even survival. I've seen recruits that were considered stars get that smug look wiped off their face with both barrels on their first job. The most important thing I'm going to try to teach you is this: solid training will give you the skills you need to be good at this work, but good and dead is still just dead. Knowing when to set that training aside and allow your instincts to take over will make you unstoppable.

I am unstoppable. I owe much of that to experience. So, in order to truly prepare you for what you're getting yourself into, this handbook will chronicle, in great detail, my final assignment. Within this account, you will see the job as it really is, not as it is in Bob's theoretical world of "typical scenarios." I'm sorry, but there are no typical fucking scenarios when you're planning and executing the murder of a high-profile, heavily guarded individual. Bob will train you and then train you to rely on your training. This is a military approach, and it works well in military operations — for the most part. I will teach you to think like a predator and master the improvisational tracking skills predators use to execute a clean kill and survive. There's a big difference between these approaches, and the only times I've really come close to death were in the beginning, when I was drinking Bob's Kool-Aid by the gallon.

In addition to providing a play-by-play of my final assignment, this handbook will also be a field reference manual with some simple, memorable rules to follow, backed up by real-world examples. In my nearly eight years of active assignment—yes, I started wasting people at seventeen—I have thirty-four kills. I may not have seen it all, but pretty goddamned close.

ABOUT THE AUTHOR

Shane Kuhn is a writer, director, and producer with twenty years of experience working in feature films, documentaries, and advertising. He is a cofounder and executive board member of the Slamdance Film Festival, and a member of the Writers Guild of America. He lives in Colorado and works as vice president of creative services for a San Francisco–based media and special events company. He is the author of *The Intern's Handbook*, bought for film by Sony Pictures and Original Film, and *Hostile Takeover*, the second book in the John Lago thriller series.